PAMELA PALMER

HUNGER UNTAMED

A FERAL WARRIORS NOVEL

AVON

An Imprint of HarperCollinsPublishers

This is a work of fiction. Names, characters, places, and incidents are products of the author's imagination or are used fictitiously and are not to be construed as real. Any resemblance to actual events, locales, organizations, or persons, living or dead, is entirely coincidental.

AVON BOOKS
An Imprint of HarperCollins*Publishers*
10 East 53rd Street
New York, New York 10022–5299

Copyright © 2011 by Pamela Palmer
Excerpts from *Desire Untamed, Obsession Obtained, Passion Untamed, Rapture Untamed* copyright © 2009, 2010 by Pamela Poulsen
ISBN 978-0-06-179471-1
www.avonromance.com

First Avon Books paperback printing: March 2011

Avon Trademark Reg. U.S. Pat. Off. and in Other Countries, Marca Registrada, Hecho en U.S.A.
HarperCollins® is a registered trademark of HarperCollins Publishers.

Printed in the U.S.A.

10 9 8 7 6 5 4 3 2 1

Ariana . . .

She looked as she always had, her skin luminous, her rich brown hair falling in soft waves to her shoulders, framing a face of delicate beauty and indomitable strength. Her back straight, her chin raised almost in challenge, her arms loose at her side as if ready for battle.

His heart contracted, squeezed by an agony he could barely breathe through.

But this wasn't his Ariana, was she? The woman standing before him now was a stranger. Her lush mouth was pursed and hard.

Her eyes locked on him—sharp, piercing eyes that flashed with an inner fire. A queen's eyes.

A warrior's eyes.

Praise for the FERAL WARRIORS

"A wild ride . . . Thrilling."
New York Times bestselling author Anya Bast

"Magic and passion run wild
in this steamy paranormal series."
Publishers Weekly

"Fans of out-of-the-ordinary paranormal romances
are going to add Pamela Palmer's
Feral Warriors series to their keeper list!"
New York Times bestselling author Maggie Shayne

By Pamela Palmer

HUNGER UNTAMED
RAPTURE UNTAMED
PASSION UNTAMED
OBSESSION UNTAMED
DESIRE UNTAMED

To Kyle

Acknowledgments

Thanks, as always, to Laurin Wittig and Ann Shaw Moran—friends, critique partners, and sisters of my heart who read and edit everything I write, keep me sane, and guide and guard these stories like a pair of loving godmothers.

Thanks, also, to my editor, May Chen, who lets me do (nearly) anything I want, but never lets me get away with anything. Couldn't do it without you. And thanks to the entire team at Harper Collins/Avon Books—in particular, Amanda Bergeron, Pamela Spengler-Jaffee, Wendy Ho, and the fabulous art department. And to my copyeditor, Sara Schwager, who always asks the right questions.

A big thanks to my agent, Robin Rue. It's wonderful working with you!

And a very special thanks to my readers for embracing the Feral Warriors and sharing your enthusiasm with me. I love hearing from you and love your questions, even if I can't always answer them without giving too much away!

To my family, my love and gratitude. Always.

Prologue

Upon the bloody battlefield she took form, a woman of mist and light. As she turned to flesh and bone, the cold wind tore at her tunic, stinging her cheeks and whipping dark tendrils loose from her braid to fly across her eyes. Beneath clouds as thick and gray as waves on an angry sea, Ariana, Queen of the Ilinas, raked back her hair and scanned the field—a battle between men and animals. Shape-shifters.

Feral Warriors.

Only twenty-six true shifters remained in the world when once there had been thousands. Twenty-six, each of a different line, a different animal. Jungle cats and bears, a horse, a wolf, a huge fox, along with others unsuited to the field of battle who fought in their human forms—an eagle and hawk among them. The Feral Warriors fought their ancient enemy, the Mage.

Melisande, her second-in-command, appeared from the mist beside her, delicate features turning hard with distaste as she surveyed the battle before them. "He wants you to watch him kill?"

"He is my mate, Melisande." The rebuke was no less harsh for its quietness.

Ariana knew the reprimand would do no good. Melisande had bitterly disapproved of her queen's taking a mate at all, let alone a shape-shifter. Indeed, all her maidens had been unhappy with her decision. A decision they would simply have to live with, for Ariana loved her Feral beyond measure.

"I do not know why Kougar called me," Ariana admitted.

Swords clanged, a Mage cried out in pain as the huge fox ripped off his arm. Even as she watched, the lion leaped, separating another Mage's head from his shoulders in a spray of blood.

Sleet began to slice from the sky in small, stinging pellets.

A large, golden cougar broke from the battle and ran toward her, his cat's body sleek and beautiful as he ran across the frozen field. He'd known the moment she appeared, just as she felt him now through the mystical link that bound them together for eternity. The mating bond.

As the cat neared, he slowed to a walk, then began to sparkle in a rainbow of colored lights. A moment later, a man walked in his place, fully clothed in his dark blue warrior's tunic, knives and a sword strapped to his belt. The Feral Warriors were, as a whole, larger, stronger, finer than any other males on Earth. Kougar—their chief and her mate—was, without doubt, the finest of them all. His hair was as dark as her own, his beard close-cropped, his eyes as pale as ice, yet lit with a fierce and tender flame.

Warmth slid through her blood.

Though his eyes remained warm as he reached her, Kougar frowned. "Two more of your maidens attacked us as we prepared to strike, my love."

Ariana's jaw dropped. "No. They know I'll not have it! Where are they?"

"Horse cut off the hand of one, Snake the arm of the other. Both turned to mist and fled."

Their limbs would regrow quickly, as all Ilina limbs did, but the process would be painful. Of far more concern was the fact that they'd attacked the Feral Warriors at all despite her direct orders against it. Dammit. Her maidens had never accepted her mating a Feral.

Melisande threw Kougar an antagonistic look. "How many Ferals have you lost this day?"

"None."

"A shame."

Ariana shot her friend a hard look. "Mel."

Kougar sketched her lieutenant a brief, mocking bow. "Your sweet nature brightens any battlefield, Melisande."

"Go to hell, Feral."

Ariana eyed her second. "Why are my maidens

attacking the Ferals? I gave a direct command . . ."

Melisande lifted her hands. "I swear 'twas not my doing." Her gaze flicked to Kougar. "As much as I might approve." Melisande met Ariana's gaze again, her eyes turning worried. "There's been talk of wildness in the temple. I dismissed it, but perhaps I shouldn't have. Some may have been infected by dark spirit."

"Goddess, I hope not." There was no cure for dark spirit, no way to destroy it except through the deaths of the ones infected. "Find them."

Melisande nodded, giving Kougar one last parting shot. "Why don't you do us both a favor and go die in battle?" With a flick of her hand, Melisande faded to mist and left.

Kougar shook his head. "That one would try the goddess herself." He rubbed his chest with his fist, right over his heart, as if he had, indeed, been injured.

"Are you all right?" she asked.

His fist stilled, his eyes registering surprise as if he'd been unaware of what he'd been doing. "I'm fine." He stepped forward, his large hands gently cupping her shoulders as the battle raged far behind him. "What of your maidens? This is four in as many days who've attacked us. Dark spirit rarely claims more than one at a time."

Ariana shrugged though she was more than a little concerned herself. "I'll handle it."

Frustration flashed in her shifter's eyes, sparking along the bond that connected them. His hands contracted.

"I'm your mate, Ariana. I'm here to help you shoulder such difficulties."

Her own temper flared, and she cocked her head at him. "As you let me help you? I offered to fight beside you today, and you denied me."

"Of course I did. This is our war, not yours."

"And the Ilinas are my responsibility. Not yours."

As the cold wind kicked up, carrying with it the shouts and cries of battle, Kougar glanced behind him. "I must get back. Go. Be safe. Later, we'll discuss the role of a male in his mate's life."

"Later, we'll fall into one another's arms and forget talk altogether."

A knowing smile curved Kougar's beautiful mouth. "Of a certainty, we will." He pulled her close and pressed his open mouth upon hers, sweeping his warm tongue between her hungry lips. The kiss lasted only seconds, yet it left her feeling both weak and powerful.

As they pulled apart, a wry smile lifted her mouth. The argument always ended the same.

Once again, Kougar rubbed at his chest, his own mouth tightening.

She gave him an exasperated look, and he shrugged. "A twinge in my chest is all."

"The mating bond pinches?"

Kougar smiled. "So say my men, but no. Never." His hand slid beneath her jaw and he kissed her again, his tongue sweeping into her mouth on a promise. When he pulled back, she thought she might drown in the depth of the love in his eyes.

Ariana stroked his cheek. "Be safe, my beast."

His eyes crinkled. "Always." In a single move of power and grace, he turned and dove through a spray of sparkling lights to land on four paws. In a flash, he raced back into battle.

Her heart beating with pleasure and love, Ariana relaxed into her natural mistlike state, thought of her castle in the Crystal Realm, and moments later felt the gold-and-jeweled Grand Corridor take form around her, the ceiling high above. Kougar often told her she looked like a ghost in her mist state, her body visible but not corporeal. He preferred her flesh and blood. And when he pulled her against his hard body and kissed her with passionate tenderness, she absolutely preferred it, too.

She glanced around in surprise at the absence of her maidens. The Ilinas only numbered one hundred forty-one and not all lived in the Crystal Realm, far removed from the rest of the world. Long ago, the Ilinas had built the Crystal Realm, little more than a castle, in the energy belt that circled high above the Earth, known as the Syphian Stream. A castle in the clouds accessible only to those who could turn to mist and their guests. Or captives.

One of her maidens hurried into the Grand Corridor from a side hall. Getrill, her face a mask of concern, saw her. "You're back."

"Where is everyone?"

"The gardens."

Ariana started back, suspecting the two maidens injured on the Feral battlefield were the cause of her friend's concern. They were certainly causing her own. What in heaven's name was she going to do about them? Though it was the queen's right and responsibility to destroy a maiden turned to darkness, how could she possibly kill one of her own? One of her sisters, her friends?

She was halfway to the gardens when a scream broke the quiet of the passage.

Ariana froze, then willed herself to the site, turning to mist in order to cross the distance in an instant. She reached the inner garden to find Melisande, Brielle, and more than a dozen of her maidens circled around another. On the ground, writhing in pain, lay the sweet-natured Angelique.

For a moment, Ariana stared, confused. Angelique's limbs were intact. She wasn't one of the two who'd attacked the Ferals. Instead, Angelique's eyes glowed with a wildness Ariana had never seen. A wildness that crawled with evil.

"What happened?" Ariana's words vibrated with the fear that was beginning to invade her heart and blood.

Melisande looked up, her face alarmingly pale. "I don't know. She just returned from the temple claiming that the maidens down there are kidnapping human males and torturing them. They're plucking out their eyes as they ride them, Ariana. Laughing as the males' cries of release turn to screams of agony."

"What?"

"She was one of them, Ariana. *Delightful fun,* she called it. I saw the excitement in her eyes."

Angelique screamed again, her back bowing in a painful-looking, unnatural contortion. And froze, her skin turning a deathly gray.

"No!" Brielle cried.

Ariana stared with shock and understanding as deep inside, she felt the rending of the life fiber that connected them. The same kind of fiber that connected the queen to each of her maidens.

Angelique was dead.

But even as the shock of that severing tore through her heart and mind, she felt another. And another. And another. Octavia, Zerlina, Serafina. Gone, gone, gone.

Ariana swayed, her mind turning white with shock. *"They're dying. They're all dying."*

Around the gardens, her maidens cried out with grief, feeling their sisters' deaths. It was moments before Ariana realized the wails of grief had changed. That her maidens were beginning to dance. That their eyes had taken on the same glowing wildness she'd seen in Angelique's.

Ariana stared at them, her gaze flying from one to the next— Getrill, Brielle, Marinn—as understanding dawned and horror crashed over her.

No, no, no.

"Ariana?" But even as Melisande asked the question, a sly smile broke across her mouth, her own eyes igniting with the glow of evil.

Ariana's blood ran cold.

Goddess help them all.

Kougar shifted back into his human form as the Wind rode to him atop Horse, his dark hair whipping in the gale. As the Wind leaped down, Horse shifted back to man in a spray of sparkling lights until the pair faced him, shoulder to shoulder, his oldest and closest friends.

Across the battlefield, the other Ferals shoved and congratulated one another on a battle well fought, a few of the cats wrestling in their animals.

"We destroyed the last of the orbs," the Wind informed him. "'Tis done. The Mage have fled."

"Good. Let's get—"

"Kougar!" The shout came from the other side of the battlefield, a shout of warning, not jubilation.

Kougar met the questioning gazes of his friends, then shifted into his cat, running on all fours back to the site of the battle before shifting back. He found his warriors gathered warily around something . . . or someone. When they parted to let him through, he found a woman lying on the ground in obvious pain. Another of Ariana's mist warriors, though she'd turned corporeal. Only corporeal could they be injured or killed.

"Not again," Kougar muttered. His gaze pinned the polar bear shifter who'd called to him. If he'd attacked her, there would be hell to pay.

The Feral shook his head, hearing his chief's unspoken question. "She appeared before me moments ago, Kougar, her sword drawn. But she fell almost as soon as she appeared. None of us touched her."

"What's going on?" Horse asked, as he and the Wind joined them.

Kougar shook his head as the Ilina looked up at him with eyes that should have been filled with pain, but instead gleamed with an evil joy.

"Death is upon us," she cried. "The Ilina race is no more. The darkness . . . consumes us all!"

With her mouth still forming the last word, she froze, her flesh turning gray as the winter sky.

"She's dead." The disbelief in the Wind's voice pounded inside Kougar's skull, along with the mist warrior's last words.

The Ilina race is no more.

She was crazed, of course. But a shaft of unreasoning concern bolted through his chest.

He needed to see his mate.

Slamming his hand atop his Feral armband, he thought of the Crystal Realm and whispered the words of enchantment that would take him to Ariana. If she was there. Of all non-Ilinas, he alone had access to the Ilina stronghold through the magic woven into his armband, an ability to follow her to the Crystal Realm because of their mating bond.

He felt the magic sweep over him and steeled himself for the dizzying ride. A moment later, the magic disappeared as if it had never been, leaving him where he'd started, on the field of battle, surrounded by his men.

He scowled, but the beat of his heart grew to a thud as the certainty that something was wrong, very wrong, swept over him.

As he pressed his hand over the armband, whispering the chant a second time, pain hit him like a battle-axe. The force of it drove him to his knees, slicing through his chest, nearly cleaving him in two.

"Kougar!" The Wind gripped one of his arms as Horse grabbed the other.

Goddess, goddess, goddess.

His mind imploded. His heart tore beneath the assault.

The mating bond, that bright crystalline cord that had joined him to Ariana, heart to heart, soul to soul, shattered. The brilliant glow inside snuffed out as if it had never been.

"*No!*" He roared the word, the blast of sound echoing over and over in his head. "*She's gone. Ariana is gone. Dead.*"

He couldn't breathe. Pain consumed him, burning, searing pain. His claws and fangs erupted as the need to rip someone . . . anyone . . . to bloody shreds roared through his body on a tide of grief-driven rage.

"*Stay in your skin!*" Horse's voice drove a spike through his head, slashing through the wildness building inside him.

"Ease down, my friend," the Wind urged. "Ease down. This isn't the place to let it out. Let's get you home."

Kougar's senses began to shut down. Colors faded to gray before his eyes, smells all but disappeared. The severing of the mating bond created havoc within him. All he could feel was the burning, searing pain that consumed him, heart and mind.

His body would continue to live, for he was all but immortal.

But his life was over.

Chapter One

Present day

Kougar prowled on four paws through the streets of Harpers Ferry, West Virginia, sliding in and out of the night shadows of the nineteenth-century buildings that rose against the moonlit sky on steps as silent as the pre–Civil War human dead that filled the cemetery on the hill. He'd wandered this town alone since the battle four days ago—a battle between the Ferals and Mage and three wraith Daemons the Mage had managed to release.

The Ferals had won, of course, but the victory had been devastatingly hollow. Two Ferals, Hawke and Tighe, had disappeared into the Mages' spinning vortex, a spirit trap that would separate men from animals, killing both in a matter of days. Seven, now. That's all they had left unless the Ferals saved them.

And there was only one way to do that.

One person alone had ever been able to breach a Daemon spirit trap and come out alive. A woman who could turn to mist at will. The Queen of the Ilinas.

Kougar growled low in his cat's throat, hatred burning through his mind.

Only one woman could save his Feral brothers and their animals.

Ariana, his soulless bitch of a mate.

He'd thought she was dead. For a thousand years, he'd grieved for her until twenty-one years ago when he'd learned the truth—that Ariana and her race had faked their extinction after being infected by dark spirit. The knowledge had slain him until he'd remembered that the woman he'd once loved was long gone, lost to the dark spirit that had consumed her soul.

His beloved Ariana would never have betrayed him like that.

When he'd learned she was still alive, he'd refused to seek her out. The last thing he'd wished to see were soulless eyes peering out of his beloved's face. But four days ago, everything changed with Hawke and Tighe's capture. He had to find her, to force her to breach the spirit trap and free them.

The problem was, he couldn't reach her.

On cat's feet, he darted between two narrow brick buildings and ran up the night hill, frustration beating a harsh rhythm in his blood. The sound of the two rivers that flanked Harpers Ferry carried on the air, broken by the rumble of a train approaching in the distance. The sounds began to escalate suddenly until even the chirping of the insects turned to screeching in his ears.

Goddess, his senses were screwed up. Ariana's severing of that supposedly permanent mating bond had damaged him, leaving him half-alive, his emotions frozen, his senses all but dead for a millennium. Until five days ago when, trapped by Daemon and Mage, he'd come close to dying. In the darkness, Melisande had appeared with her usual scowl and, for a reason he couldn't fathom, reconnected the mating bond between him and Ariana. Apparently, his *wife* still needed him alive.

With the bond reconnected, sensation had returned in a manic, freak-show kind of way, color blazing a hundred times too bright, then throbbing and pulsing like it was about to explode, before flickering back to gray. Fortunately, the kaleidoscope had died down, most of his senses finally returning to what had once been normal. Except for his hearing.

And his emotions.

He passed through the old Harper Cemetery and headed for the Jefferson Rock, where he always ended up at some point during the night, frustration and anger burning a hole in his gut. He was starting to feel . . . too much. The wind in his face. The rocks beneath his paws. And a fury hot enough to rip someone . . . anyone . . . limb from limb. No, not anyone. *Her.* Ariana. Or at least the soulless bitch who wore Ariana's face.

Their newly reconnected mating bond was jury-rigged at best, a dull, mangled reflection of the crystalline cord that had once bound them. But it was there. And it gave him his one chance of finding Ariana and saving his friends. As her mate, he'd only ever been able to sense her presence if she was nearby . . . or in the Crystal Realm, where the Ilinas had been living since their *extinction.* Only a mate of an Ilina could travel to the Crystal Realm without an Ilina escort. And then, only if his mate was already there.

For four days, he'd waited for her to return home to that castle in the clouds, so he could catch her.

For four days, he'd waited in vain while Hawke's and Tighe's lives slowly slipped away.

Kougar leaped onto the Jefferson Rock—a small tourist landmark upon which the human, Thomas Jefferson, had supposedly proclaimed the sight worthy of a trip across the Atlantic. Kougar couldn't fault the sentiment as he stretched out atop the bit of shale in his cat's body. The breeze slid through his whiskers as he perused the dramatic, moonlit convergence of the Shenandoah and Potomac Rivers far below.

Four days ago, at the end of the battle, he'd told Lyon, his chief, that he'd return in ten days. Only that. Not where he was going, not whom he intended to find. No one could know the Ilinas were still alive. Melisande had taken it upon herself to kill anyone who threatened their secret, who knew of their existence. Except, apparently, him.

Not that the Ferals were likely to be bested by mist warriors, but they were already dealing with more than enough—the death of Foxx, the loss of Hawke and Tighe, the theft of the Daemon blade, and the Mages' newly acquired dark power and goal to destroy the Ferals and release the Daemon plague back into the world.

The last thing the Ferals needed was ambushing mist warriors added to that list. No, he'd return to Feral House only after Ariana had freed Hawke and Tighe. And she would, dammit. He'd see to it.

Failure was not an option.

If only she'd return to the Crystal Realm!

Something fluttered briefly in his chest at the site of the decrepit mating bond, and he stilled, his cat's pulse lifting, then kicking up to Mach five.

Got her. Finally, Ariana had returned to the Crystal Realm.

Kougar sent his newly keen senses into the woods in every direction, then, certain he was alone, leaped off the rock and shifted into his human form. Through the battle-damaged shirt he still wore from four days before, he reached for the gold cougar-head armband that circled his biceps.

As his fingers closed around the cool metal, he stilled, slammed by the realization he was about to see Ariana for the first time in a thousand years.

Goddess.

Taking a deep, unsteady breath, he closed his eyes and concentrated on the mating bond, whispering the ancient words of connection. As the words left his lips, he felt a familiar spin of dizziness, a momentary sensation of weightlessness, then solid flooring beneath his feet.

Smooth flooring, not ground.

While his vision cleared, the scent of pine hit his nose, slamming him with a rush of memories. He blinked, gooseflesh rising on his arms as he found himself standing in the archway of the Grand Corridor of Ariana's palace in the Crystal Realm. The wide expanse of emerald floor stretched out before him, framed by walls of crystal twenty feet high, rising to a ceiling painted with murals of women indulging in a multitude of delights, carnal and otherwise. Along the walls, torches flickered, setting the crystal aflame with an inner fire.

He'd once thought this hall the most beautiful in existence. It was a sight he hadn't seen in a thousand years, and standing there had his heart thrumming in his chest.

How many times in those first few days after he thought Ariana dead had he tried to get here, to reach her while he'd prayed over and over that she was somehow, miraculously, still alive? How many times had he visited this place in his dreams, dreams in which Ariana still lived? Dreams in which he'd stood beside her, in which he'd saved her.

How many times?

But she'd lost the battle before he'd known there was a battle to fight, and he hadn't been here when she'd needed him. Maybe if he had been, he could have helped her vanquish the darkness and return to him before it consumed her soul. Now it was far, far too late. Given enough time, dark spirit always consumed the soul.

Slowly, he started down the corridor, memories attacking him from every direction. Making love to Ariana in her chamber. Making love to her in the garden. Making love to her beneath the waterfall. Goddess, he'd never been able to get enough of her, nor her of him. Even though the Ilinas had disapproved of his marriage to their queen, his Ariana had loved him. For two short years, they'd been blissfully happy.

He stilled as a familiar warmth bloomed within the misshapen excuse for a mating bond.

Ariana.

At the feel of her nearness, his heart began to beat a hard, erratic rhythm. At the certainty he was about to see her again. And the certainty that it was going to hurt like hell.

Hatred for the woman she'd become, for the evil thing who'd destroyed his mate, crouched, snarling inside him as he strode toward her chambers. The cool, crystalline air parted before him as if seeking to escape the menace that radiated from his pores.

"Ariana!" He shouted her name, his voice deep as a roar. There was no sense in stealth, not with the mating bond reconnected. Just as he felt her, he knew Ariana had known the moment he'd arrived.

Melisande drifted out of the nearest passage, mistlike, her blond braid hanging over one shoulder, her sword drawn. With an expression hard as flint, she blocked his path. "You're not welcome here."

Kougar lifted a brow at the petite mist warrior. "You reconnected the mating bond. Had you forgotten that meant you couldn't keep me out?"

"No, but I'd hoped you had."

He was about to barrel through her when a woman stepped into the passage behind her, flesh and blood, a woman as familiar to him as the beat of his own heart. His feet stopped without his awareness. His heart seized for the space of three beats, then took off like a flock of birds in a wild flight.

Ariana.

In so many ways, she looked as she always had, her skin luminous, her rich brown hair falling in soft waves, framing a face of delicate beauty and indomitable strength. She stood in that achingly familiar way, with her back straight, her chin raised almost in challenge, her arms loose at her sides as if ready for battle.

"The queen will not see you, Kougar," Melisande snapped.

"She already has." Emotions careened inside him—the passionate, tender love. The searing pain of losing her.

His heart contracted, squeezed by an agony

he could barely endure. Deep inside him, his cat gave a joyous yowl. His soul sang at this proof that Ariana lived, at this miracle that the woman he'd loved more than life, that he'd mourned for a thousand years, once more stood before him.

But she wasn't his Ariana, was she? The woman before him was a stranger. For a moment, just a moment, he thought he glimpsed emotion in her once-beloved face. A mix of joy and agony that mirrored his own. But he blinked, and it was gone, and he knew he'd been mistaken.

Now that he looked at her clearly, he saw that her lush mouth was pursed and hard. Her brows dipped in the middle over cold eyes the brown of a wild cherry tree instead of the blazingly bright Ilina blue they'd once been.

Her gaze locked on him with a piercing sharpness she'd always possessed. Both queen and warrior, she'd been fire and sword, able to slay any opposition with a single look. But those sharp eyes that had once softened for him, melting with love and heat, now stared at him with a stranger's cold reserve.

His mind reeled at the sight of her, his heart an erratic thrum in his chest. He longed for the lack of feeling he'd lived with for a millennium, the insulating numbness he'd felt for so long. Instead, his heart split asunder all over again.

She wasn't dressed as Melisande, in the ancient mist-warrior garb of tunic and pants. Nor was she garbed in one of the jewel-toned gowns she'd often preferred. Instead, she wore blue scrubs that fit her slender form, and white shoes, as if she played at being a doctor or nurse. At being human.

For a moment, her dress confounded him until the reason clicked sickly into place in the pit of his stomach.

Darkness always fed on pain and fear. Where better to find pain in this day and age than in a human hospital? She was nothing but a parasite feeding off the misery of others. Was that why she hid the unnatural brightness of her eyes behind brown contacts? Because she spent so much time trolling the human world?

Despite the plain clothing, despite the dark circles beneath her eyes and the contacts hiding their true color, she was still achingly beautiful. Even if that beauty was truly only skin-deep.

"Leave us, Melisande," Ariana ordered quietly.

Melisande glanced over her shoulder. "Ariana . . ."

"You knew it would come to this, Mel, when you reconnected us. You knew, sooner or later, he'd find me."

"He's known you lived for twenty-one years."

"I said, leave us," Ariana snapped at her second-in-command.

On a huff of displeasure, Melisande disappeared.

Ariana remained where she was, as if rooted. Staring at him. Again, he thought he saw emotion dart across her eyes and sensed she was struggling for control. As if she were as thrown by this meeting as he was.

Even from here, he could smell her, the unique

scent that had always reminded him of lilies of
the valley. The scent tumbled him back in time to
long, glorious nights lost in the pleasures of her
body. He clenched his fists against the needs warring inside him. Part of him longed to haul her
into his arms and feel her against him one more
time. A stronger part wanted to rip out her soulless heart. And the unstable emotions careening
inside him made one or the other an all-too-likely
possibility.

With a low growl in his throat, he fought for
control.

He'd come for one thing and one thing only. To
save his friends. But standing within reach of the
woman he'd thought dead for a millennium, he
found himself wanting more. And needing answers.

"*Why*, you soulless bitch?" The question came
out as a snarl. "Why sever the mating bond? Why
make the world think you were gone? Why make
me think you were gone?"

A shadow passed over her face, her mouth tightening as if in pain though he knew that to be a lie.
The soulless felt no pain but the physical.

She swallowed visibly, her expression hardening to granite. "I severed the bond because
I could. Once I embraced the dark spirit, I had
no need of you, Feral. No desire to touch you or
be touched by you again. And I still don't. The
Ariana you knew no longer exists. And *I* have no
interest in you."

Even though her words didn't surprise him, her

cold dismissal turned like a blade in his gut, igniting his fury.

His hands fisted until the blood began to throb in his palms. "Why did Melisande reconnect the mating bond?"

She looked away. "A perverse bit of mischief. Go away, Kougar. There's nothing for you here."

As her gaze returned to his, brown contacts blocking any glimpse into her thoughts, he struggled to hold on to his thinning control. And felt it slipping through his fingers—fingers about to erupt in claws.

Ariana flushed hot, then cold, as she stared at Kougar, at her mate, at the man she'd loved for a thousand years.

She'd forgotten how tall he was, how broad his shoulders, how muscular his arms, as he stood before her now in a white-collared shirt and black pants, clothes torn and bloodied as if he'd been fighting. She'd forgotten how his presence filled a room, how it filled the entire castle, until she could hardly breathe through the need to be in his arms, to feel his body sliding against hers, sliding into hers.

He couldn't know.

Never had she struggled so hard to control her emotions, to hide what was in her heart and head. Never had doing so caused her so much pain as it did now as Kougar stared at her with eyes as pale as ice, filled not with tenderness but with pain and a growing fury. Not with love but hatred. A hatred she must fan.

Her stomach clenched and churned. What she was doing was cruel beyond measure. But she had no choice. Her cruelty just might keep Kougar alive.

Soulless, soulless, soulless.

The chant pounded in her head as she focused on keeping her expression closed and hard even as emotions clawed at her in a wild battle—longing and fear. A storm of devastating love and aching grief that had lived within her for an eternity.

Inside, her heart trembled, on the verge of an emotional meltdown. She narrowed her eyes, dropping her lids to mere slits, trying to hide the sheen of disastrous tears even as she fought back the emotion, fought for control.

Goddess, she loved him. She'd never stopped loving him even when she'd hated herself for it, for the destruction that love had wrought. So many dead. So much grief.

But the danger wasn't past for the Ilinas.

And thanks to Mel, Kougar was in danger again, too. Damn, Melisande! She never should have reconnected the mating bond without Ariana's knowledge. Without her consent!

Mel knew Ariana wouldn't approve, which was why she'd gone behind her back. Melisande might not care if Kougar, or any Feral, lived or died. But Ariana did. Too much. And he would die if that poison started flowing again. The only thing saving him was the miserable, mangled state of their mating bond.

And she *must* keep it that way.

Kougar took a threatening step toward her. Within the flaying hatred in his eyes she saw flashes of a pain that nearly drove her to her knees.

"Why are you here, Kougar? Why now if you've known I was alive for over twenty years?"

"You're going to free two of my friends from a Daemon spirit trap."

Oh, sweet goddess. She couldn't help him.

Struggling for control, she yanked the icy mask tighter over her features. "No. I'm not. I don't give a damn about your Ferals." Which was partly true. Most of his men had been as opposed to their mating as her maidens had been. Only Horse and the Wind had ever been friendly to her. But whoever the two were who were lost, they were Kougar's men. If she could, she would certainly save them. For him.

But she couldn't help him. And she couldn't keep up this pretense much longer! She had to get him to leave.

Lifting her chin, she gave him her haughtiest, coldest look. "Go, Kougar, and don't come back. You're not welcome here."

In a flash, his anger ignited. She'd pushed him too far.

A chill of fear skipped down her spine as his eyes turned the pale gold of a cougar's, as fangs dropped from his mouth. One moment he was standing still, the next he lunged, grabbing her around the throat with a wickedly clawed hand. Fiery pain exploded as his claws pierced the sides of her neck, as warm blood ran down into her scrubs. As he slammed her back against the wall.

Too late, she fought him, her instincts off, her gut-deep belief he'd never really hurt her causing her to move too slowly when it suddenly became obvious he would.

"You *bitch*." The words were a growl in his throat, his furious face mere inches from her own as his hot breath wafted over her chilling flesh.

She began to tremble from a combination of shock and the knowledge that without her unique Ilina weapons, she was virtually helpless against his far superior strength. If he chose to rip out her throat, she couldn't stop him.

That alone wouldn't kill her. Ilinas, like all immortals, healed almost any wound within minutes. Only if he took her heart would she die. But if she died, so too would her maidens. Her life force would dissipate, spreading to the other Ilinas. And with it, the poison she'd protected them against for a thousand years.

As badly as she wanted to protect Kougar, her first responsibility must be to her maidens.

"Kougar." Her voice gurgled with the blood in her ruptured windpipe.

He flinched, his gaze dropping to her neck, to where the blood ran in rivulets, soaking her top. Almost as quickly as he'd attacked, his claws and fangs retracted, but he didn't pull away. His large hand remained closed around her throat as her pulse beat against his palm.

His gaze locked on hers and held as her wounds healed, as the pain in her throat died a quick death. And still he watched her, pale eyes probing, digging too deep. She tried to look away and couldn't, her parched heart drinking in the sight of the man she'd longed for, whom she'd missed, and loved, for a thousand years.

In so many ways, he hadn't changed. His hair was much shorter than he'd worn it in those days, his beard trimmed to encompass only his mouth and chin. But he'd always exuded a powerful pull on her physically, nearly overwhelming in its intensity, and that hadn't changed. For a thousand years, she'd blamed herself for giving in to her feelings for him. But standing within the heat of his body, enveloped by his raw, masculine scent, snared by the power of his eyes, she remembered all over again how impossible he'd been to resist.

But she must resist him now. His life absolutely depended on it.

He released her neck but continued to crowd her, forcing her to meet his glittering diamond-hard gaze. "You're going into that spirit trap, Ariana. You're going to get them out."

She swallowed the words of regret. The soulless regretted nothing, and he must believe her soulless. "No. I'm not."

He growled low in his throat, the sound of an

animal, his hand tightening around her throat. "Seventeen Ferals died in one of those traps six hundred years ago."

Seventeen. Her mind reeled.

"Horse died. You could have saved him. You could have saved them all."

Sweet goddess, Horse had been one of his oldest and closest friends. What must it have done to him to have lost so many in a single blow?

"Now the Ferals number only nine, or will once the new fox comes forth. The Mage have acquired dark power and are coming too damn close to freeing the Daemons. *We cannot lose two more.*"

Her heart ached, her fingers clenching at her sides as she fought to hide the sorrow fisting in her chest and present a callous front.

She swallowed, clearing the blood and emotion from her throat, layering her voice with ice. "I couldn't have helped them, Kougar, even if I'd known. Even if I'd wanted to. And I can't help the ones in there now. You're mistaken if you believe I can breach a spirit trap."

Only by turning to mist could she possibly get into the trap and out again. And if she did, her maidens would die.

She could see Kougar's anger mounting. She could feel the pulse of it battering her through the mating bond. "The Ilina queens possess that ability, Ariana. You know it as well as I."

"Queens of old, perhaps, but not I." She needed to get away from him. Even if she hadn't seen him in centuries, she knew this man. No one had ever lived who was more tenacious.

With his friends in trouble, there was no way he'd simply turn his back on her and leave. No way. He'd hound her and threaten her, demanding she help him until he finally broke through her façade and discovered the truth.

That she still loved him. That she'd always loved him.

A truth that would, quite literally, kill him.

Chapter Two

"I'm not the woman you knew, Kougar," Ariana snapped. Even through the contacts, her eyes stabbed at him. She'd never been one to give up or give in.

Kougar crowded her against the wall. Though their bodies didn't quite touch, her body heat permeated his clothing, sinking into his skin. His hands fisted, slick with her blood as his gaze fell again to the red smear that had soaked into the neck of her shirt. Never had he expected to actually touch her, let alone hurt her. Ilinas were notoriously quick to turn to mist when threatened. Yet she hadn't. And despite his fury, drawing her blood had shaken him.

"You ask the impossible, Kougar." She slid her

hands between their bodies, grasping her wrists as she murmured something beneath her breath.

Too late, he recognized the chant he himself used to travel back and forth to the Crystal Realm.

An instant later, she was gone, and he stood alone in the Grand Corridor.

"Ariana!" His angry shout hit the walls, echoing back on him over and over. He couldn't follow her. And his awareness of her through the mating bond told him that she was no longer in the Crystal Realm.

Four days he'd waited to catch her. *Four fucking days!*

Fury detonated within him, and he slammed his fist into the nearest wall, shattering no fewer than half a dozen bones in his hand. With a roar of pain and frustration, he held the hand still for the long seconds it took to heal, as the emotion swirled, then drained away.

She'd claimed she couldn't help him. Which wasn't all that surprising since he could hardly expect the soulless to possess compassion.

But nothing about that confrontation had gone as expected.

When he'd attacked her, she hadn't turned to mist. He'd been almost as surprised as she had that his claws had found purchase in her neck. And when she left just now, instead of simply turning to mist and disappearing as any other Ilina would do, she'd murmured a spell of transport, like a non-Ilina. As if she couldn't turn to mist.

And an Ilina queen who couldn't turn to mist certainly couldn't breach the spirit trap. If she'd been irrevocably injured or altered in some way, in *that* way, his only chance to save Hawke and Tighe was gone.

No fucking way.

"Melisande!" His voice echoed through the crystal hall, over and over. "Brielle!"

He waited, his muscles rigid, his breath tight in his chest. As he opened his mouth to yell again, Melisande appeared, hovering before him. A slip of angry female.

"Why isn't she turning to mist?" he demanded. "Why does she need a transport spell?"

Cold eyes flinched, but Melisande's expression remained defiant. "She's not your concern."

"Like hell she isn't! She's the only one who can save two of my warriors. Why did you reconnect the mating bond, Melisande? *What's the matter with her?*"

The woman's chin lifted. "Find another way to free your men, Kougar. You'll get no help from us."

His fangs and claws erupted, and he lunged at her, reaching for her throat as he had Ariana's even though she was already mist and he knew his claws would go right through her. For his efforts, she zapped him with her Ilina energy, lighting a fiery pain in every molecule of his body.

He struggled against the agony and, with a growl of pure fury, threw himself backward, out of that energy-induced inferno, slamming against the wall behind him. As he straightened,

Melisande stared at him, her aura reddish orange, her sapphire eyes flashing with an anger to match his own.

"Don't *ever* touch me, Feral," she hissed between bared teeth. "If I didn't think it would hurt her more, *I'd kill you.*"

He growled between his fangs, drawing on his full size and power to intimidate. "Then tell me what I want to know. Why isn't Ariana turning to mist?"

"Because she can't."

"Why not?"

"The dark spirit . . . changed her."

Melisande's words almost made sense, but the blond Ilina had always been a lousy liar, and she was lying now.

"Tell me the truth!"

Instead, she disappeared, leaving him once more alone in the hall. It was all he could do not to slam his fist into the wall a second time. It wasn't over. It was *not* over.

So long as Hawke and Tighe lived, he would never give up.

Yet his hands were all but tied. He couldn't stay in the Crystal Realm more than a day before he started weakening and had to return to Earth, but once he left, he couldn't return until Ariana did. And unless he missed his guess, she'd stay away as long as she could now that she knew he'd come after her.

Which meant he had to find his answers immediately. Before he was forced to leave.

As he turned to begin the hunt for an Ilina who would tell him what he needed to know, something on the floor caught his eye. A flash of white—a card in protective plastic splattered with a single drop of blood. He bent down and picked it up. Turning it over, he stilled. Ariana's pensive face stared back at him from a photo ID that read ANNA SMITH, R.N.

A nurse. Not just pretending. Was she living among the humans, then? If she truly couldn't turn to mist, then of course she was. No corporeal creature could live long in the Crystal Realm. Not even an Ilina.

He stared at the card, then tapped it against his hand, a savage smile lifting one corner of his mouth.

The hunt was on.

Deep below Feral House, Wulfe watched as Esmeria, the most gifted of the Therian healers, touched the forehead of the human male lying unconscious in one of the three now-occupied cells in the Ferals' prison block. Long ago, all Therians had been shape-shifters, before the race had mortgaged most of its power to defeat the High Daemon Satanan and his horde. Now, only one each of nine of the ancient shifter lines still retained the power of his animal and the ability to shift. The nine known as the Feral Warriors.

"It's time." Esmeria glanced at him as she rose, running fingers through her short, dark hair. "I'm amazed these humans have been able to last five days without food or water. That energy Olivia fed them must have been powerful stuff."

The humans had survived the battle from hell in Harpers Ferry five days ago, only to face an uncertain fate when the Ferals had realized they couldn't steal their memories. And goddess knew, they'd seen too much—shape-shifting Ferals, three Daemons that hadn't existed in the world in millennia, and the gruesome deaths of three of their friends.

During the battle, Jag's new mate, Olivia, had fed them all a potent life energy, the humans included. The Ferals never killed needlessly, but neither did they hesitate to take the lives of humans who in any way threatened the anonymity and safety of the immortal races. Humans could not be allowed to carry tales of shape-shifters into the human communities. Too many odd occurrences might start to make sense to the more open-minded, and a witch hunt of colossal proportions could too easily ensue. The mortals, with their firepower, could end up destroying the only ones who could save them from Satanan's hell if the Mage succeeded in freeing him and his Daemon horde as the idiots seemed determined to do.

No, humans whose minds couldn't be cleared were a danger the Ferals could not tolerate. And yet, after so much carnage on that field of battle, none of them had had the stomach to end three innocent lives. So they'd brought the trio back to Feral House in hopes that the energy they'd consumed would wear off and make them once more susceptible to mind-clouding. They'd kept them unconscious as long as they could.

Esmeria stepped out of the cage. "All three are in need of liquids and some real sustenance, though nothing critical. Just feed them the next time they wake up. Since the unnatural energy is starting to wear off, you may be able to clear their minds now." The woman shrugged. "Or it might take another few days. It's impossible to know."

When Esmeria had gone, Wulfe shucked off his pants and shifted into his wolf. He curled up on the cool stone floor, where he could watch two of the captives and hear all three. The humans had been put in separate cages divided by thick stone walls. He lay in shadow, out of sight, in case any of them awoke suddenly.

Nearly an hour later, he heard footsteps on the stairs, his wolf's hearing identifying the one approaching by both scent and sound. His chief, Lyon.

Wulfe shifted back into his human form but didn't bother to pull his pants on. He wasn't a Feral who could keep his clothes on when he shifted and would just have to take them off again when he returned to wolf—the far more comfortable form for lying on the floor of the prison block.

Lyon appeared from the long passageway that led from the mansion's basement. When he reached him, Lyon extended his arm in greeting, as the Ferals always did. Touch was an important need to the Therians, particularly the Ferals, with their ties to the animals within them.

"Any change?" Lyon asked.

"They're still out. Any word from Kougar?"

The chief of the Ferals shook his head, a low growl rumbling from his throat. "I *hate* not being able to do anything for Tighe and Hawke. I trust Kougar to do what he can, but there's no way to know if he'll succeed. *We can't lose them.*"

Lyon stared into one of the cages. "The sooner we get these three stripped of their memories and out of here, the better. I don't like that they're here. And I sure as hell hope you can get into the male's memories if it turns out he's blind, as you suspect."

Minds were clouded and memories stripped by staring into the eyes. A blind person offered no easy entry. Possibly, no entry at all.

Wulfe shrugged. "I'll do what I can." Tighe would do better. He was the best at clouding human minds. But Tighe wasn't here and, goddess help them, might never be again.

The soft rustle of clothes on stone told him one of the humans was stirring, and he shoved back the grief that tried to crowd him at the thought of his friends lost in that spirit trap.

The blonde was the one stirring. He'd taken watch enough times over the past days to be well acquainted with which human lay in which cell. The blind male, who'd been ignored by the Daemons even though he'd been staked with the others, was in the cell out of his direct line of sight. The other two were females—the one with the lip ring who looked to be still in her teens, and the blonde who, he was certain, was older than the other two by at least eight to ten years. She was thirty, or close to it, her limbs long, her face pretty but for the three-inch gash one of the Daemons had opened in her cheek.

Wulfe had healed the cut enough to stop the bleeding, but she was going to have a hell of a scar. And if anyone knew a thing or two about scars, it was he. He rubbed his jaw, feeling the soft brush of day-old whiskers. Whiskers that did little to hide his own disfigurement—the hideous marks that had long ago transformed him from a male women admired into one from whom they ran.

At the sound of a soft feminine groan, he and Lyon both stiffened. "You'd better talk to her, Roar," he said quietly, reaching for the jeans he'd tossed against the wall. "She doesn't need any more terrorizing."

Lyon grunted. "I don't have much luck with terrified humans . . . or females who think they're human." Wulfe knew Lyon referred to the night he'd plucked their new Radiant, Kara, out of her human world with all the finesse of a bear in a flower garden. She'd adjusted beautifully, but apparently that had been one hell of a night. For both of them.

He and Lyon eyed one another, each looking to dodge this particular task, each certain the prison block was about to erupt in screams and/or tears.

"We need Kara," Wulfe muttered, pulling on his pants.

Lyon nodded, relief flooding his eyes before he turned back to the passage that led into the house. "I'll get her."

"Use your cell phone."

"It won't take but a few minutes."

"Coward."

"Not denying it." With a quick, feral grin, Lyon disappeared into the passage, leaving Wulfe alone with the waking human female. *Dammit.*

Safe in the shadows, Wulfe watched as the woman struggled to sit up, working her way back to full consciousness. Her blond hair was straight and mussed, her casual clothes wrinkled, but not visibly damaged. Confusion clouded soft gray eyes beneath knitted brows as she looked around. Lifting a hand, she touched the wound on her face and winced, then jerked and slowly turned to stone.

Remembering.

Her jaw dropped, her eyes at once flaring and tightening with pain and a horror few humans had experienced in the last five thousand years, and none had lived to tell about.

Here it comes. Wulfe tensed, prepared for a flood of tears and a few good screams, even before he showed his ugly face.

But no tears came. Instead, she shot unsteadily to her feet, grabbing the bars of her cage. "Xavier?" Her voice was hoarse with lack of use and raw with fear. "Xavier!"

The fear wasn't for herself, he realized. Not directly. He noted the modest diamond solitaire on the third finger of her left hand. Was the male her intended mate, then?

Her agitation grew as the seconds passed without answer. And while he could tell she was struggling to hold on to control, she was losing. The tears were beginning to spring up in her eyes though they'd yet to fall.

"Xavier!"

He'd been hoping to leave the woman to Kara. Like most males of his acquaintance, he took off . . . or wanted to . . . at the first sign of tears. But this one was fighting them so valiantly, he found he couldn't let her suffer.

"Is Xavier blind?" he asked from the shadows.

"Yes." The word burst from her lips, her gaze spinning toward him. Hope and fear shone in her damp eyes.

Damn. He was hoping he'd been wrong about the blind part. "He's unharmed, unconscious, as you were. He's in one of the other cells." From the angle of her cage and where the blind male was lying in his, he doubted she could see him.

Her forehead dropped to the bars, her shoulders bending as if crumbling beneath the weight of her relief. After several, deep, trembling breaths, she straightened again, once more spearing him with that gaze that he found oddly . . . visceral.

"Who are you?" By the tone of her voice, he wondered if she feared he was one of the Daemons.

"We're the ones who rescued you. You're safe now."

"Then why are we caged?"

Good question. And he couldn't see any reason not to tell her the truth. "We can't set you free until we're able to take your memories of us and all you've seen."

She was silent for a moment, as if processing that. Would a human believe memories could be taken? Then again, after all she'd seen, she was likely to believe anything.

"Then you'll let us go?"

He hesitated. "Yes." There was no sense in scaring her. But it was unlikely Xavier was going anywhere. Alive.

"Let me see him. *Please.*"

Ah, crud. Where is Kara? "Someone will be down soon . . ."

"*Please.*"

He'd given her hope that her male was alive, but no proof. And she clearly needed that proof. Hell. "All right. But . . ." *I'm ugly as sin.* "I'm not going to hurt you."

He sighed and stepped out of the shadows, watching her carefully, surprised when she seemed almost . . . relieved. Well, hell, of course she would be. She'd probably feared he'd be a Daemon.

The band of tension eased from his chest, and he strode to her cell and unlocked her door. She was out like a shot, brushing past him. Spying the male, she surged forward, clinging to the bars of the male's cage while Wulfe unlocked the cell door. The moment he swung it open, she bolted inside and fell to her knees beside the young man.

"Xavier? Xave?" Her hand went to his throat, to his pulse. As she clearly felt what she was searching for, she sank back on her heels, gripping one of Xavier's hands, the tension flowing out of her.

"Is he your mate?"

She turned to meet Wulfe's gaze, looking at him as if seeing him for the first time. But still no revulsion or fear crossed her features. "He's my brother."

Had the other human male been her mate, then?

As if reading his mind . . . or his expression . . . she shook her head. "My fiancé wasn't there." Remembered horror swam through those soft gray eyes. "The others . . . Jill, Mary Rose. They're dead, aren't they?"

He hated to add to her misery, but the knowledge lived in her eyes. There was no sense in lying to her. "Three died. Two females and a male. The remaining female is the one in that cage." He motioned across the block.

Her head snapped around where she could see the one with the lip ring clearly, but her expression didn't change. She clearly felt no relief.

"You don't know her."

"I . . . yes, I know her, or at least I know who she is. Her name is Christy. I only met her today. Her boyfriend is Mary Rose's brother. Was." She swallowed hard. "He was."

She'd handled all she could take, he could see

it in the faint shaking of her shoulders and the way she was beginning to hunch over with pain. Though five days had passed, she thought it had all happened today.

"What's your name?" he asked quietly.

"Natalie." Her voice was thickening with tears. "Natalie Cash."

"I'm sorry, Natalie."

A fat tear dripped from her cheek. Then another. Wulfe gripped several bars of the cage as he watched her struggle with the grinding grief, and loss. He'd expected to want to run at the first sign of tears. Instead, he felt a compulsion to move forward, not back. To try to comfort her, which was a laugh. He wouldn't even know where to begin.

Her crying grew worse, and she bent over, wracked with sobs.

If only he'd been able to take her memories in Harpers Ferry, she wouldn't have to suffer like this.

He straightened. Esmeria had said enough time might have already passed. He might be able to take them now.

Easing his big frame into the cell, he squatted beside her, hoping he didn't scare her by getting too close.

"Natalie?"

She straightened, looking at him with tear-drenched eyes, her hand going to her face as she choked on another sob.

"Look at me. Look into my eyes, and let's see if we can't make you forget."

Her head jerked. "I don't . . ." The sobs wouldn't leave her, and she quit fighting both of them and looked into his eyes as he'd requested.

He cupped her tear-damp jaw, his gaze dropping to the thick, grotesque gash across her cheekbone, then back up. Staring into gray eyes as deep as a storm-tossed sea, he attempted once more to cloud her mind and steal her memories, but as before, on the battlefield, nothing happened.

With a frustrated sigh, he released her and rose as she curled in on herself, swept away by the chaos of her emotions.

Kara and Lyon finally arrived, and he went to join them.

"No luck?" Lyon asked.

"No."

Kara made a sound of misery. "She's suffering, Lyon. Can't you steal her emotions as you did mine?"

"She's human."

Kara looked at him askance. "So? Until a few weeks ago, I thought I was, too."

Lyon caught Wulfe's gaze, his trepidation about going anywhere near a crying female clear in his expression.

Wulfe gave him a wry look. "This one's okay. Come on. She could use your magic touch." Lyon was the only one of the Ferals with that particular gift to any substantive degree.

He walked into the cage first and once more squatted beside the grieving woman. "Natalie? This is Lyon. He's going to help you. Give him your hand."

The woman struggled against the tide of tears, gasping as she straightened again, her gaze moving from Wulfe to Lyon with wary uncertainty.

Lyon held out his hand. "I won't hurt you."

Taking a deep, shuddering breath, she slowly placed her hand in Lyon's much larger one. Almost at once, the tension began to visibly drain out of her, the tears subsiding. "What are you doing?" Even her voice sounded almost clear again.

Kara came to stand in the doorway of the cell, a water bottle in one hand, a small bag of crackers in the other. "He's a healer of sorts. He helps heal broken hearts."

Lyon grunted. "I take emotions."

Kara smiled softly. "It's often the same thing. I'm Kara. I'm sorry for all you've been through." She handed Wulfe the water and crackers.

Wulfe screwed off the top of the water bottle and handed it to Natalie.

The woman took a long drink, her intrigued gaze returning to Lyon beneath tear-spiked lashes. "That's amazing, what you can do. I feel . . . okay, now. Like I can handle this."

The moment Lyon released her, she dug into the bag and pulled out one of the crackers. Her gaze swung to Wulfe. "How long have I been asleep? I'm starving."

"Longer than you think. Eat up."

Lyon rose and joined Kara at the cage's door, his arm going around his mate's shoulders.

"Esmeria says only one bottle of water and a few crackers this first time," Kara told him. "She needs to take it slow."

Within minutes, the crackers were gone and the water bottle empty.

Lyon steered Kara out of the cage. "She needs to sleep, Wulfe."

"Agreed."

Natalie's gaze snapped to his, wariness leaping into her eyes. "You're going to knock me out again. I watched what you did to Xavier and Christy. I know you did it to me."

He didn't deny it. "It won't hurt you, and the less you hear, the better for you and us both. I'll leave you in here with your brother if you'd like."

Her tension slid away. Slowly, she nodded. "All right."

Sliding his hand to the side of her warm neck, he found the spot beneath her ear with his thumb and pressed. He caught her as she collapsed. Beneath the acrid scent of fear and sweat that still clung to her, he smelled another. Her own scent. A calm gray-eyes scent, like a warm summer breeze.

Lifting her into his arms, he laid her on the opposite side of the small cage from her brother so the male wouldn't accidentally kick her when he woke, as he was sure to do soon.

As Wulfe left the cage and locked it behind him,

Lyon lifted a brow. "She didn't appear to be afraid of you."

"Why would she be afraid of Wulfe?" Kara asked.

Wulfe looked down at his chief's mate from his seven-foot height with his badly scarred face, and saw nothing but genuine puzzlement. Not for the first time he marveled at their good fortune in being blessed with this woman as their Radiant.

With a smile, he hooked his arm around her neck and pulled her to him for a hug as he met his chief's gaze. "Think of all she saw that day."

A quick smile of understanding flickered across Lyon's face. "Daemons. You're flat-out pretty compared to them."

Wulfe grinned, releasing Kara.

Lyon nodded toward the unconscious male. "Who is he to her?"

"Her brother. And she confirmed it. He's blind."

All hint of amusement left his chief's face. "Shit."

"Yeah." He felt the same way about the prospect of killing the male. But he wasn't sure how they were going to avoid it.

"Well, we don't have to do anything about them today. Do you want someone to spell you for a while?"

"No, I'm good."

Lyon clapped him on the back, slipped his arm around Kara's shoulders, and turned to leave.

Wulfe went to stand by the cage with the brother and sister, his gaze lingering on Natalie's tear-streaked face. A lightness filled his chest at the thought that for once, he looked damned close to normal. At least in the eyes of this woman. It was a novel experience.

Behind him, he heard the other female, Lip Ring, stirring. He turned slowly, watching as she sat up, as she opened her eyes and stared at him.

As she screamed.

Chapter Three

"Hi, Mr. McCloud. How are you feeling today?"

As Ariana strode into the ailing patient's hospital room, the elderly human looked up. Eyes tight with pain lit with pleasure at the sight of her.

"Hi, pretty girl. Did you finally transfer down here to the oncology ward?"

"No, I'm still in maternity." The poison inside her leaped to feed on the poor man's pain. Goddess, she hated feeding on others' misery, though it didn't hurt them. She took nothing from them and gave back what she could. "I'm off work and heading out, but I wanted to stop by and see you, first. I hear you're leaving us tomorrow."

He nodded, his face a mask of resignation. "Hospice. There's nothing more they can do for me here."

Stage-four bone cancer. Not only was he the quickest feed, but she'd learned he had little family and far fewer visitors than the others on the ward. So they gave to one another, though only she understood the true nature of the exchange.

An Ilina's natural energy was pleasure, not pain. But the poison inside her was another matter—a living thing that demanded the misery. Long ago, she'd discovered that the hungrier the darkness became, the less able she was to control it.

She gripped his frail hand. "I'm sorry."

"Me, too." He was silent a moment, then visibly shook off the pall. "Tell me about the Orioles. I hear they won."

As much time as she'd spent among humans these past centuries, she'd come to know and understand them well. She never failed to be humbled by the depth of their courage in the face of impending death.

"They did. They beat the Mets seven to six." She'd never acquired much of a taste for human sports, but Mr. McCloud was an avid baseball fan, and she kept tabs on the games so she'd have something to talk with him about. Something that might take his mind off his own terrible pain.

"You should have seen them in '96. What a team." While Mr. McCloud regaled her with stories of the Orioles' pennant race, the poison inside her exhausted body feasted.

For most of her years in exile, she'd acted as a midwife or maternity nurse, her Ilina nature feeding off the joy of childbirth even as the dark poison gorged on the accompanying pain. But sometime over the past couple of years, the balance had tipped. Either she was growing weaker, or the darkness inside her had grown in strength. Her feeding had had to grow along with it.

Deep inside, she felt a fluttering of panic that she was losing control. The fear that, after all these years of struggling to hold on, her strength would fail before Melisande caught the Mage sorcerer and forced an antidote from him.

And now, to make the disaster complete, Kougar was back, demanding explanations and aid she couldn't provide, their mating bond reconnected and endangering his life all over again.

She felt beaten, pummeled by emotions that had her torn between screaming and crying ever since Kougar walked back into her life three days ago and turned it upside down. She ached at the pain she knew he was in over the impending deaths of his friends. Yet she could do nothing. Nothing but ensure that he continued to hate her.

Letting his friends die ought to seal that hatred for eternity. Maybe someday she'd be able to make it up to him, when this nightmare was finally over. When they were both free of the threat of the poison.

It would happen. Melisande would find the bastard. Though she'd been saying that for nearly a millennium, she couldn't give up hope that someday this would all be a bitter memory. For a long time, she'd thought Kougar would be part of that future. Now she wasn't so sure.

If she didn't keep him hating her, he wouldn't be alive to see any future at all.

As the elderly patient's voice slowed, his eyes beginning to droop, Ariana patted his hand. "Get some rest, Mr. McCloud. You have a busy day tomorrow."

His eyes softened. "I won't see you again, pretty girl. Thank you for brightening an old man's last days."

Ariana bent down and brushed his cheek with her lips. "You'll have the best seats to all the games, soon."

His eyes crinkled. "From on high. I'll save you a seat, though you won't be needing it for a good many years."

He had no idea. She'd already lived nearly thirteen hundred and might live thousands more, despite her current inability to turn to mist. Killing an Ilina queen required cutting out her heart, which took a speed and slyness few possessed.

Ariana smiled softly, sadly. "Save me that seat." With a squeeze of his hand, she grabbed the purse she'd left on the chair by the door and headed home, her heart heavy, but the poison back under control. For a while.

The night was cool, a light fog blurring the edges of the streetlamps that lit the parking lot. As she made her way to her car, she shrugged, trying to ease the tension twisting her neck muscles, a tension she laid firmly in the lap of the mate she'd hidden from for a thousand years.

She strode through the parking lot, her gaze

skimming for movement, noting only a pair of young parents hurrying toward the Emergency Room with a feverish-looking toddler in arms. Ariana's inner radar had long ago become finely tuned to threats of any kind, but she sensed none. Not even the Feral who'd become the biggest threat of all. He wasn't anywhere near. Yet.

As she'd dressed for work two days ago, she'd discovered her name badge missing, and she was all too afraid she'd lost it in the Crystal Realm when Kougar attacked her. If she had, he'd found it. All she could do was hope that he wouldn't be able to use it to track her down since the hospital's name wasn't on it. But she felt far from safe.

Kougar was nothing if not determined.

For the past two days, she'd monitored the mating bond, seeking any sense of his drawing closer than normal, but she'd felt nothing. That didn't mean he wouldn't find her, only that he hadn't yet.

If she could just avoid him for the next week or two, until his friends caught in the spirit trap had died, she felt almost certain he'd go away and leave her alone again. Something inside her twisted at the callousness of that thought. The loss of so many Feral Warriors since she and Kougar had last been together was a tragedy. She'd known none of the shifters well, but Horse and the Wind had always treated her with kindness and even gratitude for the happiness she'd brought their friend. She was sorry she hadn't been there to save

Horse when he'd been caught in that spirit trap with the others. Sadly, it was the very fact that she'd come into Kougar's life that had ensured she couldn't save his friends. The Mage would never have attacked the Ilinas if they hadn't feared that the Ilinas might join forces with the Ferals against them.

She unlocked the door of her ten-year-old beige sedan, climbed in, and tipped her head back against the seat. Slowly, she unwrapped the bandage that covered her right wrist and the silver cuff set with six blood red moonstones, a cuff that she'd worn since that day she'd tried too hard to save her maidens and taken too much poison, then lost it all. The moonstones shored up her defenses, keeping her from accidentally turning to mist. Her boss wasn't fond of the bandage but preferred it to her flashing the jewelry. It was a compromise they could both live with.

With the bandage off, she pulled on the cardigan she'd left on the front passenger seat against the night's chill, started the car, and headed home. Over the years, she'd purchased three different homes in the D.C. area, rotating between them, careful to change her home and identity every fifteen to twenty years so the humans wouldn't notice that she never aged.

Each of her houses was situated at the outer edge of where she could sense Kougar and draw strength from the bond that had never entirely been severed between them, at least on her side.

She was careful to stay away from the Therian enclaves, where another immortal might spot her, though she doubted any would ever recognize her. Few Therians still lived who were over a thousand years old.

The drive to her current home, her favorite of the three, a small three-bedroom Cape Cod located in downtown Baltimore, took only ten minutes. She drove into the narrow drive and turned off the ignition, the sweet scent of spring flowers welcoming her as she stepped out of the car and made her way up the pavers to the front door.

Kougar's presence remained at a distance, not as far, perhaps, as Feral House in Northern Virginia, but a good distance, nonetheless.

All that mattered was that he wasn't here.

With another shrug, trying to loosen some of the tension in her neck and shoulders, she inserted the key into the lock and let herself into the dark living room. The streetlights illuminated furniture and shadows, revealing nothing out of the ordinary. Nothing moved. No sound carried to her ears. But as she closed the door behind her, a faint tingle pricked her skin, tripping her pulse. Telling her she was being watched.

Her breath caught. *She wasn't alone.*

But even as the adrenaline surged, her mind calmed. Even without her Ilina's energy, she was stronger than a human woman, equal in strength to any human male. And after a thousand years, her hand-to-hand combat skills were excellent.

She could handle him, whoever he was. Because he wasn't Kougar.

The intruder moved, faster than any human.

Shit.

She grabbed for her bracelet, to escape back to the Crystal Realm. Before she could reach it, an iron-strong hand clamped around her wrist, yanking it away from her body as a second snagged her other wrist.

He was too strong. Too fast. Too big.

Feral Warrior.

Crap, crap, crap. Damn Kougar. He'd known she'd be able to sense him and had sent another in his place.

With a swift backward kick, she slammed her heel into her assailant's knee and might as well have hit a brick wall.

"Do your worst, Sugar."

She slammed her head back, hoping to hit his nose, but he was too tall and she barely clipped his chin. "Where's Kougar?"

"On his way."

Double shit. She tried to twist out of his grasp, and for a moment thought she was succeeding until she realized he'd used her own momentum against her. Before she could stop him, he picked her up and pushed her against the nearest wall, wrenching one hand wide from her body. She'd forgotten how strong the Ferals were!

The cold bite of steel snicked around the wrist of her outstretched arm. And though she struggled, her second wrist quickly met the same fate. And then he was gone.

A moment later, she heard the click of a lamp, and light flooded her living room, illuminating her captor. Like the Ferals she'd known in the past, he was tall, broad-shouldered, muscular. A man women of all races noticed . . . and most lusted after. His hair was in need of a good cut, his pants camouflage, his black T-shirt revealing the golden armband that wrapped around his upper arm, an armband with the head of some kind of predatory cat.

The shifter pulled out his cell phone even as he watched her with curious eyes. "Got her. Now are you going to tell me who she is?" A brief look of disgust passed over his features as he put the phone away.

"Verbose, the man is not. So who are you, Sugar?" the Feral drawled. "Why are you so important that I'm babysitting you instead of making love to my new mate?"

She didn't answer, her mind furiously searching for a way out. Within the throbbing, erratic mating bond, she felt Kougar beginning to move toward her. *Hells bells.*

The shifter studied her. "You're not Mage. Number one, you don't have the copper rims around your irises. Number two, Captain Death didn't warn me not to let you touch me, and he would have if you'd been Mage." He gave a brief scowl. "Probably."

.

She cocked her head at him. "Captain *Death*?"

His mouth kicked up on one side. "The man's cold as, and delivers it mercilessly. Always has." His expression turned serious, his gaze flicking down over her scrubs. "I don't know what he wants with you, Florence Nightingale, but for your sake, I hope it's nothing more than a quick roll in the hay."

"Who are you?"

"I'm Jag. You've got to be Therian. You're stronger than a human, though not by much."

Smart-ass. "Kougar's making a mistake, Jag. A grave mistake. You need to let me go."

"Nice try, sweetheart. Do I have *idiot* engraved across my forehead?"

If only she still had the ability to turn to mist. With her hands cuffed, she was all but helpless. There was nothing more she could do but wait for Kougar, then hope she could manage one more escape.

Kougar strode up the front walk of the small bungalow, certain he had the right house. He could feel Ariana inside as strongly as any beacon, small bursts of anger pulsing through the mating bond. His plan to capture her had worked like a charm. Now came the hard part—forcing her to free his friends from the spirit trap.

Opening the door without knocking, he strode into the living room to find Jag on the sofa, his feet propped up on the coffee table, a baseball game on the television. Ariana stood with her back to the wall, her wrists caught in manacles Jag had attached to the wall.

He had to hand it to Jag. He'd carried out Kougar's directions precisely, though attaching her to the wall was a small bit of brilliance that was all Jag's. The drill he must have used sat on the coffee table.

Ariana's eyes speared him with fury. She was dressed again in medical scrubs, a black sweater over them this time. The clothing might be drab, but there was nothing plain about the woman wearing them. Her dark hair was up in a casual knot, her slender neck exposed and beckoning. Goddess how he'd loved to kiss her neck, to trail his mouth and tongue over the silken length from her shoulder to her ear, feeling her shiver, hearing the soft moan of pleasure in her throat.

Would this woman without a soul react to his touch the way his beloved had? Goddess, did he really want to know? No, he didn't. He wanted only one thing from her, and that was the rescue of his friends.

But as she watched him with hard, wary eyes, her mouth and chin stony, he knew it was going to be a battle all the way. He could hardly appeal to her compassion, not when the woman possessed none. Not anymore.

The cougar inside him leaped like an overeager pup, as if he longed to be free to race to her and lick her face. As if she were truly Kougar's mate and not some soulless look-alike.

She's not ours, Cat. She hasn't been for centuries.

"Release me, Kougar." Her eyes snared him, piercing in their intensity, even behind the brown contacts. He felt them stabbing, probing. Stroking the places deep inside him that had yearned for her for too long.

"Leave, Jag."

Out of the corner of his eye, he saw Jag rise lazily to his feet. "Just when things were getting interesting." But the shifter turned off the television, picked up his drill, and sauntered to the front door, closing it behind him.

Pulled by forces beyond his control, Kougar moved slowly toward Ariana, drawn against his will. His body throbbed with alternate bursts of cold and heat, his newly awakened emotions pingponging between hatred and a need to touch her that tore at every shred of control he possessed.

Closing the distance between them, he watched her, noting the shadows of thoughts and emotions she tried to hide. Her breathing was as unsteady as his own, a pulse kicking at the base of her throat. Though her anger was written all over her face, in her eyes he saw worry, dark hunger, and rank exhaustion. But no true fear. Which told him that pounding pulse was all for him. That the need he felt to touch her wasn't one-sided.

Which was good, very good, since the only way he knew to force her to turn to mist was to arouse her to it. To make her lose all control.

He grabbed her jaw, and his cat made a low growl of approval.

"Let go of me," Ariana hissed, her eyes flashing like those of a cornered beast ready to strike.

"No."

His hand shook as he held her jaw, her scent rising to ensnare him in sensual memories and painful longing. She was turning him inside out. His Ariana, yet not. She smelled the same, looked the same—or she would once she took those contacts out. She felt the same beneath his hand. But she wasn't the woman he'd loved.

Goddess, he needed to get away from her. To forget her.

But first, she was going to save his friends.

He tightened his grip. "Why do you think you can't turn to mist? What's the matter with you?"

She jerked her chin as if trying to dislodge his grip, her eyes flashing at him. "Dark spirit slowly eats away an Ilina from the inside out. Didn't you know?"

Kougar studied her. Melisande had said as much, but his instincts now, as then, told him there was more to it.

"You can turn to mist, Ariana. You're going to."

"No."

Again that flash of . . . defiance? Desperation?

He didn't want to see it.

Her mouth tightened, the full, unpainted mouth he'd dreamed of for a thousand years. His arms ached to pull her closer, yet his mind rebelled. She wasn't the woman he'd loved!

His cat clawed at him, urging him to claim her.

Ariana stared at him, flaying him with her

gaze even as she began to tremble beneath his hand. Her nostrils flared as she took a shuddering breath. Heat sparked in her eyes, igniting an inferno inside him.

He was losing the battle. "I have to taste you."

Her jaw tightened as if part of her wanted to object, but another part wouldn't let her say the words.

It wouldn't have mattered anyway. He dipped his head and pressed his mouth to hers. The feel of her lips against his, the achingly familiar taste of her released a floodgate of need and grief and desperate longing. At that moment, it didn't matter who she was, what she was. Ariana was back in his arms, her mouth opening beneath his, her tongue welcoming the desperate stroke of his own.

Her taste wasn't quite right. How he knew that after all this time, he didn't know, but didn't question. She still tasted as she always had, of crystal streams and summer nights, but overlying the sultry sweetness was another taste. A taste of darkness, and darkness had a taste all its own. A sharpness, a tang that was not unpleasant. But then darkness was often all too seductive.

His hands framed her face, his fingers weaving into her hair as he feasted on her mouth. His senses swam, his heart breaking. The feel of her beneath his hands, the taste of her kiss, the scent of her hair all rushed together, swamping him with memories, pummeling him with so many emotions he couldn't make sense of any of them.

His hands began to shake, a deep quaking

setting up inside him. How many times had he dreamed of having her in his arms again, of feeling her lips against his, her small breasts pressed against him? How many times had he longed to taste her kiss just one more time? To watch her spread her thighs and welcome him into her body? His Ariana. His woman. His mate.

But she wasn't, was she?

His Ariana—his bright, beautiful Ariana with the shining soul was not in his arms.

He tore his mouth from hers, released her, and stepped back. His hands were still shaking, his world tilting precariously. Whirling away from her, he strode to the window with harsh strides, his chest feeling like it was about to implode.

Goddess, he needed this over. He needed this woman . . . this *thing* . . . out of his life.

Pressing his hands to the window frame, he dipped his head and took deep, unsteady breaths. Every instinct he possessed told him to go, to get the hell out of there before she destroyed what was left of his sanity.

But he'd come for a reason. He had to force her capitulation, force her to enter the spirit trap. That was all that mattered.

Slowly, he turned back to face her. She watched him with eyes as deep as the darkest well, her mouth damp and full from his kisses. His body tightened, desire eclipsing everything else. He hated her. But, goddess, he wanted her.

He strode to her as he'd left her, his strides long and angry, but when he gripped her face this time, his fingers were steady. "I'm going to . . . fuck . . . this body of yours." He'd almost said *make love to*, but there was no love involved. Not anymore.

She swallowed visibly, the pulse pounding in her throat. But she didn't deny it.

He squeezed her jaw. "You're going to turn to mist, Ariana."

"If I do, I'll just escape you."

His grip tightened. "I'm aware of that. But then you'll return and help my friends, because if you don't, I'll give away your secret. I'll tell the immortal world you still exist."

She paled, and he felt a moment's hesitation as that old, fierce protectiveness tried to rise.

"You can't. You can't betray me, Kougar. The mating bond won't allow it."

He shoved off the protectiveness, reminding himself she wasn't the woman he'd loved, ignoring his cat's hiss of denial. "I'll find a way, never doubt that. And when I do, you soulless bitch, I'll destroy you and yours. I swear it. Unless you help me."

Her gaze never wavered from his. Shadows of fear slid through her eyes, then dissipated, replaced by a weariness that almost plucked at his sympathy.

"Do your worst, Kougar." Her words throbbed with exhaustion. Defiance, he would have understood, but not this. His threat hadn't hit its mark. Why not? Because she didn't believe he could betray her? Or because she truly didn't believe he could make her turn to mist?

The latter sent a frisson of fear skating down his spine. If he couldn't make her turn, his friends were dead.

Falling. Falling.

Hawke felt as if he'd been tumbling for hours, perhaps even days. One minute he'd been digging the heart out of one of the Daemon's throats, the next, the ground had fallen away, the earth opening to swallow him in a swirling red vortex.

He'd lost all sense of feeling, of sight, of sound. And the sense that he'd never landed was messing with his mind.

As was the fact that he had no idea where he was. Or how to get out. Inside him, his hawk let out a fierce and angry cry, clearly not liking this any more than he was.

Tighe had been right there beside him as the earth opened. Had he, too, fallen?

Tighe? Tighe! Lyon? Anyone?

They'd only be able to hear his telepathic call if they were in their animals. Would he be able to hear them if they responded? He couldn't even feel his body, though he knew his heart must be pounding, rivulets of sweat running down his neck. Everything primal inside him roared with a need to escape this forbidding darkness.

But he refused to panic. The same thing had happened inside the Mage stronghold in Harpers Ferry, from what he'd heard. Those Ferals who'd been caught inside had been unable to communicate with anyone. But they'd gotten free, and he had to believe he would, too.

Goddess help him if there was a Daemon in here as there had been in that other place.

Goddess help them all if the other Ferals had fallen, too. He'd only seen Tighe go down, but that didn't mean others hadn't been caught.

If only he could feel his body. Feel *something*.

He got his wish as sudden, searing pain tore through his mind. Not an external attack, but a pain that originated from within and radiated outward like a bomb going off in his brain.

Even as he ground his teeth against the raw agony, he welcomed the proof that he was still alive.

Sounds brushed his mind, the odd sound of a horse's whinny, and the growl of what sounded like a bear. Farther away, he heard other animal sounds. The low roar of a jungle cat and the cry of another bird of prey.

He listened with confusion until realization dawned. *Animal spirits*. Icy shock splayed across his mind.

The spirit trap. The very trap that had swallowed the seventeen.

His heart stuttered. It wasn't possible. The seventeen had disappeared in Scotland, not West Virginia. But what if that vortex hadn't been the trap itself but a wormhole to the original?

Dread curled deep in his mind.

Ferals didn't come out of spirit traps alive.

The seventeen had walked into one centuries ago and died, their bodies spit out days later. Their animals had never again returned to mark another.

Now he knew why. *The animal spirits were still here.*

And if he and Tighe didn't find a way to escape, their animals were about to meet that same terrible fate.

Chapter Four

Ariana's pulse pounded as Kougar's powerful body, dressed in all black, crowded hers, not quite touching her, but close enough that his heat called to her on the most primitive level.

She stood with her back pressed against her living-room wall, manacled, her body flushed and ready, desperate for the feel of him inside her even as her careening emotions threatened to sweep her away. The thought of him taking her in anger, in hatred, destroyed something inside her, yet on a purely physical level, her body reacted to his as it always had. Opening, turning moist and hot. She wanted him. Desperately.

That kiss . . .

She'd almost forgotten what it was like to be gripped by the powerful essence, the passion, that was Kougar, caught in the vise of his strength, drowning in his warm, masculine scent, a scent she'd never forgotten.

His kiss had left her shaking, bringing back all those old feelings in a rush of memory. A pleasure that rushed through her body, opening her, strengthening her, making her blood sing and her body long for his. But the storm of feelings he'd dredged up were so much more complicated.

She'd loved this man with an intensity that had left her blind to the danger, to anything but keeping him in her arms. It was that love for him, the insanity of their being together, that had brought such destruction. Such death. Such catastrophic joy.

He watched her, his pale eyes burning with a cold, carnal light as he plotted her seduction. *I'm going to fuck this body of yours,* he'd said. A chill danced over her skin, a fear that he'd see her bracelet. Because she was all too afraid he knew about red moonstones, that they kept an Ilina from turning to mist. If Kougar saw her cuff, he'd be furious.

Which meant she had to make certain he was too focused on getting inside her to notice anything else. Her true goal was to get him to free her hands. And the moment he did? She'd call on the transport magic woven into that cuff and be gone.

He reached for her, his fingertips trailing down her neck, sliding slowly, sensuously with a gentleness she knew he didn't feel. But the memory of how he'd once touched her in just this way, with aching tenderness, sparked a longing inside her for those lost days. The feel of his warm fingers on her skin sent tremors of desire vibrating down into her body.

He'd always given her such pleasure. She needed that again. The mere thought of his thick erection sliding inside her had her body melting, *wanting*. Five minutes in his company, and all she could think of was taking him inside her again.

But not like this, not for the reason he intended. Always in the past, as she'd climaxed around his swollen shaft, as he'd pumped his seed inside her, she'd turned to mist. It had been glorious for them both, a true melding of body and spirit.

That's all he wanted from her, now. To force her to turn to mist. He had no feelings for her anymore. Goddess, he thought she was soulless. He hated her.

And he'd hate her even more when he realized she would never save his friends.

Watching her with those pale eyes, he dipped his head, his mouth replacing his hand, his warm lips caressing her sensitive neck, his soft beard tickling her skin. She shivered, the need growing. As if he sensed her weakening, he grasped her waist, his hands sliding beneath her shirt, his fingers cool against the heat of her skin.

She inhaled deeply, arching at the delicious touch of him. Goddess, she had to get control. Already, her breathing was turning shallow, her breasts aching for the feel of his hands. Or mouth.

Think, Ariana. Seduce him. Seduction came as easily as breathing to an Ilina. Pleasure—her own and others'—was a necessary source of strength for a mist warrior. The challenge was to avoid falling into the seduction herself.

"Let me see you." Her voice sounded husky even to her own ears. "I want to see you, Kougar." At the thought of him removing his clothes, her body began to give off the mating scent few immortal males, and no human, could resist.

His eyes darkened. Her own quick glance below his waist told her his body was more than ready.

Behind her contacts, her eyes began to tingle in a way that told her they'd started to sparkle with sexual heat—another natural seduction she hadn't felt in far too long. There'd been no one in a millennium whom she'd wanted to seduce. But her eyes would do little to attract him hidden, as they were, behind the contacts she'd worn for years in the unlikely event she stumbled into the path of an immortal who might recognize her too-blue eyes for what they were—Ilina eyes.

"Release one of my hands, Kougar. My contacts are growing uncomfortable."

"No." The word came out rough, little more than a growl. "Leave them in." His own eyes had turned silver, his pupils dilated. His breaths were becoming as shallow as her own.

It was a game they both played, now. Maintain as much control as possible while seducing the other. It was a game he wouldn't win. But could she?

"Let me see you, Kougar," she said huskily. "Take off your shirt for me."

He ignored her, his mouth moving lower, to the flesh bared by the vee neck of her scrubs. His hands rose beneath her shirt, his fingers brushing against her abdomen, then sliding up and over her breasts to claim them. The feel of his hands on her, cupping her, squeezing her, had her arching into his touch and gasping with true pleasure.

He released her suddenly, and she made a sound of dismay before she could stop herself, then quieted, holding her breath when he reached behind her to unfasten her bra. A moment later, he pushed the lacy garment up and out of his way, covering her breasts, skin to skin, her sensitive nipples brushing the rough curve of his palms.

Her head tipped back at the achingly right feel of his touch. She reveled in the roughness of that touch, which revealed his own growing need. He dipped his head, pushing her shirt out of his way with an impatient tug, and sucked the fullness of one hungry breast deep into his mouth.

Ariana moaned, her hips rocking, her body hot and wet, burning to be filled by this man whose touch she'd missed so desperately. "Kougar . . ."

Still suckling her breast, he grasped the waistband of her pants with hands as unsteady as the pounding of her heart and pushed them down over her hips. With a low growl, he released her breast, meeting her gaze with eyes like hot steel before he stepped back and turned his attention to her feet. With quick, efficient movements, he pulled off her shoes and socks, then yanked her pants down her legs and off.

She stood shaking before him, wanting what he was about to give even as her heart rebelled.

His breathing shallow and erratic, he rose and met her gaze again, a rich, carnal promise in his eyes. And a hard determination that told her that he was still firmly in control. Ripping that control from him was never going to happen. This was his game, his experiment—to see if he could make her turn to mist.

And he was going to fail.

But oh how her body looked forward to the trial, even as her heart ached at the callousness of it. She longed to tell him the truth—that she'd never lost her soul. That she loved him still and always had.

But the truth was far too dangerous. All she could do was play this out and keep him safe, the wreckage of her heart a price she gladly paid.

The breaths tore into Kougar's lungs, the oxygen barely reaching his brain as all the blood in his body pulsed and throbbed between his legs. He pressed his pelvis against hers, a hiss tearing between his teeth at the damp heat he swore he could feel even through the fabric of his pants. As if his cat had taken over, he found himself rubbing his cheek against her hair, marking her with his scent even as her own scent made his blood pound a deep, thunderous beat.

He was losing control.

He'd meant to excite Ariana to release, taking her with his fingers or his mouth, forcing her to turn to mist, proving to them both that she could—that she was either a liar or, at the very least, mistaken. But the moment he'd started to touch her, his need for her—for the woman she used to be—crashed over him like a pent-up wave.

He had to get this over with to prove his point and secure her cooperation. Then he'd be done with her once and for all. But his body wanted more. His cat growled at him to claim her completely, to make her his again as she'd once been. And the soft feelings he'd lived with for so long demanded that if this was the only time her body was to be his again, he savor every moment.

It was a mistake to give in, he knew that. The more he tasted her, the more he touched her, the more he remembered. And the deeper the pain corkscrewed into his heart that this wasn't the Ariana he wanted.

Nothing would bring his love back to him. Joining with her fully would only drive that fact home. But he could touch her. He could see her. And, dammit, he needed to see her—the queen, not the nurse. His glorious Ariana. One last time.

Drawing claws, he ripped her shirt down the middle, then her bra. Then he shredded the sweater and shirt from shoulders to wrists in one quick move that left her skin unscathed. As he reached her right wrist, his claws clinked against metal, a bracelet of some sort.

With a quick tug of destroyed fabrics, he bared her from the waist up.

Her breasts lifted on a gasp as she stood before

him in nothing but a scrap of white lace panties and the silver bracelet winking at her wrist.

His chest contracted, his heart taking a hammerblow as he stared at the body of the woman he'd loved for so long, this body he'd once known every inch of, every freckle, every taste.

She was glorious. More beautiful even than he remembered, her breasts perfectly shaped, her waist small, her hips sweetly rounded, and her legs lithe and shapely. He'd loved touching her in bygone days. Loved trailing his lips and tongue over every inch of the skin now revealed to his hungry eyes. How he longed to kiss her shoulder, trailing his lips down her arm, over the curve of her elbow, all the way to her wrist. . .

He stilled as his gaze, which had been following his thoughts, snagged on that bracelet. A silver cuff set with . . . *red moonstones.*

Fury stirred as a growl rumbled in his chest.

"Kougar, wait!"

"You *bitch.*" Moonstones kept an Ilina from turning to mist. No wonder she was so certain he couldn't turn her. She'd have convinced him she couldn't help, then disappeared on him yet again. Leaving his friends to die.

He grabbed for the bracelet.

"Kougar, don't!"

With a single furious move, he unsnapped the manacle that bound her to the wall, pried open the offending bracelet, and tossed it across the room.

"No!" A desperate horror sliced through Ariana's voice, her skin turning suddenly, deathly pale. "The cuff." Her eyes clutched at him, wide and terrified. "I'll tell you everything. Just give me the cuff!"

Kougar stared at her, part of him wanting her to suffer as he was suffering. Another part of him, driven by the cat inside him, desperate to protect her from whatever was causing her such distress.

Even knowing what she was, the sight of her anguish was a blade twisting in his gut. With a frustrated burst of air, he went to retrieve the bracelet from the rug by the foot of the sofa.

Returning to her, he clasped it back around her wrist. At once, the tension left her on a shuddering sigh as she collapsed against the wall behind her, eyes closed. "It's okay, it's okay, it's okay," she murmured, the litany, a desperate mantra.

He kept hold of her wrist, suspecting the bracelet held the transport magic she'd used to escape him before, and he wasn't letting her go again. Not until he knew what the hell was going on.

Suddenly, she stiffened, her eyes flying open, eyes filled with shock and terror.

"Ariana." Though one manacle kept her chained to the wall, he grabbed her as her knees gave way beneath her. "Tell me."

Her gaze lifted to his, her eyes deep wells of horror. "*He knows.*" A tense quaking invaded her body.

Kougar felt like he'd walked into the middle of a

movie he knew nothing about. He lifted his hand, cupping her face, his thumb brushing her cheek. "Who knows, Ariana?"

"I have to get to my maidens, Kougar. They're in danger." Her voice trembled, her eyes almost wild. "You have to let me go!"

"Tell me what's going on."

She struggled against his hold, thrashing wildly. "Let me go!"

Inside, his cat yowled with distress. His gut knotted at the anguish in her eyes. But if he let her go now, he might lose his only chance to save Hawke and Tighe. He couldn't be certain where she'd go. And if it wasn't the Crystal Realm, he wouldn't be able to follow.

He tightened his grip on her jaw, forcing her to look at him. A sheen of perspiration dampened her too-pale skin. "You're not going anywhere until you tell me what's going on, Ariana."

He waited as she struggled to pull herself together though her breaths remained ragged, and her lips pressed together with a faint tremble that told him she was close to tears. She blinked hard, pulled in a shuddering breath, and met his gaze.

"Who knows?" he prompted quietly.

"A Mage." She tried to look away. "The moonstones have kept him from finding me. He'll attack us."

Kougar frowned. "I didn't think anyone knew you were alive." Those who knew the truth had a way of dying beneath Melisande's sword. Or being dragged back to the Crystal Realm to die there.

"He didn't. Now he does."

Kougar stared at her, struggling to fill in the blanks. Since when did the Mage attack Ilinas?

"He's attacked you before?" He stilled. "When, Ariana?"

She glanced at him, but couldn't hold his gaze. "A hundred years ago."

"You're lying." Goose bumps erupted on his arms as understanding crashed over him. "Not a hundred years ago, but a thousand. Am I right?"

When she didn't answer, he squeezed her jaw harder. "Am I right?"

"Yes! Yes, it was a thousand years ago." She met his gaze, truth and anguish in her eyes. "He all but destroyed us. The moonstones were all that's kept us safe. I don't know why he couldn't sense me through them, but he couldn't." Tears began to roll down her cheeks. "But now he knows."

Kougar reeled at the implications. "It was never dark spirit that attacked you, *but a Mage*?"

His breath lodged in his throat as his world flipped upside down, as Ariana rewrote thousand-year-old history in the space of seconds. Twenty-one years ago he'd learned the Ilinas weren't extinct. That Ariana still lived. Twenty-one years later, he was still reeling from that revelation. But this rocked him even more. Because if Ariana hadn't been attacked by dark spirit . . . *she wasn't soulless*. The woman he'd loved still lived.

His hands began to shake.

"Why didn't you tell me?"

Her lashes swept down, tears running down her cheeks. "Kougar . . . it was a long time ago."

"Why didn't you tell me?"

"Because I should never have mated with you in the first place!" Brown eyes snapped open, desperation and anger in their depths. "If I'd never taken you to mate, the Mage would have had no reason to attack us. Nearly two-thirds of my maidens died, Kougar." She shook her head, a bleakness in her eyes that mirrored that rushing through his heart. "If he attacks again, all will die. He'll win."

His head pounded. Only one thing shone through the chaos, crystal clear. *She wasn't soulless.*

The hand holding her wrist spasmed. With his other, he gripped her chin, forcing her to meet his gaze. "Take off your contacts."

"I need both hands."

And the moment he released her, she'd try to escape.

"Open your eyes wide."

She made a grunt of annoyance but didn't fight him as he released her jaw and plucked out the soft discs, one after the other, tossing them on the floor.

"Look at me."

She lifted her gaze to his with a slow, thick sweep of dark lashes. Defiant eyes. Brilliant blue eyes he'd drowned in once upon a time. And in those eyes, her soul, Ariana's soul, shone brightly. His cat had known all along.

His chest caved as if beneath the swing of the sledgehammer. The woman he'd loved wasn't gone at all. She never had been.

He should feel relief. Maybe even joy.

Instead, he couldn't breathe. Everything he'd believed for a thousand years was a lie. That she'd been infected by dark spirit and destroyed her race. That she'd died. *That she'd loved him.*

She'd wounded him physically. Emotionally. *Intentionally.* With a cruelty beyond comprehension. Then walked away.

He stared at her, at the stranger he'd loved, his mind trying to rewrite those two short years they'd been together.

His cat growled at him, but he ignored the beast. Yes, he'd been right. This Ariana *was* the woman he'd mated all those years ago. But she'd never been the woman he thought she was. That woman would never have ripped his heart out of his chest and walked away, leaving him injured by a severed mating bond, leaving him to grieve for a millennium. The woman he'd thought she was would never have been so cruel.

Raw anger sparked into flame.

She lifted her free hand, reaching for her bound wrist. *She meant to escape him.*

He grabbed her, fury seething, tearing at him like finely honed blades, ten times worse than the

fury he'd felt before. This was the agony of betrayal.

His hand clamped around her wrist too tight,
her fine bones close to breaking beneath his grip.
And he didn't care. White-hot pain seared his
mind and heart. Everything he'd believed was a
lie. His marriage. His love.

Goddess. He couldn't breathe. Tipping his head
back, he struggled for control, struggled to think.
The past couldn't be undone. But the future. . .

He released her wrist to grab her shoulders in
the same punishing grip. His jaw ached from
the clench of his teeth. "You're going to free my
friends."

"I can't! I can't turn to mist."

"Why not?" he roared.

"The poison. If I turn to mist, I'll release the
poison into my maidens. They'll die."

He stared at her, seething. Aching. And came to
a decision.

"We're going to figure out what we have to do to
free you from the magic, then you're going to save
my friends. After that, I don't give a damn what
you do or where you go."

"I have to go to my maidens."

"You're coming to Feral House."

"No!" She bared her teeth at him with a hiss.
"I'm not going there with you."

His eyes turned to steel. "Yes. You are." He
jammed his thumb beneath her ear, then caught
her as she collapsed against the wall, unconscious.

He'd loved her once, body, heart, and soul, and she'd betrayed him, consigning him to purgatory for a thousand years. Never again would he willingly allow her into his life. When this was over, when Hawke and Tighe were safe, she could go to hell.

Chapter
Five

Ariana jerked awake to the feel of powerful arms lifting her amid a cool night breeze. She blinked at the sight of the unfamiliar landscape of thick woods pierced by the early light of dawn. Kougar's scent hit her, and it all came roaring back—the confrontation in her house, his removing the moonstone cuff. *Hookeye.* Her heart began to pound.

The Mage she called *Hookeye* knew she was alive.

Carrying her, Kougar closed the door of an expensive-looking sports car with his hip. Her wrists were bound together with duct tape, no doubt to keep her from reaching her bracelet and disappearing on him again.

She'd known the moment she saw him standing within the walls of the Grand Corridor that his reappearance in her life was going to spell disaster. But she'd never guessed it would happen so quickly.

Goddess, she had to warn Melisande and the others!

"Kougar, let me down," she commanded, staring at the hard, shadowed lines of his arresting face. "Let me go. My maidens could be in danger!"

"Have you turned to mist?"

"No, of course not."

"Then they're safe. Isn't that what you implied?"

"I can't be sure." But he was right. The greater danger was that Hookeye would pump more poison into the mating bond itself. Too much for her to control.

She squeezed her eyes closed against the fear that threatened to overwhelm her, then opened them again on a shuddering breath. All she could do was hold on and fight the poison attack when and if it came. And she would fight. To the end. She hadn't held on for so long only to give up now.

As Kougar carried her across a wide, circular drive lined with vehicles, her gaze took in the monster of a house looming before her. No, not a house. A mansion, with dormers on the top floor and black shutters framing each of the windows. Though sunrise was still a good half hour away, light glowed from all the downstairs windows and several of the upper ones—three brick stories lit up like a prison after an escape.

A prison full of shape-shifting Feral Warriors.

Her pulse faltered, perspiration dampening the

back of her neck. No one but Kougar knew the Ilinas still existed. Now he was about to wrench that secret wide open.

At least before he'd kidnapped her he'd taken the time to dress her in the pair of jeans she'd left hanging on her bedroom doorknob and a fitted red T-shirt from her closet. If she wasn't mistaken, he'd even found her a bra.

At the base of the stairs leading up to a massive front door that was easily half again as wide as most, and a good eight feet high, Kougar dropped her bare feet to the walk and grabbed hold of her arm.

She fought him as he tried to propel her forward.

"Kougar, no. Let me go to them, let me see for myself that they're all right. Then I'll come back."

He didn't reply, which was answer enough. He didn't trust her.

And he shouldn't. The moment she got free, she was leaving. The Ferals would try to force her to turn to mist and save their friends, regardless of the consequences. If her race perished as a result, it would simply be an unfortunate case of collateral damage.

She had no reason to trust them. Not since the Daemon War had the two races been allies, and both their peoples had disapproved of her and Kougar mating. While she'd loved Kougar, she'd never really trusted any of the other shapeshifters, with the possible exception of his two closest friends. And at least one of them, she knew, was dead. No, the Ferals weren't going to have it their way. No way in hell would she allow them to sacrifice her people to save their own.

Kougar led her up the front steps and through the wide door, ushering her into a high-ceilinged foyer. Lights from a large, crystal chandelier sparkled upon the heavy green-and-gold floral wallpaper that belonged to a bygone age, while twin staircases curved downward in a sinuous dance, drawing the eye to the floor, where a lush painted mural enchanted with all manner of mythical creatures.

As Kougar closed the door behind them, two large men strode into the foyer, each eyeing her with surprise and no small amount of curiosity. One was badly scarred and huge. The other, a man with a tawny mane and nice clothes, gave off an air of command that made her suspect he was one of the leaders of the warriors. And they were definitely Feral Warriors. Even if she weren't in Feral House, she'd know that the men were shifters by the sheer, raw power they exuded.

Jag descended one of the twin stairs, a petite redheaded woman at his side. He gave a grunt as his gaze landed on Ariana. "Already bringing her home to meet the family?" His brows drew together as he stared at her. "What's with the neon baby blues? I'd have noticed eyes like that."

Kougar ignored him, ushering her toward the nearest hallway. The men followed, the one she'd nailed as one of the leaders calling out, "War room. Now!"

Moments later, Kougar propelled her into a

large wood-paneled room with a huge conference table ringed by upholstered executive-type chairs. The rips in the cushions of a couple of the chairs and the occasional cracks and dents in the wall paneling gave telling evidence that this particular office space belonged to men who were not quite civilized.

Kougar pulled out a chair for her, then shoved her into it, reminding her that his anger was alive and well. She felt his anger like a physical ache that lodged itself between her shoulder blades, right where she imagined he'd like to stab her.

When Kougar took the seat beside her, she glanced at him in surprise. She would have thought the chief would stand at the front of the room, but perhaps their ways were different. As the others followed them into the room, she saw it was the man with the tawny mane and rust silk shirt who took that place. A man who wore the mantle of leadership like a comfortable cloak.

Her palms were sweating, but there was nothing she could do about it with her wrists bound together. Nothing but wait for Kougar to rip her world to shreds.

She glanced at him stonily. "When did you stop being chief?"

Kougar's eyes were cold when he met her gaze. "The day I lost my mate."

Ariana stared at him, his words sinking in slowly. The death of one's mate was known to cripple many an immortal, but because of Melisande's intervention, she'd never suffered unduly from the severing of the mating bond. She'd assumed Kougar hadn't either. He'd been a strong, natural leader back in those days. What must she have done to him, for him to have been unable to continue? Her stomach gave an involuntary cramp. She'd never considered she might have injured him like that.

Goddess, they'd hurt one another in so many ways.

And he was about to hurt her all over again.

She leaned toward him, gritting her teeth. "Don't do this, Kougar. Let me go."

He met her gaze, his eyes like flint, then turned away.

"Damn you." She clenched her hands into fists, watching as others filed into the room, recognizing none of them from the old days. Jag and the redhead entered first, followed by a bald Feral with what appeared to be a snake earring hanging from one lobe and a viper's head armband curving around his upper arm.

As a tall, dark-haired woman walked in, grief and battle in her eyes, the chief greeted her, compassion in his voice. "Delaney."

The woman gave a nod. "Lyon."

All took their seats around the table, each eyeing her with avid curiosity. Was it so unusual for them to bring a stranger into their midst?

"Where are the others?" she asked Kougar softly.

"Paenther's the only one not here."

Goddess, no wonder they were so desperate to retrieve the two from the spirit trap. He'd said their numbers had dwindled, but the evidence was shocking. Five Feral Warriors in this room when once there had been more than two dozen.

"The Wind?"

"Dead. His son is one of those in the spirit trap."

The breath went out of her with the unwelcome ache at the losses he'd suffered. "I'm sorry."

When everyone had taken a seat, the chief, Lyon, turned to Kougar. "The Shaman is on his way, as you requested." His amber gaze flicked to Ariana, then back again. "What's this about?"

Kougar remained still and silent for ten long seconds before reaching up to stroke his beard once, twice. His hand returned to his chair's arm while those around him watched. And waited.

Finally, he spoke, his voice low, yet as rich and hard as mahogany. "This is Ariana, Queen of the Ilinas."

Gasps and other sounds of disbelief erupted like scattershot around the room, half a dozen gazes spearing her, staking her to her chair.

Kougar turned to her, his eyes like flint. "My mate."

As quickly as the noise erupted, it receded as if Kougar's words had sucked the room dry of sound, turning the space silent as a morgue. The only sound was her heart pounding in her ears.

Every eye widened, every jaw dropped, the silence growing thicker, heavier, until it bruised her skin, until it pressed against her rib cage and threatened to crush her lungs.

Still, they stared.

"Holy *shit*," Jag exclaimed, shattering the awful tension. "You're *married*?"

And suddenly everyone was talking at once.

"The Ilinas have been extinct . . ."

"Did you *know*?"

"Is she the only survivor?"

"Silence!" Lyon took control. Though the talking stopped, the room was anything but quiet as the Ferals leaned forward, their expressions confused, wary, excited.

Kougar's voice slid into the void. "A millennium ago, the Ilinas were attacked by a sorcerer's magic, a poison that killed many of them." Quickly and succinctly, he relayed what little she'd told him.

When he was done, Jag shook his shaggy head, his expression ripe with disbelief. "You've known all along the Ilinas were alive?"

"No." The word was hard, clipped. "Like everyone else, I thought they were dead. I only learned the truth twenty-one years ago."

"The mating bond . . . ?" The scarred man's words were low, his tone pained.

Kougar met his gaze. "Severed, Wulfe."

The sympathetic tightening of the other Feral's eyes stabbed Ariana with guilt.

"That shouldn't be possible."

"She's Ilina." Kougar's tone said they were worse than dirt.

"You left Harpers Ferry to find her," Lyon said. "You think she can help us save Tighe and Hawke."

"I did."

The brunette's eyes widened as they locked on her. "Dear God."

By the fragile hope in the woman's desperate eyes, Ariana knew one of those Ferals was her mate.

Ariana sighed, hating to deliver the blow. "I can't help them."

The woman surged to her feet, her expression turning battle-hard. "You have to."

A warm tingle teased the back of Ariana's neck, a feeling as familiar as the beat of her heart. *No.* The scent of pine wafted on the air, the scent of the Crystal Realm.

Kougar must have smelled it, too, for he shot to his feet. "Attack!"

Even as he roared the word, the room exploded with the flash of steel, the splatter of blood, and the roar of fury and pain.

Melisande and half a dozen mist warriors took form around the room, stabbing the Ferals with their knives, flinging painful energy. Attacking without provocation though Ariana doubted Melisande saw it that way. Brielle had no doubt felt Ariana's agitation. Her fear. And Melisande had led the cavalry to the rescue.

But if Feral blood spilled, Ilina blood would soon follow.

And Feral blood was spilling.

Kougar pulled his knives and started swinging even before the six mist warriors turned fully solid and launched their attack.

Led by Melisande, the Ilinas were out for blood, aiming for hearts and heads as the Ferals drew blades to parry the attack. Vhyper took a knife to the shoulder, moving an instant before Melisande's blade pierced his heart. Lyon took a knife to the back, but it didn't seem to slow him down.

Jag and Wulfe shifted into their animals, their teeth bared.

"Cease!" Ariana yelled, on her feet beside Kougar. Her general's tone shot through the room, stilling her maidens' blades as the women lost full substance, but not form, becoming wraiths through which a blade would pass and never find purchase.

The Ferals faced off with the wraiths, the jaguar and wolf snarling, the others' blades ready to attack the moment the women returned to flesh and blood.

Only one battle persisted. Melisande continued to fight Lyon, blade to blade. The hatred in the blond mist warrior's eyes told Kougar she was waiting for the right moment to turn her energy blast on the Chief of the Ferals. The savage light in Lyon's eyes said she was about to die for her efforts.

Kougar wouldn't care, except that Melisande's death would devastate Ariana. "Don't kill her, Roar."

Ariana lifted her bound arms straight in front of her as if preparing to fire a pistol. Kougar was about to stop her when he realized her aim wasn't on Lyon but on her own out-of-control lieutenant.

Melisande flew off her feet as if she'd been launched, turning to mist and disappearing an instant before she slammed into the wall. A neat trick.

Silence descended except for the low growling and snarling in the throats of the wolf and jaguar.

"How the hell did they get in here?" Lyon roared.

Kougar eyed the remaining Ilinas, satisfied they were firmly under their queen's control. "Mist warriors come and go as they please."

"Like hell."

Out of nowhere, Melisande reappeared atop the conference table, holding a short sword at either side, her eyes blazing with fury. A fury this time aimed at her queen.

The jaguar crouched as if to spring.

Kougar lifted his hand.

"Hold, Jag," Lyon ordered.

Melisande's form faded to ghostlike, a faint red glow around her edges. Anyone who attempted to attack her like that would think he'd shoved his fist into a light socket. Ilina defensive energy was a bitch, and damned dangerous. A human or Therian could be caught in it and dragged to the Crystal Realm to die. A Feral was too strong to be transported against his will unless the Ilinas ganged up on him. Then it was anyone's game.

Hatred lit Melisande's eyes. "They have to die!"

Ariana pulsed with fury beside him. He could

feel it through the mating bond and see it in the angry lines of her body. But when she spoke, her voice was low, woven with steel.

"Stand down, Melisande. They are not the enemy."

"They know about us, now!"

"*He* knows, Mel. Hookeye knows."

Slowly, Melisande's eyes widened, her fury evaporating beneath real fear as she jumped from the table with a soft, graceful leap to land in front of Ariana.

Kougar grabbed Ariana, gripping her upper arm to keep the other Ilina from stealing her away. Ariana's bound wrists might keep her from transporting herself, but any one of her maidens could take her, bound or not. If they tried while he held on to her, they'd have to take them both.

"How does he know?" The words were little more than a breath, as if driven from Melisande's body by a gut blow.

"It doesn't matter. He knows. I saw his eyes again."

Melisande swayed, her face turning chalk white. "It's over."

Kougar had always found it hard to like the woman, especially knowing how strongly she detested him and his entire race, but he found himself almost feeling sorry for her. Almost.

Ariana shook her head. "Maybe not, Mel. Maybe it's not over yet. The Ferals need me to turn to mist before their friends die in the spirit trap. Maybe they can help us find a way to end this." Ariana glanced at Kougar, meeting his gaze briefly with eyes that held little trust in her own words.

Melisande scoffed. "The spirit trap will destroy their friends within days."

"We've nothing to lose by enlisting their help."

A scowl darkened the mist warrior's face. "Do you really believe that?"

Ariana didn't reply, her lack of response answer enough.

Lyon's voice broke the uncomfortable silence. "Save our friends from the spirit trap, and we'll do whatever it takes to help you find a cure for the poison."

"Stupid shifter," Melisande muttered.

Ariana silenced her with a look and turned to Lyon. "You don't understand, Chief of the Ferals. The only way I can breach the spirit trap is as mist. And if I turn to mist, my maidens will perish."

Kougar felt the hope that had briefly flared in the room die a quick, agonizing death. Tighe's wife, Delaney, sank back in her chair as if she barely possessed the strength to hold herself upright.

Kara's voice broke the thick atmosphere from the doorway. "The Shaman's here, Lyon." Kara, Lyon's mate, strode into the room, the Shaman close behind her.

The ancient Therian stopped just inside the doorway, staring from one mist warrior to the next, his eyes growing wide with excitement.

"Ilinas," he murmured. "Extraordinary."

Though he looked like a fifteen-year-old kid,

Kougar knew the Shaman to be well over six thousand years old, probably closer to ten. He'd been considered one of the Old Ones when Kougar was a boy.

Lyon lifted his hand, once more demanding the full attention of those in the room. "Queen Ariana, I'm willing to move heaven and earth to save my two warriors. If that means saving the Ilina race first, then we'd better get started. But I want your warriors out of my house and your promise that they'll never return unannounced or uninvited again. Or next time, the Ferals will rip their hearts out." His hard gaze landed on Melisande. "Is that understood?"

That commanding gaze swung to Ariana. "You'll remain with us until this is over."

Ariana stiffened. "I'm safer in the Crystal Realm, where he can't reach me."

"Unacceptable."

Kougar could feel her agitation rising. He understood her need to be with her maidens, especially when she considered them at risk, but he suspected equal to that need was her distaste of the idea of staying in this house. With him. He couldn't say he was thrilled himself, yet Lyon was right to demand she remain. If they let her go, she might never return.

Ariana's jaw turned hard. "My warriors have to be able to reach me. To contact me."

"Communicate telepathically," Kougar said.

"I've been corporeal so long that I can't hear them any longer. Communication between us is only one-way. A few of them can still hear me. Or sense my emotions if they're strong. I'm sure that's why they attacked."

Brielle nodded.

"One warrior only, then," Lyon said. "Flesh and blood, and she comes to the back door and knocks. Not Melisande. She's no longer welcome anywhere near Feral House, and if she approaches any of my warriors or their wives again, it will be considered an act of war."

Melisande threw up her hands with a look of disgust.

"Return to the Crystal Realm, Mel." Ariana's voice, though quiet, brooked no argument. "All of you except Brielle."

Lyon lifted an eyebrow.

"She knows things that could be of help. I'll send her away when we're done here."

"Fair enough," the Chief said.

With an angry wave of her hand that made the windows rattle, Melisande disappeared. A moment later, the others followed, leaving only Brielle and Ariana behind.

A heavy silence blanketed the room for several moments, then Jag and Wulfe shifted back into their man forms, both sans clothes. Jag strode to the chest in the corner and pulled out a couple of pairs of sweatpants, tossing one to Wulfe.

Delaney leaned forward, her eyes gleaming with a desperate determination. "Where do we start? Tighe and Hawke don't have much time."

"Everyone, have a seat," Lyon ordered quietly.

Kougar held Ariana's chair, releasing her arm, but she shook her head, restless agitation radiating from her in waves. As she stepped away from him, Kougar tensed, ready to grab her again, not trusting her not to try to escape him.

But when she turned to him, the raw despair in her eyes turned to a physical ache beneath his breastbone, and he let her go. His gaze never left her as she walked to the window, her stride graceful and sure despite her bound hands, her shoulders bowed by the weight of her fear.

Lyon's gaze, too, followed her. "We need to know everything you know, Queen Ariana, if we're to help you."

Ariana turned to face his chief, her bearing proud, her eyes flashing with determined fire despite her agitation. Kougar doubted anyone else sensed that agitation but him. Watching her, he saw again the indomitable, fierce beauty he'd fallen in love with.

A mistake he would not repeat.

"We were attacked by Mage magic a thousand years ago." Her voice clear and strong, she continued. "I'd chosen to take Kougar as my mate, an act one of my maidens was convinced I'd soon regret." Melisande, no doubt. "Without my knowledge, she procured a Mage potion to keep the mating bond from fully attaching. We now believe that the Mage who produced the potion wove additional magic into it. Two years later, he attacked us through that mating bond."

Lyon glanced across the room. "Shaman?"

The Shaman's air of excitement made him look even younger than fifteen. "I knew something was up, but I could never have imagined this." He rose and walked toward the window and Ariana slowly, cautiously.

Ariana watched him approach with equal wariness.

The Shaman, little taller than Ariana, stopped just shy of arm's reach in front of her and held his hands out as if she were a fire he meant to warm them with.

Ariana stiffened and cocked her head with warning, but the Shaman didn't seem to notice. Backing up a few steps, he motioned her to follow, pulling her away from the window, then closed his eyes and began to circle her, his hands still up as if warding off a blow.

The Shaman frowned. "It's Mage magic. An abundance of it, thick and powerful, yet it doesn't seem to be harming her." He opened his eyes and stared at her. "How long have you held it like this?"

Ariana glanced at Kougar, her stance open as if she prepared to defend herself, her gaze wary. She clenched her jaw, turning back to the Shaman as he continued to circle her slowly, his face a mask of patience and concentration. "A millennium, though it's grown stronger in the past couple of years."

The Shaman nodded. "No doubt because the Mage have acquired dark magic. If I had to hazard a guess, I would say the change occurred when your sorcerer lost his soul and acquired that dark magic for himself. If his magic is connected to you, and it seems to be, it's been growing stronger."

The Shaman's mouth pursed, and he turned abruptly to Brielle. "Now you." With a flick of his hand, he motioned the other Ilina to him, but Kougar quickly intervened, not wanting Brielle anywhere near Ariana.

"No, Shaman. Go to her." With swift strides, Kougar reached Ariana, clamping a hand around her arm, unwilling to take any more chances that Brielle would whisk her away before he could stop her.

Ariana threw him a disgusted look but didn't fight him.

The Shaman's examination of Brielle took less than a minute. When he was done, he was frowning.

"Tell me everything." He lowered himself slowly onto one of the chairs, his brows knit in thought.

At first, Ariana said nothing, her stance guarded and defensive. But the Shaman was infinitely patient and waited in calm silence as her gaze met Kougar's, then slowly returned to him.

"At first only a couple of my maidens became infected. At least, I thought it was only a couple. I thought they'd come in contact with dark spirit. Those infected turned from seeking the pleasure of others to craving their pain. They attacked humans, torturing and killing for days, possibly weeks, before they died. Those residing in the corporeal world showed the symptoms far earlier, though I didn't know it at the time. But the deaths came all at once. By the time I realized what was happening, more than half my maidens were in their death throes."

"They attacked only humans?"

"No." She explained how Kougar had called her to the battlefield that day after several of her maidens had attacked his shifters. "I returned to the Crystal Realm to find all of my warriors showing signs of the darkness. Brielle was the first to suspect it was a Mage attack, and as soon as she said the words, I knew she was right. Every few days for weeks I'd dreamed of a pair of copper-ringed Mage eyes floating before me, one with an oddly shaped pupil. I called him Hookeye, and I believe he's the one who attacked us."

She glanced at Kougar, and in her eyes he glimpsed the horror of that day.

"My maidens were dying. All were infected. I didn't think, I simply acted, willing the poison into me instead of them. And it worked. At first. Until I took too much. The moment I turned to mist, the poison rushed back into them. Several dozen more died before I was able to reclaim the poison."

Kougar heard the anguish in her words, the fear that it was all going to happen again, and he felt the edges of his anger soften. Listening to her tell the tale, he could see it all happening. He could feel her terror, her confusion. He'd known the Ilinas were in trouble that day; but as always, she'd insisted on handling the situation on her own. And when the worst had happened, she'd shut him out.

But why had she severed the mating bond? That was the part he couldn't understand. Why hadn't she at least told him what had happened? Why had she made him believe she was dead?

The Shaman's expression softened with compassion. "It's a miracle you were able to retrieve the magic to save as many of your maidens as you did."

"My maidens are no longer saved."

Beneath his fingers, he felt her tremble, a faint shudder that echoed inside him, reminding him of the powerful need he'd once felt to protect her. A need that wasn't entirely gone.

"Hookeye knows I'm alive."

"How?" Lyon demanded.

Ariana glanced at Kougar, their gazes clashing briefly before she turned toward the front of the war room and told his chief what had happened in her living room, how Kougar had removed her cuff, and she'd seen the eyes again.

"He won't be able to reach you." Kougar's grip on her tightened protectively. "Not here."

"It's not the man I'm worried about. It's his poison. And he can absolutely reach me here. He can reach me anywhere."

"Shaman?" Lyon asked.

"I have to concur," the Shaman said. "It appears to me that your hook-eyed sorcerer snared you with a connector spell. Extraordinary, really."

"What's a connector spell?" Jag asked.

"Think of it as a valve inserted into the middle

of the tube of the mating bond. A valve controlled by the creator. Anytime he wishes, he can open that valve and pump more poison in."

Kougar looked at Ariana, though she didn't meet his gaze. "Is that why you severed the mating bond?" He felt as if he'd been lashed to a rack and was being slowly pulled apart as he struggled to make sense of that day, of why she'd turned her back on him and everything they'd meant to one another. "Did you sever the bond to break the Mage's connection, Ariana? To keep him from pumping more poison into it?"

She refused to turn to him, her gaze falling to the floor, the air thickening with tension around her.

"The bond was only severed on your end, Kougar, not hers," Brielle said, earning a sharp look from her queen. "She was still connected to the source of the poison. Hookeye could have attacked her anyway, which was why it was so important he not learn the truth when he thought we were extinct. Ariana is barely holding on to the poison she has. Melisande reconnected the bond a few days ago because . . ."

"Brielle." The name escaped Ariana's mouth through clenched teeth.

Hell, the poison . . .

Brielle turned to Ariana, then back to him, her fingers twined, her hands pressing against her waist. "I'm sorry, Kougar. Ariana didn't know. I tried to talk Mel out of reconnecting it, but Ariana's been struggling so much, and Mel hoped you could ease her burden."

"Is she saying what I think she's saying?" Lyon demanded. "That poison . . . ?"

The Shaman nodded. "Was Melisande aware that the poison would kill Kougar?" he asked Brielle quietly.

Kougar heard the words as if from a distance.

"Yes." Brielle flinched. "Melisande knew."

Jag's fists landed on the table. "That *bitch*."

Brielle turned to Jag. "If Ariana loses control of the poison, we all die. Her entire race. Would you not sacrifice one of us if it might save all of your own people?"

Jag snarled. "In a heartbeat, sister. I might do it anyway."

"Jag," Lyon warned.

As his Feral brothers' eyes turned toward him with dismay and shock, Kougar remembered that moment three days ago when Melisande reconnected the bond. He'd been caught in a Mage sensory-deprivation trap with several other Ferals and a pair of wraith Daemons with no way out. Melisande had come to him in that darkness and offered to save him, to give him a chance to save them all in exchange for the reconnecting of the mating bond. He hadn't wanted to do it. Not because of the poison—he hadn't known about it. No, it had been his soulless mate he hadn't wanted anything to do with. But he'd let Melisande reconnect that bond because he'd had no choice. Without the Ilina's interference, they'd have died.

Now it looked like his death had only been delayed.

Lyon met his gaze, barely banked emotion gleaming in his chief's eyes. "Explain, Shaman. How is the poison harming Kougar?"

The Shaman dipped his head. "The mating bond is woven directly into Kougar's heart. And where the threads connect, the poison flows like acid, eating away at the flesh. Literally. His immortal physiology fights to renew the decaying heart, but eventually the magic will win. And he'll die."

The room went quiet, the silence deafening, ringing in Kougar's ears. In that silence, another memory nudged him, a memory from long ago. He'd felt pain like the Shaman described, pain centered right where his heart sat, a long, long time ago. A thousand years, to be precise—that day on the battlefield that he last saw Ariana. He'd rubbed his chest against the discomfort, and she'd remarked on it.

Understanding hit him in a silent blast, the piece that had been eluding him—the reason she'd severed the mating bond.

"You knew."

Ariana flinched.

Kougar jerked her around to face him, searching those blue eyes for the truth. "You knew the poison was going to kill me. *That's* why you severed the mating bond."

He gripped her shoulders and felt her body shaking beneath his hands. By the set of her mouth, he could tell she wanted to deny it. But the truth was in her eyes, glistening in her unshed tears.

She hadn't severed the bond, as she'd claimed,

because she was done with him. Not because she hadn't loved him. Not even to save her maidens.

She'd done it to save *him*.

"*Tell me.*"

"Yes."

He stared at her, his world flipping end over end all over again. In some part of his mind he knew that this should make a difference, that it should quell his anger at her.

But deep inside, anger churned and grew, rising like lava about to explode. Because knowing she'd done it to save him just made her betrayal cut all the deeper. She'd saved him, carved out his heart, then walked away, leaving him to choke in a pool of his own blood. *Not once* in a thousand years had she contacted him to let him know she was still alive. *Not once* had she sought him out.

If she'd shared her burden with him, if she'd told him what she was up against, he'd have found that damned Mage. He'd have protected her. He'd have ended this!

"I was right the first time," he said, his voice low and cold. "When I thought you soulless."

She flinched, and he didn't give a damn.

"If we kill the sorcerer, can we kill the poison?" Lyon asked.

The Shaman took a long, slow breath. "You might destroy the magic. But it's equally possible that killing the one who created the poison will keep you from ever disabling it."

With a low growl, Kougar released her, needing distance. And perspective.

How dare she claim she'd done all this to save him!

He spun away, stalking to the window, while behind him, the Shaman addressed Ariana.

"The Ilinas have always known far more than most, given the memories you're able to pass down from queen to queen. I'm surprised you've nothing in your knowledge arsenal to battle this magic and its effect on you, Queen Ariana."

"Believe me, I've looked," she replied softly. "We tried everything I could come up with, and nothing worked. Melisande has been working tirelessly to track down Hookeye, but she's never been able to find him. To this day, we don't know who he is or what he looks like other than his eyes."

"We have contacts within the Mage," Lyon said. "We'll find him. In the meantime, since that mating bond was severed once, can it be severed again?"

"Kougar?" The Shaman's query had him turning away from the window.

With a low growl, he returned to the spot he'd stood moments before and allowed the Shaman to grip both his and Ariana's wrists at once. The Therian closed his eyes, tipping his head back as if sending a prayer directly heavenward.

He released them, shaking his head, and stepped away. "Whatever magic kept the bond from fully attaching the last time is gone. The attachment is complete this time. Permanent, though somewhat of a mess—twisted and collapsed in on itself. The flow of poison is very slow at the moment, little more than a trickle. Even so, it's quite deadly."

Dammit. To. Hell.

On one level, Kougar didn't entirely care. He'd lived a long, long time, the last thousand years in a numb, colorless wasteland of an existence. But the Ferals needed him. They couldn't afford to be down yet another warrior in the months it might take his cougar to mark another.

No, he wasn't about to give up this fight.

"How long does Kougar have?" Lyon asked.

The Shaman met Kougar's gaze. "The way it is, a few months at best. If the bond opens fully, and the poison flows freely, possibly as little as a week. I'm sorry, warrior."

A week.

Kougar's teeth ground together as he dipped his head in acknowledgment, a furious quaking setting up deep in his muscles. A week was all he needed. Because if he hadn't found a way to stop the poison and allow Ariana to turn to mist by then, Hawke and Tighe would be dead.

But he'd have more than that week. The bond wasn't going to open because he'd have to care for that to happen.

He was going to kill that Mage, disable his magic once and for all, and save his friends. Then, mating bond be damned, he wanted Ariana out of his life. For good.

Chapter
Six

A week.

The words hung in the air of the now-silent war room, but Kougar acted as if he hadn't heard. The anger in his eyes, anger directed at her upon her admission that she'd severed the mating bond to save him, hadn't abated even a flicker.

Goddess, she'd hoped if she could keep the mating bond in its current mangled state, he might survive the poison. Now the Shaman was giving him only a few months, at best.

This shouldn't have happened!

She could wring Melisande's neck for going behind her back. And she would if not for the fact that she knew Mel had only done it to help her. To help them all.

But, dammit, she would not see Kougar die.

They had to find Hookeye fast. Not that they hadn't been trying. Goddess, they'd been trying for centuries.

Maybe the Ferals could help. Maybe they really would succeed where Melisande had failed. Ariana's fingers clenched into fists. She had to keep that mating bond closed tight and give Kougar as much time as possible. Time enough to save his life, even if they weren't in time to save his friends.

A muscle leaped in Kougar's jaw as she watched him, his arms and shoulders rigid as steel. Fury enveloped him like a red haze.

"Under the circumstances, Kougar," Lyon began, "I think it might be better if one of the other Ferals guards Queen Ariana. The longer that mating bond remains closed, the better."

A low animal growl rolled from Kougar's throat as his hand circled her upper arm, biting into her flesh. "It'll stay closed." Beneath his tight grip, she felt a fine vibration, a volcanic anger ready to blow.

Anger at her or Hookeye? Or the fates for handing him down a death sentence? Probably all three, and there was nothing she could do to make it better.

"Then meeting adjourned," Lyon said. "Get some rest, if you can. Kougar, I'll let you know the minute we find something on that Mage."

Yanking her with him, Kougar steered her out of the room and down the wide hallway toward the foyer.

She wasn't entirely certain herself why she'd never contacted him. For a while, her situation had been impossible. But later . . . she wasn't sure. She'd never made the active decision to stay away from him. For a thousand years, she'd loved him, missed him, and always intended to go back to him. Someday.

But even if she knew what to say to ease his anger, she wouldn't say it. His anger was keeping him alive. For now.

He steered her through the foyer and up one of the curved stairs to a long hall that, like much of what she'd seen of Feral House so far, looked like it had been decorated a hundred years ago. The green-and-gold wallpaper of the foyer had given way to walls papered in swirls of gold peacock feathers on a beige field, covered in paintings of all styles and types—landscapes, medieval portraits, battle scenes. Electric sconces hung at regular intervals like oil lamps of old. She'd always loved the style of that era. The gilt and color pleased her Ilina eye.

Kougar stopped at one of the doors that lined the long hallway, opened it, and pushed her none-too-gently inside what was clearly his bedroom.

His bedroom. Could their reunion have played out any differently in her head? How many times had she imagined his reaction when she found him again, his face wreathed in joy, his eyes gleaming like silver like they used to whenever he saw her. She'd imagined him lifting her, like he had in those days, until they were eye to eye as if she weighed nothing, then kissing her as if he'd been holding his breath all that time and would only breathe again when their lips were fused. He'd always made her feel as if she were his sun and his moon when they were together, though those times had been all too seldom and those two years far too short.

But the reunion of her imaginings was nothing like the reality. There were no smiles. No sweet kisses. No softness at all. Only anger and hopelessness, and death hanging like a low, dark cloud over their heads.

Harsh fingers released her arm, leaving the flesh throbbing. Behind her, the door closed with a bang that rattled the windows. Ariana turned, ready to face her accuser; but Kougar paced away, violence seething beneath the animal grace of his walk.

Without warning, he yanked the straight-backed wooden chair out from his desk, lifted it, and sent it crashing down on the broad wood surface, splintering into a dozen pieces. As chunks of wood clattered against the wall and onto the floor, he threw what was left of the chair across the room, then arched as if in terrible pain. Hands fisted at his sides, he threw back his head and let out a roar filled with such fury that she knew she should be quaking with fear. But along with that roar, she heard pain. A pain she'd caused.

Guilt twisted inside her. She'd never meant to hurt him like this. But, dammit, he wasn't the only one who'd suffered!

His fangs and claws erupted as he started toward her, stalking her with eyes turned the yellow of a jungle cat.

Ariana held her ground, her wrists still bound before her as she faced him. Inches away from her, he stopped, staring down at her from his great height like an animal about to strike. Though her heart pounded in response to his fury and the memory of the last time he'd drawn claws on her, up in the Crystal Realm, she wasn't afraid. Not of Kougar. No, she was getting mad. He acted as if she'd carelessly tossed him aside, and nothing could be further from the truth.

His lips drew back in a snarl over teeth clenched tight, his fangs long and sharp. *"You. Put. Me. Through. Hell."*

She lifted her chin, meeting that fiery gaze, giving rein to the anger that was building inside her, knowing that the best thing she could do for both of them was to feed his own.

"Join the club!" She met him nose to nose, glower for glower. "I wasn't the one who insisted we mate despite both our peoples' being dead set against it. I wasn't the one who insisted we were fated for one another!" She punched the rock-hard plane of his abdomen with her bound hands. "I wasn't the one who pushed and pushed . . ."

He snarled. "You think this was all my fault? You blame *me*?"

"I blame us both! *Ninety-six* Ilinas died because I let you talk me into a mating that should have never been. It was both of our faults." She punched him again. "If you'd left me alone, my maidens would be alive. The Mage would never have turned on us. I wouldn't have lost *ninety-six* of my friends, my sisters, then spent nearly three hundred years tending the remaining forty-four, most of whom were barely alive. My world was destroyed!"

She slugged him again. "I put *you* through hell? I used to dream I could change the past, dream that I'd turned and walked away instead of letting you kiss me that first time. For a thousand years, I've rued the day we met!"

She was as angry as he was, her chest heaving, her eyes burning with righteous fire and unshed tears. Somewhere in her diatribe he'd retracted his claws, and he grabbed her shoulders hard, his eyes once more pale, sparking with fury, and something more. A passion of a different kind.

"You haven't rued that day half as much as I have." But the tone of his voice had changed, turning husky. He curved his hand around the back of her neck, pulled her to him and crushed her mouth beneath his in a kiss filled with anger and frustration, and hot, searing need. He didn't want to be kissing her, she was more than sure of that.

Ariana struggled against his hold, trying to escape the kiss that was already sending drugging warmth flowing into her blood. The kiss changed from one of possession to one of passion in an instant, and she was lost.

She gave herself up to the kiss, reveling in the power of the man and the need that sparked like an electric wire in a raging storm. So much lay between them. So much grief, so much pain. But, goddess, she'd missed him. Missed his demanding, yet gentle touch, his warm, masculine scent, and the feel of his hard body moving against hers.

Passion exploded. Pleasure engulfed her, flowing through her like warm honey as their lips parted, and his tongue swept into her mouth. Unlike the kiss he'd forced on her in her home, this one contained no true hatred, only an anger that was already washing away in the passion. His mouth gentled, his hands gripping with a growing hunger as sharp as her own.

In her blood, the passion dissolved in a sweet rush, shifting into an essence more important to an Ilina than food. Normal pleasure strengthened. A tasty dinner, a beautiful ballet, even a little quality time with her vibrator. But what she felt in Kougar's arms transformed. She'd forgotten. A moan trembled in her chest. Dear goddess, she'd forgotten.

For so long she'd needed a man. *This* man. Though she'd taken a few lovers over the centuries, Kougar was the only one she'd wanted.

His mouth left hers, dipping to her neck, and she tipped her head back, absorbing the exquisite feel of his mouth on her body. She needed to touch him, to slide her fingers into his hair and hold him as he held her, but her bound hands were pinned between their bodies.

"Unbind me, Kougar. I need to touch you."

He ignored her, kissing her neck, his hands sliding to her waist, to the fastening of her jeans. Her pulse vaulted. He shoved her jeans and panties down over her hips in a single tug, then thrust his hand between her legs, entering her with a single, quaking, seeking finger.

Her body melted. "*Kougar. More.* I need you inside me."

She wasn't sure what happened, only that the moment the words left her mouth, he pulled away. His finger left her, his expression turning back into a hard, brittle mask. Without a word, with a coldness she didn't entirely understand, he turned and walked to the window, where the morning sunlight poured into the room, gleaming on the chair wreckage that littered the floor.

He spoke, his back to her, his words flat and devoid of the anger of a moment ago, and all the more cutting because of it. "When we kill that damned Mage, and I'm free of this poison, I'm out of your life, Ariana. And I want you out of mine."

"Done." And she meant it. She *meant* it.

Goddess, had she blamed him all this time without consciously realizing it? Had she been punishing them both by staying away from him? Even if it wasn't the only reason, she couldn't deny it had undoubtedly played a part in staying her hand all those times she'd thought of seeking him out.

She took a deep breath and let it out on a ragged sigh. There was no going back, only forward. What was done, was done. All they could do now was try to find Hookeye before he attacked again.

As if Melisande hadn't been trying for hundreds of years. Hopelessness pressed on her as she stared at Kougar's rigid back. He was going to die. The poison would take him, just as it had taken so many she'd loved. And when it did, now that the mating bond was well and truly attached, she was going to suffer.

Even if she hated her mate, the bond's rupture would damage her.

And she didn't hate Kougar.

But neither did she love him as she once had, with that certainty, that wholehearted exuberance. What she'd once felt for him had long ago become twisted with dark layers of grief and horror and anger. Instinctively, she knew the best thing was for her to keep it that way.

Then maybe, when Kougar died, she wouldn't feel like she'd died, too.

Chapter
Seven

Kougar gripped the window frame until he heard
the wood creak beneath his fingers. He was losing
it, the emotions that had been all but dead for a
millennium turning into a wild storm inside him
as he struggled for control. He wanted to shake
Ariana until her teeth rattled for severing the
mating bond and walking away from him. He
longed to yell at her until his throat was hoarse.
And he yearned to make love to her. Goddess, he
needed to make love to her.

And that would be a monumental mistake.

Already, his body was a living inferno from just
a kiss and the quick slide of his finger inside her.
He hadn't meant to touch her like that. He hadn't
meant to touch her at all, but he was losing control. All he could think of was tearing off Ariana's

clothes and making love to her until neither of them could think . . . or stand.

And he didn't want that!

From the moment he saw her again, he'd needed to be inside her. From the moment he'd ushered her into his bedroom, even through his rage, he'd shaken with the need to toss her onto the bed and follow her down.

Goddess, all he wanted was her out of his life again!

Yet deep inside him, his cat clawed to reach her, to claim her. Not as *he* wanted to, with his cock deep inside her, but as his mate. *Their* mate.

No. Not again. They might not be able to sever the bond again, but that didn't mean he had to care what happened to her. He didn't have to love her. He'd done that once, and it had damn near killed him.

He refused to fall for her again.

But his body burned, hot and throbbing, desperate to be inside her. It wasn't going to happen. He wasn't having sex with her. He refused to lose control like that with her again. But his body *burned*.

Turning, he found her watching him, her jeans once more up around her hips, though not zipped. Those too-blue eyes watched him, the fire he'd set in them banked but not out. Not nearly out.

Goddess.

He walked to his desk and dug through the wreckage until he found his scissors, then crossed to her and removed the tape binding her hands none too gently.

She rubbed her wrists, her eyes sharp with annoyance.

He was a fool. A fucking weak fool.

"Take off your clothes." The words came out of his mouth, little more than a growl, and he knew he was lost.

"*Now*, why are you mad?" Anger flared in her eyes even as she pulled off her T-shirt and tossed it on the chest at the foot of the bed.

"Because I don't want you. Because I refuse to fall back into that soul-sucking trap of needing to be inside you every moment of every day."

He closed the distance between them and once more yanked her jeans down over her hips, taking her panties with them.

She stared at him, her face a mask of heat and confusion. "Then what are you doing?"

"Losing control."

Her Ilina mating scent—that lush, intoxicating fragrance Ilinas used, at one time, to lure males into their sensual traps—began to spin its magic, lighting fires in every part of his body. If he hadn't been hard as a rock already, he would be now, though he doubted she released the fragrance intentionally. Ariana had always lost control of hers at some point in their lovemaking. Usually, the moment he started to undress her.

He shoved his hand between her legs. She moaned and ripped open his shirt, sending the buttons flying. He drew his claws and reached for her bra, but she grabbed his wrist before he could slice through it.

"Bras cost money." She removed the filmy lace, exposing her fully to his gaze once more.

As he reached for the soft mounds of her breasts, her hands went to his belt; but he grabbed her wrists, stopping her.

"No." Instead, he picked her up, intending to toss her onto the bed.

But Ariana had never been a woman to give in meekly. She kicked out of his hold to curl her bare legs around his waist, flinging her arms around his neck, leaping onto him like a wildcat on the attack. An erotic, sensual attack. His arms pulled her closer as she fused her mouth with his, devouring his. Pebbled breasts teased his skin, slender fingers raked into his hair, cutting him with memories.

She'd always slept without clothing in those days, and he'd loved to surprise her in bed. She always seemed to sense him coming, and she'd greeted him just like this, flying into his arms, curling herself around him like a wild cat claiming her mate.

Memories flayed him of those idyllic days even as anger burned inside him at Ariana, the Mage, the fates, for stealing them away.

As he cupped her buttocks, digging his fingers into the soft flesh, desire flamed higher.

Her mouth moved to his jaw, to his neck. "Let it

go, Kougar. Let the anger go and feel the pleasure. Just feel. Just this once."

She rubbed the tight nubs of her nipples against his bare chest, and he was lost. Naked and warm in his arms, she was living, lily-of-the-valley-scented fire, and he wanted her with a need that stripped him of all control.

Holding her with one hand, he slid the other between her legs, finding again the source of her heat. Goddess, but she was hot and wet, ready for him as she'd always been. The sex had been the best part of those two years.

Conflicting emotions crashed inside the walls of his chest. He wanted to hurt her as she'd hurt him, until she cried out with the pain of it. And his arms shook with the need to free himself and shove his cock inside her until they both screamed with pleasure.

But he wasn't completely out of control. Not yet. Pulling her off him, he tossed her onto the middle of the bed, shaking with the need to follow her down.

Ariana stared up at Kougar as he stood beside the bed. His emotions pulsed down the mating bond, pounding at her even when he wasn't touching her. Her breaths were shallow, her body on fire from the feel of his hands and his gaze, and the sheer magnitude of her own desire for this man.

She wanted him, needed him, in so many ways. But the tight line of his body and the rigid set of his jaw made it all too clear he didn't want to give in. Though seduction was as innate to any Ilina as breathing, she wouldn't employ such tactics. If he came to her, it would be through his own free will, not her machinations.

They'd already hurt one another in too many ways.

So she waited for him to make the decision, watching the battle in his eyes. The small flare of frustrated anger told her it was over.

She'd won.

He pulled off his ripped shirt, revealing the beautifully sculpted, lightly furred chest she'd loved so well. Claw marks tore across his abdomen— red welts that looked new though he'd had them since the day he was first marked to be a Feral Warrior well over a thousand years ago. Watching her with predatory eyes, he climbed onto the bed, moving between her parted legs like a cat on the prowl. His eyes were steel, his powerful shifter's body as dangerous as it was beautiful as he bent over her and lowered his face to her breast, watching her the entire way down.

He claimed her breast without gentleness, his passion barely controlled, sucking the fullness into his mouth on a hard, desperate tug that sent pleasure arcing through her body and down into her core. As if he felt her need, his fingers reached between her legs, stroking her damp, swollen flesh before two dove inside, claiming her with sure, hard strokes.

Another hard surge of anger hit her through the

mating bond, puncturing the intense pleasure, telling her he hated his own weakness in needing to touch her. This wasn't the way it used to be between them. This wasn't the way it was ever supposed to be, but she'd ended all chance for anything more when her world had come crashing down around her, and she'd left him thinking her dead.

The pleasure, though intense, was hollow. Still, she needed the strength it would give her to battle back the darkness that attacked her from within.

His bearded mouth left one breast damp and throbbing, to claim the other. Her fingers caressed his short hair as she thrust her hips against his hand, forcing his fingers deeper and deeper inside her.

How could so much pleasure leave her feeling so empty?

He released her breast, pulling his fingers from her, only to replace them with his mouth. His tongue delved into her inner depths, drawing a moan from her throat. His hands slid beneath her hips, lifting her, splaying her wide as he devoured her, his tongue moving out of her to circle the tight knot of nerve endings.

Clasping the bedspread, she hung on against the rising passion tearing through her body.

He pleasured her. Goddess, he pleasured her, but there was no tenderness. If he'd been fully in control he wouldn't be touching her at all, she was sure of it. And the knowledge that he touched her against his will filled her with a sweeping sadness, an ache in that part of her heart that had always belonged to him, despite all that had happened.

With his mouth working her clit, he shoved the two fingers back inside her and within moments she came with an exploding rush of ecstasy and emptiness. Once upon a time, when she and Kougar were in love, she'd often started to turn to mist as she'd climaxed and would have to battle it back until he followed. Then she'd let the mist overtake her just enough that he'd sink into her body, making them truly one. He'd loved it when she did, the sensation moving and powerfully erotic for both of them.

But there was none of that this time. Even if she weren't wearing the moonstones, she doubted she'd be compelled to turn to mist. While her body metabolized the pleasure of their joining, the lack of closeness, not to mention the enmity, left her feeling bereft.

Kougar rose slowly from between her legs, wiping his mouth with the back of his hand, watching her with catlike intensity. Without a word, he rose with that animal grace and padded to the door in the back corner of the room. The bathroom, she realized, as he went in and closed the door behind him, shutting her out.

Flinging her arm across her forehead, Ariana stared up at the ceiling, her body pulsing with glorious release, her chest hollow. With her hands free, she reached for the moonstones but couldn't bring herself to chant the magic of transport. The

Ferals had promised to try to help her, and though she hadn't expected to trust them, she found that she did. She sensed a strength and honor in Lyon to rival that which she'd always seen in Kougar. And she'd be a fool to turn her back on their offer of help, especially with their friends' lives such a powerful force driving them to succeed.

Yes, she would stay, and hope the Ferals triumphed where she and her maidens had failed. Kougar's enmity was a small price to pay for the chance to save her friends, and the man she loved, even if he no longer had any soft feelings for her in return.

Ten centuries she'd spent outcast by her own hand, wandering the human world, living on her own. Yet in this crowded house, the man she'd once been mated to in the next room, she'd never felt so alone.

Chapter Eight

Kougar shucked off his pants, took himself in hand, and pumped off into the sink with a few quick strokes, then braced his hands on the counter and forced the air back into his lungs, willing his heart to cease its crazed beating.

The taste of Ariana, the scent, the sound of her low whimpers as she rose, and her cry as she released—each of them tore at his control, every one sliced open the cold mass of aching muscle that had long ago become his heart. He'd wanted to climb her body and sink inside her so badly it had become a burn in his quaking muscles. But every instinct he possessed told him that taking her, possessing her like that again, would be a mistake of monumental proportions. Never had he taken her that his love for her hadn't grown stronger, and loving her again, even a little, would only open the mating bond, hastening his demise.

And even if they succeeded in capturing the Mage and curing this poison, if he wanted any hope of walking away whole, he had to keep some measure of distance between them. Not that burying his face between her legs was distance. But he remembered all too well what happened when they came together, when they released together. Maybe it wouldn't be anything like that now that there was anger and distrust between them. Now that the mating bond was little more than a twisted wreck. But he wasn't taking any chances because if he tasted even a shadow of that perfection again, he'd never be able to walk away. He'd never be free of her.

He turned on the shower and stepped under the cold spray, letting the chill sink into his body and douse the heat that refused to abate, willing it to freeze his heart and the unwanted emotions that careened inside him after being dead for so long. He didn't want them. Didn't need them. Especially now, with Ariana back in his life.

Finally, he turned off the shower and grabbed a plush bath sheet, drying himself thoroughly. What he needed was a run in his cat. But the sun was up, and he couldn't leave Ariana behind. If she was even still here. It had occurred to him she might not be since he'd left her unbound.

But as he stepped through the door, he found her asleep on his bed. The sight of her like that— curled up atop his satin sheets like a diamond on a sea of dark red—tugged at that aching mass of flesh in his chest. His cat gave a howl of frustration that he refused to claim her and take her once more to mate.

He stepped closer, drawn to her against his will, until he stood over her, close enough to watch the rise and fall of her chest. And the soft lock of hair curled atop her cheek.

Goddess, she is so beautiful.

From out of nowhere, a thread of joy surged through his battered heart, and he reveled in the miracle of her survival. He fought it back, fought to reclaim the anger that had threatened to consume him such a short time before, but it was gone. Instead, her voice echoed in his thoughts, telling him of ninety-six maidens she'd had to send to the next world while trying to save those few remaining. For the first time he began to understand the enormity of her loss and the magnitude of what she'd faced. As hard-pressed as he was to not forgive her for not telling him she was still alive, on some level he found himself doing so.

For long minutes, he stood there, perfectly content to watch her sleep. But he needed sleep as well. He'd gotten little the past few days as he'd tirelessly tracked her down. It was the perfect time to rest, while Lyon and Paenther hunted for Hookeye's trail.

He eyed Ariana, torn between shifting into his cat to sleep on the floor and joining her in the bed. With a sigh of disgust, he dropped the towel and pulled on a pair of silk sleep pants that might possibly deter him from claiming what he really wanted. Then he lay down beside her, careful not to touch her.

But she stirred and rolled over, moving to him unerringly in her sleep as she'd often done, as if a thousand years hadn't passed. Before he could catch his breath, she pressed against his side, her head on his shoulder, her arm sliding across his torso, one knee lifting to rest on his thigh.

For half a minute, he lay still as stone, his muscles shaking as he struggled between pushing her away and pulling her into his arms. The latter won.

He turned to her, his arms going tight around her as he pulled her against his heart. He had to squeeze his eyes closed against the tidal wave of emotion that threatened to rip his feet out from under him—the overpowering joy that the woman he'd loved more than life, and thought dead for so long, was alive, her breath warm against his shoulder, her hair tickling his chin, her heart beating strong and sure beneath his hands.

Hatred, then anger, had fought the celebration of his heart. They'd tried to silence his cat's rejoicing. But in the stillness of the room, Ariana sleeping safely in his arms, that soul-deep joy knocked him to his knees. Moisture burned his eyes. From the moment he'd seen her again, he'd been struggling to keep his distance from her, struggling not to let himself care again.

Not to let himself love her again.

The problem was, despite the decrepit state of their mating bond, he'd never stopped loving her.

And it was a problem, a huge one. Even now, he felt the mating bond begin to unfurl, a low burn setting up in his chest where the poison began to trickle through.

Even if they got another chance, they were too different to make a go of this marriage. Their worlds were too far apart, and their loyalties had always been too firmly entrenched with their own instead of one another. If he found a way to save Hawke and Tighe that risked the lives of her maidens, he'd take it. Without question. Not only would he do whatever it took to save his friends, but the Feral Warriors were all that realistically stood between the world and Satanan. The Ferals had to survive for the sake of far more than their own desire to live. But that argument would do nothing to assuage Ariana's grief if it came to that. Nor her hatred of him for letting it happen.

No, they had no future together. Even if they defeated Hookeye, another villain would only take his place. Now that the Mage knew the Ilinas were still alive, they'd seek to steal their souls as they had others'. Or destroy them, as Hookeye had almost done. And might still do. No, he and Ariana had no future. They'd never had one.

But the feel of her in his arms again was heaven after a millennium of hell.

Wulfe heard voices as he slipped through the mirrored door of the workout room into the hidden stone passage and headed back to the prison block deep below Feral House. Not voices, he amended.

One voice. Xavier's. If that kid was awake, he was talking. Which beat the hell out of Lip Ring's screaming. As it turned out, those screams of hers weren't reserved for him alone. Lyon had tried to take her terror three times, then given up, which might not bode well for their ability to take her memories when and if the energy Olivia had fed them finally wore off. The teen girl's mind seemed locked in a loop of terror. Not that he could really blame her, given what she'd seen.

As he strolled through the passage, he rolled up the too-short cuffs of his button-down, trying to get comfortable. It wasn't like he'd gotten dressed up. He hadn't tucked in the shirt and was still wearing jeans. He just . . . felt a little more civilized-looking in a collared shirt.

He'd taken guard duty down there on and off for the past couple of days; but never again had he managed to catch Natalie awake, though he kept hoping to. Both Lyon and Jag claimed she was doing fine. Wary and watchful, but calm, all things considered, even as she stuck as close to her brother as a momma bear to her cub.

Xavier went quiet, and Wulfe assumed Lyon had knocked him out again. But Xavier's next question, which carried to Wulfe clearly, proved otherwise.

"So, are you going to be able to let us go, or do we know too much?"

"And what do you think you know?" Lyon asked with deceptive softness.

"I know the earth opened up. I know there was

some serious magic shit going down. I know there were large wild animals prowling around who suddenly turned into men."

Even before he reached the cellblock, Wulfe heard the low growl in Lyon's throat. "How could you possibly know that?"

"I heard you, Dude. When you don't have eyes, you see through sounds, and I saw the change. Besides, Nat told me she saw you shift." A pause. "You don't have to kill me, you know, even if you can't take my memories." Clearly, he'd heard too much. "I'm a decent cook. I can wash dishes. I can help out around here, man."

Wulfe didn't have to see Lyon's face to know he was groaning. Disposing of dangerous humans was so much harder when you couldn't help but like them. Especially when the only danger they posed was to the anonymity of the race.

"I'll think about it. Lie down, Xavier. You're going back to sleep."

"I'd rather stay awake."

"Nevertheless . . ."

By the time Wulfe walked into the cellblock, Lyon was locking the brother and sister's cage, Xavier once more unconscious.

Lyon eyed Wulfe's shirt with a lift of his brow. "Going somewhere?"

"Go to hell," Wulfe muttered. "The women?"

Lyon gave him an amused look but didn't razz him further. "That one," he said, nodding toward Lip Ring's cage, "woke in her normal bloodcurdling manner about half an hour ago. She'll be out the rest of the day. The other hasn't woken yet, but should soon. Call Kara when she does, and she'll bring a tray."

When Lyon had left, Wulfe shucked off his clothes, shifted into his wolf, and curled up on the floor to watch. And wait. An hour later, Natalie finally began to stir. Wulfe shifted back and pulled on his jeans. As he buttoned the shirt, he felt like a fool. He usually wore T-shirts since they stretched comfortably to fit his monster-truck size. He used to dress up a little for Beatrice from time to time, hoping to please her, though he never had. His now-dead mate had never been able to see past his scars.

But Natalie hadn't seemed put off by him. He scowled. She hadn't seemed *terrified* of him. She might still have been revolted. Revulsion could be masked.

Hell.

Natalie sat up groggily, her hand sliding to Xavier's pulse before she was even fully awake. She looked better. Much better now that she was no longer battling the terror and anguish as she had been that first time. In fact, she seemed almost calm.

That was the first word that came to mind when he thought of her. *Calm. Lovely* was the second, despite her unkempt appearance. Her hair fell to her shoulders in tangled golden waves framing a face of strength and depth and compassion. The only thing jarringly out of place was that wound across her cheekbone.

Cautiously, he stepped out of the shadows.

Natalie looked up, her wary gaze softening slowly. "Hi," she said, a hint of a smile lighting gray eyes.

A smile. He felt like laughing, but contained the urge, settling for a small smile of his own. "How are you feeling?"

"Since the last time I saw you? A thousand times better."

"Good."

She nodded, but her expression sobered. "We're still in the cages, though. How long has it been? Since the . . ."

"A week."

Unhappiness clouded her eyes. "My mom and my fiancé are going to be frantic. Have we hit the news? Are they looking for us?"

"You're all the humans are talking about around here."

Dark blond brows drew together. "Humans. And you're not. But of course you're not." She looked down, then back up again. "Werewolves, or were-animals?"

"We prefer the term shape-shifters."

"What were those . . . flying creatures that attacked us?"

Daemons. "Nothing to worry about anymore. They're dead."

"And there aren't any more of them?"

"No." Not yet, not unless the Mage found a way to free more of them, but she didn't need to know that. "Are you hungry?"

That smile flitted across her face again, pleasing him more than it should. "Starved."

Wulfe pulled out his cell phone and speed-dialed Kara. "I have a starving guest down here. Lyon said you might have a tray with Natalie's name on it?"

"Coming right up." Kara's cheery voice carried to him through the phone. "Or down, I guess I should say. I'll be right there, Wulfe."

A few minutes later, Kara appeared with a tray laden with a full three-course meal—salad, ham, potatoes, and a sweet-smelling cherry cobbler that had been sending their stomachs into wild tumbles of hunger all morning. Kara left, and Natalie dug into the salad as if she was indeed about to expire from lack of food.

He wished he could let her out of her cage for a while when she was finished eating. She had to be sick and tired of being locked up. A walk through the woods came to mind, but it was the middle of the day, and he wasn't kidding when he'd told her they were all over the news. Human law enforcement had found the bodies of Natalie's three friends where the Ferals had left them, more than a mile from the actual site of their deaths. They'd left the Mage bodies on the field of battle, warding the area against human senses for the few days it took the earth to reclaim them. Immortal bodies might live centuries, but they decayed to dust quickly.

"Can you shift into anything you want?" Natalie asked when she'd clearly taken the edge off her hunger.

"No." He didn't elaborate.

Her pretty mouth twisted. "The less I know, the better, right? It's hard not asking questions when there's so much I want to know." Her eyes moved over his face as if studying his scarring. "You intrigue me," she said quietly.

He turned away, feeling like he'd just been shoved under a microscope. "Finish eating," he said gruffly.

When she had, he took her tray, then motioned for her to stand. She was tall for a woman, probably close to six feet, though he still towered over her by over a foot. She might be slender, but she was no stick-thin model. The woman had curves. His man's eye noticed, but his body paid little attention. His mate, Beatrice, the Ferals' previous Radiant, had been dead only a few months. And while their mating had never been what he'd hoped for, he'd loved her. And the severing of their mating bond had ruined him in ways he was still trying to figure out.

Even if he were whole and normal, it wouldn't matter. The woman standing in front of him wore another man's ring. Another's mark.

"Let's try this again."

Calm gray eyes met his. "To clear my memories?"

"Yes." He reached for her jaw, but she touched his hand.

"Wait. In case this works, I just wanted to say thank you. To you and your friends. I know you had as much reason to want those things dead as we did, but I overheard you talking out there. I know we saw things we shouldn't have and that our lives hung in the balance for a while. Thank you for saving us."

He nodded, meeting her gaze, yet oddly reluctant to continue. Once he captured her memories, he'd have to knock her out and take her back, and he'd finally just gotten a chance to talk to her again. Whatever her reason for not being put off by his looks, it was a novel experience he wasn't quite ready to end.

His gaze fell to that jagged cut on her cheek, his thumb lifting to trace it lightly.

Natalie flinched.

Wulfe jerked his thumb back. "It still hurts."

"Not too much."

Which was a blatant lie.

Her brows drew down. "How bad does it look?"

"Not as bad as mine."

A genuine laugh escaped her throat, utterly delighting him. She caught herself with a groan, though wry humor continued to light her eyes and tug at her mouth. "I'm sorry, but that wasn't quite the reassurance I was looking for."

He grinned at her, amazed at how easy she was to be with.

To his surprise, she lifted her hand, almost touching his face, before lowering it again. As she did, her smile died, her expression sobering. "I'm sorry for all you must have suffered."

He grunted. "It was a long time ago." And the suffering hadn't been his. Not until later. Much later.

Without thinking too much about what he was doing, he made a decision. "Hold still. This may be uncomfortable for a moment, but I won't hurt you." When her eyes gave him the go-ahead, he said, "Close your eyes."

She hesitated only a moment before doing as he asked. He opened his hand, covering her wound, and half her face, with his palm.

"What are you doing?" she asked quietly.

Beneath his palm, her heart beat, throbbing beneath the surface of her skin. Once more, her scent wrapped around him like a warm summer breeze.

"I'm something of a healer." Sometimes. His own cheek began to burn and throb with surprising misery. How did humans stand the pain that took so long to go away? "How do you feel?"

"The pain's gone." Her voice held a note of wonder.

Lifting his hand, he peered at her cheekbone with keen satisfaction. The wound was gone completely now, her cheek unblemished.

She opened her eyes, blinking. "How did you . . . ?" Her gaze locked onto his cheek, to the throbbing, aching wound he knew to be there, now. Her hand flew to her own cheek, then rubbed, as if seeking . . . anything.

"What have you done?"

Wulfe shrugged. "What's one more?"

But he saw no gratitude in her eyes, only a keen dismay. "No, no, no." Her brows knit. She grabbed his face between her hands without fear, staring at him, at the cut that would mark him as all the others had. To his amazement, her fingers slid gently over his scarred cheeks. "You took it."

Her voice was breathless, stunned. She stared up at him, pain in her eyes. "*Why?*"

He frowned, confused by her reaction. The last thing he'd meant to do was upset her. But the truth was, he didn't have an answer. He wasn't sure why he'd done it. Maybe he just didn't like seeing her suffer when he could help. Or maybe he hadn't liked the sight of that ugly scar on her pretty face.

What difference did it make? Women were so damn hard to please.

He turned away, breaking her soft hold on him and ending the discussion. "Lie down." The words came out harsher than he'd meant them to.

But when he turned back to her, she was still standing where he'd left her, still staring at him. Although her brows were still drawn, her eyes no longer flashed with pain but something infinitely softer.

"Will you heal?"

"Of course."

"But it'll scar you."

"Like I said, what's one more?"

"Plenty." The softness in her eyes deepened, a fine film of moisture making them shine like diamonds. "That may have been the most unselfish thing anyone's ever done for me. And I don't even know your name."

"I'm called Wulfe."

Understanding lit her gaze, the memory of watching him shift, he was certain. "I suppose that makes sense. Thank you, Wulfe."

He nodded, his jaw tight. Then he slid his hand to her neck and pressed beneath her ear, feeling a need to close those eyes that saw too much. As she fell unconscious, he caught her, then laid her down carefully on one of the pallets someone had brought down for the prisoners.

Straightening, he stared down at her, clenching his jaw at her now-unblemished beauty.

With a burst of self-disgust, he turned away.

Ariana woke suddenly, her body tensing at the feel of warm flesh beneath her cheek until she caught the wonderful, familiar scent. *Kougar's.* Her head was on his shoulder, one of his arms gripped tight around her waist, his bare chest rising and falling in a deep, even rhythm, telling her he was fast asleep.

For an achingly sweet moment, her world felt as if it had righted itself. As if the nightmare of the past millennium was nothing more than a dream, and life was as it had always been meant to be. With her waking in Kougar's arms.

Ariana jerked. Sweet goddess, what was she doing in his arms? It was the last place she needed to be. He was supposed to be hating her, not holding her!

Her heart at once melted and squeezed with fear as she slipped free of his hold and sat up. With an unintelligible murmur, Kougar rolled onto his side away from her.

Raking her hair back from her face with both hands, she turned inward and examined the mating bond. *Dammit, dammit.* As she feared, it had begun to unkink. It still looked mangled and sunken in on itself, but the poison was beginning to trickle through steadily.

Not good, not good, not good. Yet what could she do about it? She'd known this would happen if he found out the truth—that she'd severed the mating bond to save him. Sooner or later, he'd forgive her the rest. And once he did, the poison would begin to flow freely.

Pulling her knees up, she curled her arms around them. It was too late to try to arrest the opening of the mating bond. Their only chance now, as far as she could see, was for the Ferals and their Mage allies to figure out who Hookeye was and locate him. Maybe they really could. Maybe it would work. But she'd long, long ago quit believing in miracles. And this situation would take a big one.

Despair filled the room as she dipped her head and rested her chin on her updrawn knees. She hated being forced to let others take the lead in her battles; but, unable to turn to mist, she'd long ago been relegated to the sidelines. Then again, she was the one with her finger in the dike. If she allowed the floodwaters, or in this case the poison, to flow, all would die. Not the sidelines, perhaps, but the center, with all those around trying to help her hold on, trying to find a way to destroy the poison before she could no longer hold back the killing tide.

Her life hadn't been her own to control in a very, very long time. Even now . . .

She needed to call the hospital and let them know she wouldn't be in for a few days. There was a good chance she wouldn't be back at all. If the Ferals' attempt to locate Hookeye failed, if Kougar died, there would no longer be a reason for her to remain close to Feral House. Once the mating bond was truly, permanently severed, she could go anywhere—except home to the Crystal Realm.

For centuries, her existence had been a stasis of hiding and survival, searching for an answer that never came, waiting for Melisande to find the Mage at the heart of it all. In the few short days since Kougar had charged back into her life, he'd turned every single aspect of her existence end over end until she didn't know what to think, what to feel.

She wanted to be furious with him for endangering her people all over again, but she was beginning to believe the Ferals genuinely meant to help her, even if only to save their own. For the first time in forever, a flicker of hope had sparked, a rare, precious feeling that she was almost afraid to acknowledge, knowing it could be snuffed out again between one breath and the next.

If the Ferals really did succeed in finding the

Mage behind the attacks, if by some miracle, she found herself free of the poison? The thought tantalized. The first thing she'd do was return home and take up the mantle of queen-in-residence once more. It was all she'd wanted for a thousand years.

She turned to Kougar, to his strong, beloved back, rising and falling in sleep. No, being queen wasn't all she wanted. But she'd been a fool to think she could be both queen and wife. Her maidens should have been her top priority all those years ago . . . her only priority. If they had been, they'd still be alive.

That was a mistake she couldn't make a second time, no matter how much her heart ached for the man at her side.

On a sigh, she turned away from him, her gaze sliding over his room. He'd closed the drapes after she'd fallen asleep, and sunlight now fanned out from the edges of the window, thin rays escaping the darkening curtains. It was the kind of room she would expect of Kougar, she realized. Clean, neat, controlled. If she ignored the splintered chair.

The bed on which she sat was a large, mahogany four-poster, beautifully carved, probably by hand. The bedside lamp, a heavy jewel-encrusted brass. Kougar had always enjoyed fine things. Even a thousand years ago when there was so much less to choose from, he'd carried intricately carved knives and worn cloaks with silk linings.

And he'd been incredibly generous to her—

plying her with gifts of beauty that he'd known would please her Ilina's heart. Jewelry from exotic traders, gowns of the finest velvet. And flowers. Where he'd found them, she'd never been certain, but he'd rarely come to her without flowers of some kind, even if all he'd been able to find was a sprig of honeysuckle.

She'd always loved flowers, especially in those days, when she'd spent so much time in the Crystal Realm, where nothing grew. And he'd known it.

On the walls of his room hung more paintings, mostly centuries-old landscapes. Though three of his walls were tan, the one before her was a vibrant blue. The color of the summer sky, neon bright. Almost the exact shade of her eyes.

Beside her, Kougar made a sound deep in his throat, a low growl as he rolled onto his back. His body had turned rigid with tension, his arm muscles flexing, his hand fisting against his hip.

He was dreaming, and it wasn't a happy dream.

She lifted her hand, intending to stroke his shoulder and soothe him, only to pull up. What demons did he wrestle in his sleep? Perhaps she should find out. A soft smile tugged at her mouth. It had been so long since she'd joined him in one of his dreams.

Ariana closed her eyes, calmed her mind, and stepped into his dream, an ability all Ilinas possessed. She expected to find herself a spectator of some Feral battle. Instead, she blinked with confusion as she realized she was standing inside her own cabin hundreds of years ago, the night three human trappers stumbled upon it . . . and her. The coarse men had thought to slake their physical urges on an unwilling woman, and she watched as her younger self fought off two of the men at once with well-aimed kicks.

She frowned at the nonsensical sight. This was supposed to be Kougar's dream. Instead, she and Kougar both stood in the middle of one of her own memories. Dressed in the dark sleep pants he wore in the bed beside her, he passed through the center of the action like a ghost trying to fight off her attackers. They, of course, didn't even know he was there.

"Kougar."

His gaze jerked to her, then to her dream self and back again, the tension leaching from his body as understanding lit his eyes.

"It's a dream," he muttered, his voice barely audible over the grunts of the men and the snap of bone as her dream self broke one of her attacker's kneecaps.

The man yelled, crashing into the sole chair in the tiny cabin, splintering it. Goddess, she'd been furious about losing that chair. It had taken her weeks to make it.

Her gaze took in the small windowless space, the rough-hewn logs infilled with mud, the down pallet that had been her bed, now destroyed, the feathers floating in the glow from the fire. The scent of smoke and sweat and unwashed bodies choked the air.

Kougar crossed to her, pulling her tight against him with a shudder of relief. "My fists kept going right through them. I was beginning to think I'd died." His gaze skimmed her nakedness. "Walking in my dreams?"

"I could tell you were having a bad one. I thought I'd take a look." Her brow furrowed. "But this isn't your dream."

"This isn't real."

"No, but it happened. It's my memory."

His frown deepened as together they watched her fight off her assailants with sweeping kicks and elbows to the throats and noses. She might have been a woman alone, but she'd been as strong as any human male, thanks to her immortal blood, with nearly seven centuries of hand-to-hand combat experience by that point.

"When did this happen?"

"Late 1600s, in the woods about forty miles west of Feral House."

"You lived nearby even then?"

She met his gaze. "I've always lived near you. I discovered early on that even though our mating bond was severed, there was still a connection. Being near you strengthened me. I've had to be careful to stay out of the paths of the Mage and Therians, but I've never been far away."

The frown didn't leave his face. "How is it possible I'm seeing your memory?"

"I don't know."

Her dream self pulled a knife out of her boot

and slid it through the neck of one of her assailants. The trapper collapsed onto the floor.

"Good gir . . ."

Kougar disappeared from beside her, leaving her alone to watch and remember a night that had repeated itself too many times. She'd killed all three men, as she had numerous others over the centuries—men who'd thought any unprotected woman fair game. A few times, early on, she'd been overpowered and knocked too senseless to stop the attacks. But she'd killed her attackers afterward and learned to fight them off.

Watching her younger self, the excruciating loneliness of those days came rushing back. How many nights had she lain on that pallet wishing for Kougar's strong arms around her?

Too many to count.

She closed her eyes, clearing her mind even as the ancient battle raged around her, and followed her mate, landing in a room filled with screams and the scent of blood.

Like before, she found Kougar standing in the midst of another of her memories, watching her assist the Countess de Frottier as she attempted to birth her second son. They'd traveled back in time several hundred years, to the 1300s. The Ferals had been living in France at the time.

The countess's bedchamber within the castle was large but cold despite the fire burning brightly in the hearth. The velvet bed curtains had been flung wide as two aging handmaids tended her, one mopping her mistress's sweat- and tear-drenched face while the other held her hand, tethered by the countess's punishing grip.

Kougar saw her and came to stand beside her as another of the woman's screams rent the air, sharp and agonized. Ariana felt the poison inside her leap with pleasure at the woman's misery even as her dream self closed her eyes, feeling the same.

"You're feeding on her pain," Kougar said, his voice cool as he stared at her other self.

"I was then, and I am now. Midwifery always brings pain, but usually joy as well. This time there was little of the latter." She glanced at him, raising her voice over the woman's rising screams. "The poison possesses a dark hunger, Kougar. When it gets too hungry, it threatens to overpower me. So I serve its needs without hurting others. Midwifery has been the perfect solution—joy and pain. And the knowledge I was doing good in the world. I'm not a monster, whatever you want to believe. I've done the best I could with the hand I was dealt."

His gaze thawed, but he said nothing as he turned back to the scene on the bed.

The smell of blood grew stronger, the dark stain spreading on the sheets. "She's hemorrhaging. She won't last much longer."

"And the babe?"

"Both died. There was nothing I could do." But she felt again the helplessness she'd felt that night. Needing to shut out the sight of the countess's agony, she turned fully to Kougar. "Why are you dreaming my memories?"

He glanced at her with a shake of his head. "I don't know. Every time I've closed my eyes the past few days, I've dreamed like this, watching you. Even before I saw you again. I figured it was that damned mating bond."

"I'm sure it's tied to the mating bond, but I still don't understand why . . ."

He was gone.

With a sigh, she turned toward the young countess, who was in her last hours of life. "I'm sorry," Ariana murmured, then followed Kougar into a glade she remembered with soft joy—a sunlit glade painted with a profusion of wildflowers.

Kougar was waiting for her, his expression at once pensive and wry. "This is one weird-ass dream."

"Are you ready for it to end? I can wake you at any time."

Soft laughter, her laughter, carried from behind them, and they turned as one.

"It's us," he murmured. "A thousand years ago."

Dressed in one of the simple belted gowns of the day, she stood holding an armful of wildflowers. With a grin, the Kougar of old picked more and more, pressing them into her arms as her laughter grew. Soft love on his face, he crushed her and the flowers to him, kissing her with a fierce and tender passion.

Ariana's chest ached as she watched them as they'd once been, so in love.

She tore her gaze away to find Kougar watching her, not their younger selves. With a lift of his hand, he stroked her face, his eyes warm as the sun, yet shadowed by a deep sadness.

If only things had been different.

Kougar's fingers slid to the back of her neck, and he leaned down to place a soft kiss on her mouth, his lips warm and sweet, the kiss surprisingly tender. Slowly, he pulled back, tracing her cheek with his thumb, the longing she felt to return to those long-lost days mirrored in his eyes. Pulling her against him, he held her as together they watched their much younger selves slowly disrobe and join in a straining tumble of need and love.

Inside, she felt the mating bond creak and groan as it untwisted a little more.

"Kougar . . ." But as she started to pull back, he disappeared from her arms.

She stood alone in the sunny glade, the summer warmth beating down on her naked flesh despite the fact she wasn't really there. Her gaze slid over the pair in the grass, watching Kougar drive into her body with long, slow strokes, their gazes locked in a powerful vise of love.

If they could hear her, if she could walk over there, interrupt their lovemaking, and warn them of the future, what would she say? At that point, the damage was already done, the poison already sewn into their mating bond, waiting to attack.

What would she say? What would have happened if she'd taken another path after that attack and run straight to Kougar for help?

She'd never know.

With a shake of her head, she locked on to him and followed, materializing in a place, for once, she didn't remember.

Had he finally left her memories and entered a real dream?

Kougar reached for her, taking her hand in a room of some sort, the walls intricately carved, but plain stone and windowless, the ceiling high. It reminded her of a cave. Or a temple.

In the middle of the room, thick stone pillars circled what appeared to be a pool of water. The darkness was broken only by the flickering flames of small fires set in stone pots and placed between each pair of pillars, the fire casting eerie shadows on the walls.

Kougar's hand squeezed hers. "What is this place?"

"I don't know." The carving reminded her of the earthbound Temple of the Queens, the Ilinas' primary home before the attacks that had forced them into the clouds and the Crystal Realm. But the temple's chambers were decorated with beautiful inlays of gold and jewels, not simple stone.

Ariana shook her head. "This has to be a real dream. It's not one of my memories. I've never been here before."

Kougar's gaze jerked to hers. "Then who's that?"

She followed the direction he pointed, sliding away from him to peer around the pillar that blocked her view of whatever . . . or whoever . . . he was looking at. A woman. In a soft white gossamer gown, she knelt beside one of the stone pots on the other side of the pool and lit it.

Chills danced over her flesh as she stared at the woman. At herself. As she watched, the woman began walking slowly around the pillars, chanting softly in the ancient Ilina tongue. A prayer to the queens of old.

A prayer Ariana had never heard before.

"I like the gown," Kougar said. His warm hand touched her shoulder, then gripped tighter. "You're shaking. What's the matter?"

She stared at her other self. "I don't remember this place. I don't know the prayer she's saying. *I don't remember.*"

"It's been a long time."

"No," she said sharply. "We don't forget. Ilinas never forget anything. Our brains don't work that way."

How could she have forgotten so much? The place, the chant. The very fact that she'd once been there.

Her heart began to race with the implications. She swung to Kougar. "Ilinas are born knowing much of what we'll need to know in life." She was starting to feel light-headed and sick to her stomach. "Upon my *awakening*, I received the knowledge of the ancient queens. All the spells, all the magic, all the memories. It was . . . downloaded . . . right into my head. Everything that had been learned. Everything the race needed to know to continue."

He watched her sharply. "You never told me this."

"We didn't do a lot of talking in those days, did we?" She lifted her hands, raking her hair back from her face. "How many times did Brielle ask me if there wasn't something in the old knowledge that could help us? Over and over I assured her there wasn't. If there had been, *I'd have remembered.*"

She stared at him, understanding like a blade to the heart. "This is Hookeye's doing. The attack . . . the poison . . . was more insidious than I'd ever imagined. *How much have I forgotten?*"

Kougar turned her to face him, his grip tight on her shoulders. "If the poison was designed to make you forget, then there were things Hookeye didn't want you to remember. You have to get that knowledge back."

She shook her head. "I don't think I can."

Olivia paused in Kara's doorway. As the Radiant, Kara had her own palatial bedroom on the second floor, though from what Olivia was coming to understand, she slept in Lyon's room. The Radiant's bedroom had become the unofficial hangout of the Feral wives.

Olivia hesitated. Delaney and Kara were both sitting in the middle of the huge bed, Delaney crying, Kara offering comfort. And Olivia, Jag's mate for only a couple of days, was still too new to the sisterhood to feel comfortable walking in on a private moment. But before she could decide whether or not to turn away, Kara glanced up and saw her, a look of welcome blooming on her face.

"Hi, Olivia."

"Am I interrupting?"

"Not at all. In fact, I was just getting ready to come find you." Though her expression was grave, an odd, out-of-place smile played at her mouth.

Delaney wiped her damp cheeks with her hands, the same odd expression on her face. Clearly the worst hadn't happened, yet—that Delaney had ceased being able to feel Tighe through their mating bond. He was still alive.

Kara wrinkled her nose. "We're Therian-knowledge challenged."

Delaney made a sound that was almost a laugh, but when her gaze met Olivia's, her eyes gleamed like smoky brown topaz. "How does a Therian know . . . if she's pregnant?"

Olivia stared at Delaney, her mouth dropping open. "You?"

Delaney nodded.

Kara leaned forward. "Will a human pregnancy test work? I mean, she used to be human. What about a blood test?"

Olivia shook her head, understanding the strange expressions on the women's faces. Such joy mixed with the terrible knowledge that the father's life hung in the balance. "There's no need for a test." She looked at Delaney. "You already know. Within a few weeks of conception, a Therian mother always knows." She sank down on the bed beside Delaney. "You know."

Delaney's mouth compressed, her eyes brimming with a damp wealth of joy and sorrow. "Yes. A little boy. I know." A tear escaped and started to roll down her cheek. "Tighe knows."

"Through the mating bond?"

She nodded, the tears running faster. "The moment I felt my son, I felt Tighe's wonder, his absolute euphoria. Moments later, both dissolved in devastation." She choked on a sob. "He doesn't think he's ever going to see him."

Delaney shot off the bed, pacing to the window, a tense bundle of nerves. "I can't stand this waiting, this feeling him die." She whirled back to the two women, dashing away the tears running down her cheeks. "I'm going back to Harpers Ferry. I know he's not actually there, but I feel like he is. And if he dies . . ."

The field where the vortex had opened was almost certainly the place his body would be spit out.

There was nothing any of them could do but hope the Ferals found that Mage, Hookeye, and a cure for the poison that would allow Queen Ariana to save Hawke and Tighe. While there was still time.

Awake again, Kougar dressed quickly, his mind spinning from all he'd seen, from all he'd learned. His blood raced with the possibilities. Almost as quickly as Ariana announced there was no way to reclaim the ancient memories, she'd backpedaled, realizing she no longer knew what was and wasn't possible.

And he was hoping this was the miracle they'd prayed for, that within those lost memories lay the answer to saving Hawke, Tighe, and the Ilinas. And himself.

"I need to go to the Crystal Realm." Ariana pulled her jeans over her hips and zipped them up. "I have to talk to Mel and Brie."

"Call them here. To the backyard. I want Lyon to hear this, too."

"This isn't your concern." Her words dismissed him, annoying the hell out of him.

As she reached for her shirt, Kougar grabbed her arm, startling a gasp out of her as her gaze snapped to his.

He didn't say anything. He didn't have to.

Her eyes flashed. "Right. Your friends, your concern." Her tone was clipped, but her expression eased with a wry twist of her lips. "It's a hard habit to break."

Kougar's grip loosened, and he ran his hand up and down her arm, knowing he'd gripped her too hard. "Break it."

They finished dressing in silence, and he ushered her out of his room and down the stairs. As they reached the foyer, he hesitated, half-tempted to tell her to go call her maidens while he went in search of Lyon. But that required a trust he just didn't have. Instead, he took her hand as he went in search of Lyon. He found his chief in his study, working at his desk.

"We may have a lead," Kougar said, when Lyon looked up. "Ariana needs to speak with Brielle. And Melisande."

Lyon scowled.

"She'll call them to the backyard. I thought you might want to be there."

"I do." Lyon came around the desk. "Is Melisande really necessary?"

"Yes." As the three strode down the wide hall-way, Kougar filled Lyon in. "We think Ariana has lost some chunks of memory—racial memory passed down from one queen to another—either as a direct result of the Mage attack or a secondary result of the poison. Either way, if she can retrieve that memory, she may be able to find an answer that could help them. And us."

They strode through the large dining room where the long dining table sat before a wide bank of windows overlooking the thickly treed backyard. Lyon yanked open the door and, together, they stepped out onto the sunny brick patio. Birds called to one another as the midday sun beat down warmly despite the mild tempera-ture of the air.

Kougar glanced at the woman at his side. The sun glowed in her dark hair, setting it afire with red and gold highlights, drilling him with her beauty. "Call them, Ariana."

Lyon pulled one of his knives, holding it at his side with a warrior's stillness. Kougar didn't believe Melisande would attack again, but there was never any telling with that one. Moments later, Ariana's two lieutenants misted into place on a pine-scented breeze.

Melisande drew her sword, her gaze locked on Lyon.

"Ease down, Mel," Ariana snapped.

Brielle's gaze fastened on her queen. "What's the matter?"

Ariana waited for Melisande to sheathe her sword, then told them what they'd seen—the temple, the prayer. "Where is that place?"

"The Temple of the Queens, the lowest chamber, below the altar of life. Only you could go down there." Brielle frowned. "You don't remember."

"No. I've lost memories. I don't know when, or how many."

Melisande scowled.

Brielle gripped Ariana's arm. "From the time of your awakening until the attack, you returned to the temple and lit the fires in the Chamber of Life every equinox. I thought you stopped going after the attack because it was too hard on you when you could no longer turn to mist."

Ariana shook her head. "I stopped going because I didn't remember I needed to. So the memories have been gone from the beginning."

Melisande looked at her sharply. "What else have you forgotten?"

"That's the question, isn't it?" Ariana murmured.

Melisande's hand stroked the hilt of her sword, her gaze flicking to Lyon and back to her queen.

Kougar met Lyon's gaze, a fine tension running between them.

"I have to request the wisdom of the queens again," Ariana stated.

Brielle gasped. "It's forbidden for any but a new queen to request an *awakening*."

"Has anyone ever tried? More importantly, has a queen ever tried?"

Melisande snorted softly. "Only you would know that. Or would have, at one time."

"I have to try. It's our only hope."

Brielle's hands twisted together. "Ariana, Morwun's magic is powerful, even now. It might force you . . ."

"To turn to mist." Ariana looked up, eyes closed, as if seeking guidance from the heavens. "He knows, Brielle. Hookeye knows I live. I have no doubt he'll strike again, and when he does, we'll lose." Lowering her face, she speared her lieutenant with a steely gaze. "We have this one chance. We have to take it."

"I agree," Melisande said.

Ariana's gaze snapped to Kougar's. "Wish me luck."

Her words registered a split second too late. Kougar lunged forward. "I'm going with you." But the words weren't even out of his mouth before she'd touched her moonstones and was gone.

As the other two Ilinas turned to mist, Kougar growled, "Melisande, take me with you."

"No." And they, too, disappeared.

Kougar growled low in his throat. Damn Ariana. Nothing ever changed.

Lyon's growl matched his own. "Now what?"

"Now we wait and hope she succeeds."

"And hope she comes back."

Frustration seethed, but it was the knowledge that she was out of his reach, that he couldn't protect her, that was roiling his insides.

"That, too."

His fist went to his chest, rubbing at the burn inside he couldn't reach. He was starting to care again. And deep inside, the poison flowed.

Chapter
Ten

Ariana stood in the rock garden beside the small waterfall behind her palace in the Crystal Realm. The sky above was blue, sunshine glowing on the rocks and setting the air crystals to sparkling. Even if Kougar followed her, it would take him time to find her out here. And by then, she'd be gone.

She felt guilty for leaving him as she had, but he couldn't help her. He'd only insist on accompanying her, and she wouldn't let him. It was far too dangerous. Besides, it was time to put distance between them before the mating bond opened any more.

Melisande and Brielle huddled before her, gripping her hands. Ariana met their gazes one after the other.

"It's going to work."

Though she said the words to reassure her friends, it was herself who needed the convincing. Because although she'd clearly lost memories, she remembered all too well the warning that only a new queen could request an *awakening*. Anyone else who tried would invite the wrath of the first queen, Morwun, the spirit of the temple.

What form that wrath might take, Ariana didn't know. She wasn't afraid of pain. What had her trembling was the fear that she might, as Brielle feared, somehow be forced to turn to mist. That in trying to save her friends, she might kill them all.

She hugged her two best friends to her. "It's time."

"We're going with you," Brielle said quietly.

"No. I don't know what will happen when I make this request. I want you both to stay here."

Mel shook her head, the look in her eyes telling Ariana she would get no cooperation. "Brielle stays here, but I'm going with you. I'm your second for a reason."

"If anything goes wrong . . ."

"I'll be there to help you. Don't waste time arguing, Ariana. We need to get going before that Feral of yours shows up growling and making demands."

"You've forgotten how to take orders, Mel." Her tone was wry, for her friend's loyalty was rock solid.

A hint of a smile lit Melisande's eyes. "My job is to protect the queen. That's what I'm doing."

Ariana nodded. "Let's go, then. Let's find out what I've lost."

"Do you remember the Chamber of Life in the lower level of the temple?"

Ariana nodded.

"I'll meet you there." Melisande turned to mist, her form insubstantial for a moment before she disappeared.

Ariana took the corporeal's path, gripping her moonstone cuff and whispering the chant of transport as she visualized the chamber where all Ilinas were born. Moments later, she materialized within the inlaid ivory walls of the Temple of the Queens.

Around her, sconces flared. Goose bumps rose on her arms at the sight of this place she hadn't seen in centuries—the mosaic floor and the pure crystal altar standing at the very center of the circular room. It was upon the Altar of Life that new Ilinas came into the world. Upon which she herself had been born, not as flesh-and-blood creatures were born—springing forth from the wombs of their mothers as infants who must grow to full size—but through a ritual of magic that created women prepared to take their place in Ilina society within only a few education-filled months.

Unlike a flesh-and-blood woman, she remembered well the day she was born—the wonder and confusion as the maidens welcomed her as their new queen. Unlike humans and most immortals, Ilinas were born with the basic knowledge they needed to survive, including the language of their kind.

Yes, she had memories of this place, of the births of other Ilinas who'd come after her.

But of the lower chamber, the stone chamber that was supposedly hers alone, she had no memories at all.

Mel's low cry behind her had her whirling, ready to fight, but she saw no one and nothing wrong. They were alone. It took her a second to realize the problem, and when she did, her eyes went wide.

Melisande was sinking into the floor, her feet slowly disappearing into the decorative mosaic tile.

Melisande reached for her. Ariana grabbed her hands, trying without success to pull her free.

"Turn to mist, Melisande!"

"I can't! It's some kind of trap." Her oldest friend's eyes took on a rare and gut-wrenching terror.

They'd walked into a trap that could have been set by only one race.

The Mage.

Regret raked at Hawke's mind. He should have shoved Tighe away from him. He should have saved his friend.

Excruciating pain speared through his skull as his hawk screeched in agony. The pain had become a constant, now, an ever-present torment. At least he knew what was happening, though it was of no comfort whatsoever. He'd fallen into a spirit trap whose purpose was to separate man from beast. And when it succeeded? He'd be dead. The trap would spit out his body as it had the bodies of the seventeen all those years ago, leaving the hawk spirit trapped inside in perpetual agony, if the sounds of the other animals were anything to go by.

They'd been in there for centuries.

His hawk screeched again.

Easy, buddy. Calm your feathers.

But instead of soothing the spirit as he'd intended, he only seemed to inflame the creature's fury. Hawke felt the bird's anger pummel the insides of his mind, melding with the pain.

Dammit, I didn't get us trapped in here on purpose!

He had to find a way out of here. For the hundredth time, he prayed to the goddess that he'd been mistaken about Tighe's falling in with him, that Stripes was safely with the others. With his mate. For the first time in the long years he'd known the tiger shifter, Tighe radiated with a happiness Hawke envied. If anyone deserved that happiness, it was Stripes. Yet Hawke was all too afraid he was trapped down there with him, about to leave Delaney a widow.

The other Ferals couldn't afford to lose two more animals. Perhaps more? He had no idea how many had fallen into this with him.

Goddess, get us out of here. Take my life, if you must, but not like this. Let the hawk fly free to mark another. Don't let us both end like this!

Slowly, he shoved back the anger, both the hawk's and his own, forcing his mind to search for a solution. There *had* to be a way out of there. Perhaps the animal spirits themselves knew the answer if he could only find a way to communicate with them. There were at least a dozen distinct animal sounds he'd managed to identify, at least a dozen animals—several different kinds of cats, two or three bears, the screech of a bird that wasn't his hawk. And others he couldn't identify. He'd heard a deep snorting that might have come from any one of several large animals. He heard them, not with his ears, for his senses were in limbo, but with his mind.

Were they really even there? The question had plagued him from the start. He'd tried to call to them, to communicate with them, but he'd failed to get any response.

All he heard in the depths of his mind was the hawk's punishing anger. And the sound of pain.

"Get some lunch." Lyon turned to head back into the house after the Ilinas' disappearance. "Pink keeps making too much food. I think she's convinced that Tighe and Hawke might return at any moment, and she wants to be ready in case they're famished."

Kougar continued to stare at the spot Ariana had stood just moments before, frustration eating at him that she'd left. He felt her in the Crystal Realm and was tempted to follow, but he knew she didn't intend to stay there. By the time he found her, she'd be gone again, down to the earth-bound Temple of the Queens.

He hated that she refused to let him protect her, but he trusted her to return, as he hadn't before. Something had changed between them as they'd traveled his dream and her memories, together.

He joined Lyon as his chief opened the patio door. "Any word on Hookeye?" Kougar asked.

"Not yet. Skye's family has put the word out. Someone has to know of a sorcerer whose eyes had oddly-shaped pupils."

One would think. And when they got a lock on him, Kougar was damn well going to be first in line to hunt the bastard down. Meanwhile, he waited. And the waiting was killing him.

How much harder this must be on Tighe's mate, forced to wait while others tried to save the one she loved.

"How's Delaney?" he asked Lyon.

Lyon gave him a surprised look as if he hadn't expected him to remember Tighe had a mate, let alone her name. "She's on her way back to Harpers Ferry to join Vhyper."

Kougar knew that Vhyper watched over the place where Hawke and Tighe had fallen into the vortex in case they reappeared. Of course, if they did, it would almost certainly be as corpses.

"Delaney puts up a good front." Lyon started into the dining room, empty but for Wulfe. "But I've found her pacing the house at all hours, day and night."

"We'll get them back, Roar." There was an answer, and he wasn't giving up until they'd found it.

Lyon met his gaze with eyes rife with worry. "I hope to hell you're right."

As Lyon continued through the dining room and into the hall, Kougar turned to where Wulfe was making what appeared to be a sandwich. A small one. Since when did the wolf shifter bother with bread?

At the lift of Kougar's brow, Wulfe shrugged. "The humans are hungry."

Kougar stilled. "Humans?"

Wulfe bristled, a snarl in his throat. "Three of the humans attacked by the Daemons in Harpers Ferry survived, but we haven't been able to wipe their minds. As soon as we can, we'll release them."

As long as the humans posed no threat to the Ferals, Kougar didn't much care. All he cared about was Ariana's returning to him, hopefully with the answers they needed. He grabbed a plate and was piling it high with ham when he felt it, a pulse of raw emotion blasting down the mating bond, stronger than he'd felt since the bond was reattached. A blend of anger. And fear.

He dropped his plate with a clatter, closing his eyes as he tried to sense her in the Crystal Realm, but the door was closed to him. She wasn't there. *She must have already headed to that damned temple.* And he had no way to reach her. No way to communicate with any of them other than to send his emotions, his demand, roaring through the mating bond, and hope someone other than Ariana felt them and responded.

His muscles spasmed with his need to do something. Shoving through the back door, he caught a whiff of pine, felt a tingle of Ilina energy and began to breathe again.

Brielle shimmered to form before him, the look on her face telling him she already knew something was wrong.

"What happened?" he demanded.

"They're in trouble. Ariana and Melisande went together to the Temple of the Queens, but Melisande's been caught in a trap. Mel thinks it was set by the Mage. She can't be certain, but she thinks there are Mage in the temple."

Hell. "Take me to them."

"So that we can be captured, too?"

The need to reach Ariana was a live wire streaking through his blood, but he forced himself to think.

"They went directly into the temple?"

"To the Chamber of Life below the temple."

"Then you're going to deliver me outside. Far enough away that no one will know we're there and that you won't be caught by the magic."

Brielle's tight expression eased. "All right."

"Can you transport two of us?"

"Not two Ferals."

"Then get help." Kougar ran for the back door of Feral House. "Roar! Jag!" He was yelling even before he stepped into the dining room.

Lyon met him in the hallway. "What's up?"

"Ariana and Melisande ran into trouble in the temple. They've been captured."

"By whom?"

"Only the Mage would be able to capture an Ilina."

Lyon growled. "Where is this place?"

"The Himalayas."

"You've got to be kidding."

"The Ilinas can get us there. I'm taking Jag as backup."

Lyon lifted a brow. "Not Wulfe?" Hawke and Wulfe had been Kougar's partners of choice for years, now.

"We'll have to slip into the temple. Jag can downsize." And Wulfe couldn't. When he was shifted, he had only one form—huge gray wolf. Jag, like Kougar and a number of the others, had perfected the ability to take on smaller forms. He and Jag could pass for house cats, or close enough.

Jag joined them in the hallway, and Lyon filled him in.

"How in the hell are we getting there?" Jag demanded.

"Ilina."

The jaguar shifter made a sound of excited disbelief. "No shit. Hey, Chief, tell Olivia where I've gone, will you? She's with Kara."

"I'll tell her. I don't have to tell you two to be careful."

Kougar turned back toward the dining room.

"So how does this work, traveling by Ilina?" Jag asked, catching up with him.

"You'll feel like you're falling. Then you'll puke your guts out."

"Reality check, Kougar-man. Don't apply for a job as an ad man for the travel industry."

Lucky for Kougar, his link to Ariana had long ago tamped down the worst of the effects for him. But he remembered all too well his one trip to the Crystal Realm before they were mated. He'd sworn he was never traveling like that again. Jag wasn't going to enjoy himself, but there was little help for it. Ariana needed him, and he needed Jag.

Brielle and an Ilina whose name Kougar didn't know were waiting for them when they reached the patio.

The mist warriors flew at them before they were fully out the door.

"Hey!" Jag complained, then said nothing more as they were both encased in a warm, mistlike energy glow.

As long as they didn't fight the Ilinas, the energy didn't hurt unless the Ilinas wanted it to. But Kougar had never been particularly fond of the scratchy feel. It always reminded him of lying naked in hay. He closed his eyes against the blinding light, concentrating on the mating bond inside him to anchor himself against the spinning.

Moments later, he came back to himself in a bitterly cold wind that whipped at his face. On the hard, rocky ledge beside him, Jag began to retch. Ahead rose a steep, rocky path. Behind them, the cliff face dropped away, offering a view of rugged snowcapped peaks as far as the eye could see.

"I feel magic," murmured the dark blond Ilina Kougar didn't know.

Brielle clasped her hands agitatedly before her. "Mage magic. Ariana and Melisande would have transported into the thick of it."

The need to reach Ariana pulsed in his head like the pounding of drums. He started up the rocky path until the glittering crystal dome of the Temple of the Queens came into sight above him, blinding in its sunlit brightness.

The impressive structure was surprisingly large—perhaps the size of a three-story office building—and square, with a pair of thick pillars framing the entry. It sat atop a wide plateau, an iridescent ivorylike beauty capped by a crystal dome. The temple was an artist's dream, the pillars decorated with gold leaf, inlaid with sparkling gems of hundreds of varieties forming what appeared to be intricate scrollwork.

His warrior's eye took in the two sentries posted before the entrance, two men dressed in the blue tunics of Mage sentinels.

What in the hell are Mage doing here? How did they get up here? Helicopters, probably.

Brielle eased up beside him as they waited for Jag to get control of his stomach.

"This place must be warded. Humans would be able to see it from a hundred miles away, even before binoculars and satellite imaging."

"Against humans, yes," Brielle confirmed, "but

not immortals. Before the Sacrifice, the queen and her court lived here, the other Ilinas scattered in temples elsewhere in the world. But when the Therians turned on us after the Sacrifice, we were forced to flee to the clouds."

To the Crystal Realm.

"Son of a *bitch*." Jag's muttered epithet carried from below. Moments later, he joined them. "You weren't kidding about that ride. If there's another way off this perch, I'm taking it."

Kougar turned to Brielle. "Tell me how to find Ariana."

Her worried gaze met his. "The lower chambers are hidden. I have to go with you."

He could see the panic rising in her eyes and reached for her, gripping her shoulder. "Stay here. We'll find them. Just tell me what you know."

The Ilina paused, took a deep, deliberate breath, then nodded. "The temple is divided into four chambers, in the center of which lies the rotunda. The great statue of Morwun, the first queen, stands beneath the crystal dome. To reach the stairs to the chamber below, you must enter the passage directly behind the statue. At the end is a curved stair that appears to go only up. I'll tell you the words that will open the passage down, and you must say them exactly. But, Kougar, I don't know if they'll work coming from one who's not Ilina."

"Tell me the words." Kougar glanced at Jag. "Listen and memorize. I've never had an ear for Ilina."

Jag gave him a quick, half-serious salute. "Yes, sir."

Brielle whispered a string of sounds he knew to be ancient Ilina, a language that had always sounded more like music to his ear than words. And not music with any kind of logic to it.

Jag scowled. "What the hell was that?"

Kougar closed his eyes. Clearly, Jag wasn't going to be any better at Ilina than he was. "Again, Brielle."

The woman repeated the sounds. In his head he tried to mimic them and failed. *Dammit, I have to do this. It's the only way I'm going to reach Ariana.*

He tried to repeat the sounds out loud.

Brielle shook her head. "That's not it." Again, she sang the chant and again Kougar tried to mimic her with no more success than before. He felt like he wasn't hearing her properly. Like there were pieces missing. He looked to Jag, hoping he was starting to catch on.

Jag shook his head. "She might as well be speaking hummingbird."

Dammit. He'd have to figure out something else when he got in there. Without further discussion, he shifted directly into his house-cat form, bypassing his larger cougar. Beside him, Jag downsized into his mini jaguar.

Are they really going to believe two cats found their way all the way up here? Jag asked telepathically.

No. That's why we're going in together. When you get inside, head left and keep them away from the back passage. I'll go right.

Aye-aye.

As one, they darted across the open rock and up the dozen steps to the pillars. Not until they were racing between the guards did one of the sentinels do a double take.

"What's with the cats?"

"Shit. Those aren't cats. They're shifters!"

Kougar darted into the mammoth temple, heading straight for the middle and the giant golden statue of a naked woman with wild hair, lifting a sword high over her head. A woman who'd lived and ruled when humans still lived in caves. Though he sensed the presence of others in the temple, none were in the rotunda except the two chasing them, shouting for backup.

Kougar's senses went out to Ariana, but he felt her only at a distance. The lower chambers, dammit. He'd been hoping Brielle was mistaken about that.

Any sign of your queen wife? Jag asked.

Any chance you remember the words Brielle spoke?

You're kidding, right?

That's what I was afraid of.

Was that a quip, Kougar-man? Don't tell me you have a sense of humor after all this time.

Kougar ignored him. *Meet me in the back passage when you shake off your Mage.*

Already done and on my way.

Kougar darted across the ivory floor and down a passage whose walls were decorated with climbing vines of inlaid crystal and gems, to the stairwell Brielle had described. A stair that went only up. He stared in dismay at the solid wall at the base where Brielle assured him another went down. Shifting into a man, he felt for any kind of latch, for any door at all, and found nothing. If there was a door there, it was a magic one, plain and simple.

With a sharp exhale, he attempted the musical-sounding words and got two out of his mouth when he lost any memory of what came next.

"What now?" Jag asked behind him.

By way of answer, Kougar turned and gave the wall a massive kick.

"Way to keep a low profile," Jag muttered.

Kougar kicked again. And again. On the third kick, one small section of the wall began to crumble. On the fourth, his foot went through. He could feel a draft of air wafting from the opening. An opening just big enough for a house cat.

"Let's go." Kougar shifted and leaped through the small break in the wall, into darkness, hoping to hell he wasn't leading them into nothingness.

Chapter
Eleven

"Mel . . ." Ariana held her friend's hands, willing Melisande free of the magical trap, holding her from sinking farther by the sheer force of her will.

Melisande met her gaze with terrified eyes. "Go, Ariana. Go to the lower chamber. Do what you came for. Beg the queens of old for a second *awakening*."

"I can't leave you! You're still sinking."

"No, I think it's stopped. And it doesn't matter anyway. I don't matter. Only you. You're the only one who can find a way to save us."

Ariana squeezed her best friend's hands. "You matter to me. You always have, and you know it."

Melisande's mouth softened. "I know. But you may learn something down there that will solve both our problems. Now let go of me, Ariana."

Ariana looked away, her gaze raking the ivory walls, seeing a single set of stairs spiraling upward in one far corner. And none spiraling down.

"I don't know how to get down there. I don't remember."

Melisande whispered the words of the ancients, then motioned behind Ariana with a nod of her head. "There."

Ariana turned to find that a hole had appeared in the wall to the right of the Altar of Life. She eyed it with wariness, then turned back to Melisande.

"I thought you said only I could go into that place."

Melisande shrugged, her blond braid sliding over her shoulder. "I may not be able to go down there, but I've been here with you and your predecessors enough times to memorize the words." Mel squeezed her hands. "Now release me and go, Ariana. I've stopped sinking."

Ariana prayed to the queens who'd come before that Mel was right, then slowly released her grip, watching her friend for any sign of movement.

Nothing else happened. Melisande remained trapped, but sunk no farther.

"Go," Mel urged. "Quickly, Ariana, before anything else goes wrong." Melisande's voice trembled on an alien note of terror. "Before they find us."

With a quick breath, Ariana nodded, then turned and ran to the opening in the wall. Peering inside, she found a twisting stair carved of stone, just like the chamber in the dream. A stair leading into darkness. A chill skated down her spine, but she hesitated for only a second before slipping inside and starting down, using the curving inner wall as her guide.

Little by little, the stair began to lighten until finally she stepped into the chamber of Kougar's dream. The chamber was far smaller than the one above, primitive-looking in comparison, lit only by a single torch hanging in a bracket on the far wall as if waiting for her. While the floor beneath her bare feet was simple unpolished stone, up close the walls were beautiful—white sandstone thickly carved with flowering vines in high relief, floor to ceiling.

Ariana started forward, toward the small pool in the middle of the chamber circled by half a dozen pillars, classic fluted Doric. Plain stone pots the size of large flowerpots had been placed between each of the pillars, pots she remembered lighting in the dream. A scent teased her nose and her memory, an ancient scent of burning incense. With it came the certainty that the temple awaited her light.

Quickly, she strode to the torch and pulled it off the wall. How could she have forgotten this place? She knelt before the first of the pots, dipping the flame carefully inside, watching as the fire caught. Then she rose to repeat the process in the others.

She still remembered her first *awakening*, coming into her queen's knowledge, though not where it had taken place. She remembered how her mind had filled with the voices and the faces of more than a dozen ancient queens all the way back to Morwun. Queens who'd lived in a time when humans worshipped the immortals as gods and goddesses. When shape-shifters had roamed the Earth in the thousands, battling one another with fangs and swords. A time when the Mage had controlled every natural thing from the weather to the profusion of flowers growing in the fields, and the Daemons had avoided them all, living alone, high in the mountain passes, preying only on those unfortunates who wandered into their realm.

She still possessed a wealth of memories. So many that she'd failed to realize she'd lost any. What worried her was that the ones she'd lost might not help. This might all be for nothing.

When flame glowed from all six pots, she replaced the torch and returned to stand beside the shallow pool, the bottom lit with crystals, the water a rainbow of sparkling color. She'd come to request another *awakening*, but she didn't know how. Fear fluttered in her stomach.

Forcing down her rising panic, she took a deep breath. The knowledge had to be instinctive. Long ago, she'd stood like this, without any of the queens' memories. Of course, that first time she'd been young, with only a few months of living behind her. Her mind had been open, her instincts all she had to go by. Accessing what to do had been easy and natural. After more than thirteen centuries, that was no longer true.

Still, the knowledge must live inside her some-where.

Forcing herself to shut out her fears, to shut out the world, she closed her eyes and concentrated, dropping her hands loosely to her sides. Little by little, she sank deep within her own mind, down through the layers of memory of her life among the humans, through the all-too-shallow bright layer of those two years with Kougar, down through the three centuries she'd ruled the Ilinas before she became Kougar's mate.

All of a sudden, the memories began to flash and blank out like a television show that had taped poorly. Memories that weren't hers, but the queens' who'd come before her. Jagged memories with large chunks ripped away. She hadn't real-ized. From the beginning, her brain had delivered the knowledge she sought, like a dumbwaiter lift-ing the facts from the basement of her mind. It was only since she'd come down herself, that she understood the extent of the damage.

Finally, sinking deeper, she hit the ephemeral watery memories she'd been born with. Memories that appeared clean and whole.

And it was there she found the knowledge she sought.

She pulled off her clothes and discarded her weapons, then giving herself up to that ancient instinct, she stepped down into the shallow pool.

The water felt cool against her skin, bubbling oddly. How could she not remember this? She shoved the thought aside and concentrated on what she had to do.

With four slow strides, she was in the middle, the water lapping at her knees. Lifting her hands to the stone ceiling above, she called to the queens who'd come before her in the language of the ancients. And waited.

Nothing happened.

A trickle of despair broke through her concentration, and she tried to seal it off, opening her mind as instinct told her to. But the longer the temple ignored her, the harder it was to keep the fears at bay. Was Melisande all right? Had the Mage, even now, managed to break in to the lower chamber? Would Kougar come and be trapped as well?

The sharp worry and longing at the thought of him caught her off guard, slicing deep into her heart.

Concentrate.

With excruciating effort, she forced herself back down into that place of instinct and resumed the words of ritual. Over and over she begged the queens to hear her. To share their memories and knowledge with her once more.

The first bolt took her by surprise, a flash of pure energy that sliced at her shoulder like a blade, ripping her skin open from clavicle to biceps. She cried out as the pain radiated from her shoulder, washing like a wave out to her extremities. Was this how the knowledge had come to her last time? She couldn't remember!

As warm blood began to run down her arm, another bolt shot at her from the other direction, slicing down her hip and thigh.

With a curse, she began to shout. "I'm one of you, queens of the Ilinas! I need your help."

The third bolt tore down the middle of her back and she cried out with pain and frustration, losing the thread of the chant. This was no *awakening*, but an attack. Morwun's punishment for her impudence.

As if to confirm the thought, energy twisted around her, binding her in place. And when three more bolts shot at her in quick succession, tearing across her breasts and thighs and shoulders, she couldn't move, couldn't escape.

All she could do was scream.

Kougar leaped through the hole he'd kicked in the wall, thanking the goddess as his paws hit stairs. A twisting spiral of golden stairs, he realized, his cat's eyesight taking over in the dark. Behind him, he heard the soft footfalls of his jaguar companion.

Upshifting into his full-sized cougar, he flew down the stairs four at a time. Light began to reach him from below after a single turn, growing brighter as he descended, revealing the jeweled inlay work in the walls, creating magnificently intricate floral designs. One part of his mind wondered at the artists who'd created the place, but his only concern was finding Ariana.

A flash of pain, Ariana's pain, burst from the

mating bond, making him crazy with the need to reach her.

After more than a dozen turns of the stairs, he leaped into a chamber and came to a startled halt.

What the fuck? Jag pulled up beside him.

Melisande stood alone in the large, circular chamber. At first, he thought her feet had been cut off and she stood balanced upon the remaining stumps. But she was somehow fused to the mosaic floor.

His gaze rose to her face, to the defiant fury that couldn't mask the terror in her eyes. He shifted into his human form, Jag doing the same.

"Where's Ariana?" Kougar demanded.

"You shouldn't be here. You have no right to breach the sanctity of the queen's chambers." But her words held little real heat.

Kougar strode to her, in no mood for her attitude. "Tell me!"

"She's in the lower chamber."

"Show me how to reach her."

This time, her ire rose. "It's forbidden to all but the queen." Even terrified half-out of her mind, she remained defiant.

Kougar's patience was at an end. He went feral, his claws and fangs descending, though he held himself back from attacking her by the barest measure. There would certainly be no lifting this one off her feet.

A distant scream rang from deep below. Ariana's scream.

"*Melisande.*" The growl ripped through his voice.

Her resistance visibly melted, the fear for her queen getting the better of her where her fear for herself had not.

"You can't follow." Melisande lifted her hand to forestall his reaction. "I can open the door, but the temple won't let you through it. It won't even let me pass." Disgust sliced through her expression. "And you're not even Ilina."

High above, a shout sounded, followed by the smashing of stone.

"We're about to get company," Jag warned.

Melisande's temper snapped, anger fueled by pure terror. "You've led them to us!"

"Put a muzzle on it, blondie." Jag held his hand out to Kougar, palm up. "Knives? I'll hold them off." Of the two of them, only Kougar retained his clothes and weapons when he shifted.

Another distant cry of pain rang out, followed by a burst of agony blasting down the mating bond deep within him.

Kougar tossed two knives to Jag and whirled on Melisande. "Open the door!"

The blond mist warrior began to chant softly in the musical Ilina-speak. Behind the altar, a shimmering door appeared. Kougar raced for it, desperate to barrel through, but all too afraid Melisande had spoken the truth. He pulled up, attempting to slam his hand through instead. And hit solid rock.

"I told you." For once, Melisande's voice held no smugness, only a twist of defeat.

But Kougar wasn't about to give up. Again, he

heard Ariana cry out and felt her pain in that mating bond he'd been trying so hard to keep himself cut off from.

The mating bond.

Taking a deep breath, he closed his eyes and followed that bond with his mind, reaching down through the decrepit, caved-in cord, trying to touch her in some way. As he focused on her through the bond, he reached for the door again. And again, hit only stone.

From the other end of that bond, he felt her pain, her fear. And something else. A rising darkness. As if she was losing control of the poison.

Goddess. He pounded at the door with both fists, then shifted into his cougar and tried to leap through, only to be knocked back on his haunches. He sat there, his head ringing for an infuriating moment before he leaped to his feet and shifted back to man. As he'd done above the stairs, he kicked at the barrier over and over with his foot; but this one showed no intention of crumbling.

The damned temple wasn't going to let him in. *Like. Hell.*

Once more, Ariana's scream rang from below. Fear for her tore at his throat. The need to reach her rose until he thought it would suffocate him.

"Let me reach my mate!" A roar of fury and possession and frustration blasted up from his chest and out his throat, echoing through the chamber, pounding at the walls. *"She's mine!"*

He slammed his fist against the door again and again, then stopped suddenly as a weird crawling energy hit his scalp and washed down his body. Deep in his mind, a voice spoke to him. A voice he didn't know. A woman's.

Then you shall both suffer.

His gaze flew to Melisande. "Did you hear that?"

"Hear what?"

Turning back to the shimmering, unbreachable door, he knew. The temple itself, or the queen whose spirit resided within, had heard his claim and bowed to it.

In a spray of light, he shifted into his cougar and flew through as if the stone had never been. As before, he landed on tight, spiral stairs, this time of stone. The air changed as he descended to the lowest of the chambers, taking on the scent of lightning and lily of the valley. Of fear and pain.

Ariana's pain.

With his cat's agility, he tore down the stairs, a longer set than the last ones, twisting deep into the earth. With each twist, Ariana's pain grew inside him.

She cried out again. And again.

Finally, when he thought he couldn't stand it another minute, he burst into the chamber he'd seen in his dream. And into a scene of nightmare.

Ariana stood within the circle of pillars, in the center of the knee-deep pool, naked. Bloody stripes crisscrossed her breasts and thighs. Stripes that weren't healing.

As he watched, a bolt of lightning shot from the top of one of the pillars to slice across her abdomen. With a cry, she threw back her head, her face a mask of agony. She swayed unnaturally on her feet as if she were being held upright by an invisible force.

He felt her pain as if it were his own. Shifting into a man, he ran to her and jumped into the pool as another bolt struck her low across the back.

"No more!" he shouted.

The water plastered his pants to his calves and soaked into his boots. As he reached her he saw a flash of light against the ceiling and shifted to put himself between it and Ariana. Pain sliced across his shoulder blade, an electric current that raced through his body, setting every nerve ending on fire. Biting down on a groan, he wrapped his arms around Ariana's chilled, bloody body, curving himself around her. Protecting her as well as he could.

"Kougar." His name on her lips was little more than a gasp. "You can't be here."

"I'm getting you out of here."

"No. Can't . . . leave."

Out of the corner of his eye, he saw another bolt flash, and shifted to take that blow, too. The lightning tore through his left hip, slicing his pants and his flesh halfway to the bone.

Fuck.

Within the cage of his body, Ariana began to soften, her breath easing.

"Have you accessed any of the ancient knowledge?" he asked, but she didn't answer. "Ariana?" He tried to lift her into his arms, but she was caught fast by an invisible force.

Another bolt flashed and Kougar spun, Ariana tucked within the curve of his body. Whatever held her to that pool allowed him to turn her, but not remove her. Fire exploded across the backs of his thighs.

Goddamn that hurt.

He caught the next one across his left shoulder. The fourth tore through the back of his skull. He could barely think, barely breathe. His entire existence, his purpose for living, narrowed down to one thing—keeping the bolts from striking the woman in his arms.

How many attacked him, he didn't know. Time ceased to exist. He was so dazed with pain that he didn't realize the attack was over until Ariana collapsed, nearly falling to her knees before he caught her.

With a wary, cautious breath, he swung her up into his arms, then leaped clear of the pool before another bolt could flay them. He headed for the stairs, wanting only to get her the hell out of there. It occurred to him that he had no idea if she'd learned what she needed to know.

But at that moment, Ariana's safety was his only concern.

Chapter
Twelve

Ariana rose to consciousness slowly, disoriented, her body ablaze with pain. Kougar's familiar scent and the feel of his strong arms grounded her, dispersing her fear, and she sank against the warmth of his chest as she tried to remember where she was. And why.

They were climbing upward. Climbing stairs. Twisty, spiral stairs.

The temple.

With a jerk, she came fully awake, shifting in his arms, hooking one arm around his neck and pulling herself up with a blast of pain. "Kougar, no! I can't leave. It's not done. I've learned nothing."

"It attacked you."

"Morwun demanded pain as her price. Kougar, I have to go back."

But he wasn't listening, and her strength had never been a match for his. Especially now. She hurt, as if every cell in her body had been lit on fire. Her head, too heavy to hold up, fell against the side of his neck as he took the stairs at a fast climb. Even her hands and feet were beginning to prickle in the way they did when the darkness inside her grew hungry.

In her dazed mind, small memories popped forth like warm puffs of air. The metallic smell of her own warm blood as she cut her wrists to paint her body for ritual. The pleas and screams of an Ilina maiden as she curled her fingers around the traitor's heart and pulled it from her chest. The sweet pleasure of release as she rode a male she didn't recognize. Because the memories weren't hers, but those of the queens who'd come before. Scattered, confused knowledge that might prove to be of some help if she could make sense of any of it.

Moments later, Kougar burst through the warded door and into the upper of the queen's chambers, the room light and airy compared to the one below. Melisande stood where Ariana had left her, ankle deep in the floor, while Jag fought back would-be invaders at the base of the upper stair, his bare back gleaming with sweat.

"Mage?" she asked.

"Yes." Kougar's arms tightened around her. "They followed us down here."

"I can seal the door." How she knew that, she wasn't sure, but she began to whisper the ancient chant that came to her. Seconds later a wall appeared between Jag and his opponents.

The Feral sprang back in the nick of time, but the Mage surged forward. A mistake. A yell of agony filtered through the wall as his hand, sticking out through the solid stone, dropped its useless knife to clatter on the floor below.

Jag whirled, his expression fierce until it landed on her. "Did you do that? How about a little warning next time, sister? Correct me if I'm wrong, but wasn't that our only way out?"

"You've acquired new knowledge," Kougar murmured against her temple, a fine thread of expectation sharpening his words. He pulled back, and she met his gaze.

"Not enough. Not all."

"You don't know that."

"Yes. I do. I have to go back."

The air felt queer, almost bubbly, against her skin. She tightened her hold on Kougar's neck, excitement lifting her pulse. "I can feel the magic in here, the magic that trapped Melisande." Closing her eyes, she let the knowledge flow into her. "It will trap any Ilina turning from mist to flesh." She opened her eyes again, meeting Kougar's gaze. "Which is why it didn't trap me, too."

"How do you know?"

"I couldn't read the magic before. Now I can. I can block it." Softly, she began to sing one of the Ilina songs of enchantment. Slowly, she felt the magic in the chamber dissolve and the strangeness leave the air. "It's done."

"Fail." Jag nodded toward Melisande. "Peter Pan there is still trapped like an ex–Mafia boss in cement shoes." He sauntered over to Melisande, squatting at her feet. Wrapping one large hand around her ankle, he gave a small tug. "Caught fast." He looked up at the mist warrior, whose complexion had turned pasty white. "Are you sure your feet are still in there?"

Melisande scowled. "They're in there. And the moment they're free, I'll prove it to you by kicking you in the balls."

"Yeah, yeah, that's what all the girls say."

"I don't have the knowledge to free you, Mel, but no one else should get caught. If I come up with the magic . . ."

"Screw magic," Jag muttered, rising. "What we need is a jackhammer."

Kougar tightened his hold on her. "He's right."

Melisande's gaze shot to Ariana's. "You can't let them destroy the temple."

Ariana sighed. "Call Getrill, Melisande. You're a lot more important to me than the temple."

Melisande met her gaze, fear written all over her face. She was afraid Ariana was mistaken, that Getrill, too, would become trapped. Ariana could see that truth in her eyes, even if she didn't say the words out loud.

"Call her, Mel."

Melisande frowned but did as she asked, and a moment later the freckled Getrill safely formed from the mist. As her gaze took in Melisande's entrapment and Ariana's weakness, her face turned hard, her hand going to her sword.

Ariana raised a hand, reading her thoughts all too well. "The Mage set the trap, Getrill. The Ferals protect us."

The maiden relaxed only slightly.

"Take Jag back to Feral House—"

"No." Kougar interrupted her. "Jag won't be of any use by the time he gets back here." He turned to Getrill. "Knock on the back door of Feral House and tell Lyon I need a pickax and a sledgehammer. ASAP."

Getrill's wary gaze swung to Ariana, who nodded in agreement. The Ilina turned to mist and disappeared.

"It's sacrilege to desecrate the temple," Melisande muttered when she was gone; but her complaint was all but toneless, a rote objection and little more. Her desperation to be free was a palpable force, yet she held herself together with the fierceness Ariana had always admired. It was the reason the woman was her second-in-command.

"Now what?" Jag asked no one in particular.

Up above, Ariana could hear the sounds of pounding, as if the Mage were trying to find a way to break through. She stroked the back of Kougar's head.

"You can put me down now."

He eyed her without expression, then brushed his cheek against her hair. "I could." But he made no move to release her, and she leaned into his touch, perfectly content to remain in his arms a little while longer.

Inside, the mating bond opened a little more.

The all-too-familiar prickling sensation in her palms and the soles of her feet grew worse. The darkness was getting seriously hungry. Out-of-control hungry. Which made no sense at all. The more the mating bond opened, the more the grip of the poison inside her should ease, as it siphoned off to Kougar. It shouldn't be strengthening.

Was this Hookeye's doing? Fear twisted inside her even as the hunger leaped with a strength that startled her, the prickling shooting up her legs and arms like sharp little scalpels.

"What's the matter?" Kougar stiffened. "You're in pain."

She didn't answer. She couldn't. The scalpels were tearing her apart from the inside, the need to turn to mist clawing to get out. It was a compulsion that took every ounce of strength she possessed to fight.

Her heart pounded with the struggle, with the fear that this time she'd lose.

"He's attacking," she gasped.

"How?" Kougar's face swam in her vision, his eyes blazing into hers.

She clung to his neck, drawing on the small strength she gained from touching him, holding on against the darkness with everything she had as it tried to free itself to spread to her maidens. To destroy those who'd survived the first attack.

"Ariana?"

"It's the poison. More." She was beginning to shake from the effort to hold it back. *"Too strong."*

His grip on her tightened. "Tell me what you need."

"Pain. Others' pain."

In a single fluid movement, he set her on the cool floor at his feet, stripped off his shirt, and leaped at Jag, his fangs and claws erupting midair to tear a chunk of flesh from the jaguar shifter's shoulder.

The darkness inside her howled with pleasure at the shifter's pain.

Jag stumbled forward, then whirled, his own claws and fangs erupting as he went feral. "What the *fuck?*"

"Fight me," Kougar growled through his fangs. "The darkness within her feeds on the pain. Feeding it is the only way she can control it."

"Neither one of you is any good with the warnings!"

Kougar leaped again and the two part-men, part-beasts crashed to the floor, wrestling and biting, clawing and bleeding.

Seated on the cold floor, Ariana gripped her head with both hands, closing her eyes as the darkness fed, as she fought the battle inside her. Sounds carried to her—the ripping of cloth and flesh, the crunch of breaking bones, the growls and snarls. The metallic smell of blood filled her nose and slid down her throat to coat her tongue. Droplets of sweat, or blood, splattered her bare feet.

A muffled cry had her looking up and turning toward Melisande.

Ariana stared at her friend in horror. *"Mel."* Her second had a knife in both hands and was cutting her own thighs. Blood ran in rivulets down her legs, trickling across the floor, pooling near Ariana's feet.

Silent tears slid down Melisande's cheeks. Blue eyes, dark with agony, lifted to Ariana. "You need pain. I'm giving you mine. If you lose, we all lose."

Ariana's vision blurred with tears of her own, anger burning violently inside her at the Mage who'd caused such misery. She wanted him dead!

Kougar and Jag fought, clawing one another until their blood, too, began to run over the tiles as if seeking her.

Deep inside her, the poison devoured their pain and rejoiced.

A light tingle running over her skin alerted her of Getrill's return seconds before she appeared, the Chief of the Ferals at her side. With a sledge-hammer in one hand and two pickaxes in the other, Lyon fell unsteadily to one knee, his head low as he struggled against the sweeping nausea.

"Cease!" he roared at his battling warriors.

"No." When his sharp gaze met hers, Ariana explained. "Not yet. They're doing this for me. The poison inside me is demanding pain. If I don't quench its hunger, I'll lose control."

Lyon frowned but said nothing more. After half a minute, he rose slowly, dropped the pickaxes, and walked over to Melisande, the sledgehammer at his side. His gaze dropped to her missing feet, then back to her face. "I'm not entirely sure this isn't a good place for you." His tone, though dry, possessed a bite.

Melisande met his gaze, her chin lifting. A chin that dripped with tears. "I deserve that for attacking you in your home. But I thought Ariana was in trouble. There is nothing I wouldn't do for her. Nothing."

Lyon eyed her assessingly, then gave a brief nod. "Cover your face." Lifting the sledgehammer, he brought it down hard, slamming it onto the tile near Melisande's ankles. Chunks of crystal flew in every direction.

Ariana ducked her head against her knees against the flying debris.

Over and over, Lyon attacked the temple floor while Kougar and Jag continued to fight. While the poison inside Ariana fed.

Finally, the darkness inside her slunk back into the shadows, and she was able to draw a shaky breath of relief.

"It's enough," she said between strikes of Lyon's hammer.

Kougar and Jag pulled apart, Jag grinning as if he'd thoroughly enjoyed the fight. Kougar clasped the jaguar shifter's bloody, nearly healed shoulder, and together they strode to where Lyon worked. While Jag grabbed one of the pickaxes, Kougar continued to Ariana. He was a mess, flesh hanging from his cheek and shoulder, his chest and beard covered in blood. But in his eyes, she saw only concern for her.

"Are you okay?" he asked, squatting beside her.

"Yes. Are you?" She reached out, placing her hand on his bleeding chest, directly over his heart. "The poison . . ." What must this renewed attack, the flood of new poison, be doing to him?

He covered her hand and squeezed gently. "The pain in my chest isn't any worse than before. If anything, it's less."

"Why?" The pain should be worse, shouldn't it? More poison would just be eating away at his heart faster. Unless . . . "It's changed. Maybe this isn't the same poison he used before."

"You may be right. It may attack in another way this time. Or more silently." He studied her, pale eyes lingering on her mouth, his thumb tracing her lower lip, and she wondered if he'd wiped away a splatter of blood. "Either way, the original poison is still there, still eating away at my heart. I can feel it."

"Nothing's changed."

"Not in a good way, no." With a brush of her cheek, he rose and grabbed the last pickax.

Over and over, the three huge men broke away bits of the floor until finally Lyon was able to lift Melisande bodily, the solid ball of stone, crystals, and jewels still encasing her feet. He set her on the floor, holding her by one arm to steady her, and turned to Getrill.

"Are you the only ride out of here?"

"I'll call another."

A moment later, Brielle appeared beside her. Brielle's worried gaze took in Ariana's appearance, the bloody cuts that had yet to heal completely.

"I'm fine, Brie. I've suffered the punishment, but only a few of the memories have returned. I'm going back down there until I've retrieved the rest."

"*We're* going," Kougar corrected.

She met his gaze. "We're going." He refused to let her handle this alone, and yet, did she really want him to? If she were honest with herself, no. She turned back to Brielle. "I'll let you know when it's done."

Lyon grunted. "If you need help of any kind, the full might of the Feral Warriors is at your disposal, Queen of the Ilinas. Nothing is as important right now as helping you save our warriors."

"I understand."

Melisande eyed Kougar with a hard challenge. "If you let any harm come to her . . ."

"I won't."

Lyon picked up Melisande and slung her over his shoulder, ending the discussion.

Getrill took Lyon's arm as Brielle crossed to Jag and took his.

Jag grimaced. "Here goes nothing."

A moment later, the five were gone. In the sudden silence, sounds once more carried faintly through the newly sealed door. A dull pounding. A muffled shout. The hand caught in the door hung lifelessly, either severed by her magic or by the owner's own sword. She felt a moment's regret for catching the man in such a trap. But only a moment's. Not only did immortal hands regrow; but the sentinel would have killed any of them in a heartbeat if given the chance.

Kougar turned to her, his wounds all but healed, though he was still covered in blood. In his eyes, she saw concern and a fierce determination. "Are you ready to go back down there?" He bent and grabbed the shirt he'd discarded, hooking it over his shoulder.

"Yes." But as she pushed to her feet, she swayed, her strength all but gone.

Kougar swept her into his arms without discussion, and she didn't object. While the others' pain had fed the poison, it had done nothing to nourish her. She needed pleasure for that, her own or another's. If she were back in the human world, she'd dream hop, walking into men's dreams, stripping for them, playing with her own body as their hormones skyrocketed and their bodies grew hard and needy. Then she'd urge them to take themselves in hand and pleasure themselves as she siphoned off that sexual pleasure and grew stronger and stronger.

Long ago, she'd performed the acts on them herself, riding them in their dreams, drinking in their passion. But once she'd mated with Kougar, sexual acts with other men had ceased to bring her much pleasure. Kougar was the only one she'd wanted.

And she wanted him now. She hooked her arm

around his neck and pressed her forehead to his jaw.

"What do you need?" he asked quietly, as if he knew.

"The mating bond . . ." She looked up.

" . . . is going to do what it does." His eyes turned warm and serious. "There's little we can do to stop it. Unless Paenther and Skye get lucky in their search, our only chance of beating your Hookeye may be through reclaiming the knowledge you've lost. I'm not worried about the mating bond, Ariana. Tell me what you need from me, and it's yours."

They watched one another for long moments, their gazes holding one another, caressing. Connecting. She slid her hand over his healed cheek.

"Strengthen me, my warrior."

A low growl of agreement sounded in his throat. "Here or below?"

"Below. Within the circle of the pillars is where the knowledge will come to me, if it comes. That much I've remembered. I need to be there."

"All right." He brushed his cheek against her hair, a tender caress that made her chest ache.

Goddess, she'd missed him. For so long she'd lived with an emptiness only Kougar had ever been able to fill.

As he strode toward the lower stairs, she tightened her hold on his neck, leaned forward, and kissed his jaw, just behind the spot where his beard ended, then flicked the lobe of his ear with her tongue.

The shiver that slid through his hard warrior's frame sent a flow of warm power sinking into her veins. A surprising amount given the simplicity of the touch. But she'd always reacted to Kougar as to no one else. A light bite to his earlobe earned her another shiver and a low growl.

As they passed through the door and began the descent to the lower chamber, she began to sing the soft Ilina chant to seal the door behind them in case the Mage managed to break through to the upper chamber. The temple's magic shouldn't allow any to pass through, but Kougar had. And the Mage were apparently far more powerful than they should be.

As Kougar carried her down the twisting steps, she slid her fingers into his hair again, watching the play of light over his strong features. "I love the feel of you," she said quietly, absorbing the touch of his soft, springy hair between her fingers. "I love the way you smell."

"You like the smell of sweat and blood?"

She smiled, marveling that she could, given the circumstances, but being in his arms made their situation seem not quite so dire. Leaning forward, she placed another kiss on his jaw.

"You couldn't smell bad to me."

His hold on her tightened as he stepped off the bottom step into the chamber and she knew he worried that the temple would attack her again. He carried her across the stone floor slowly, as if they had all the time in the world, then set her down beside the pool, close enough that she could reach out and trail her fingers in the water.

Kougar knelt at her feet, his gaze drifting down her still-naked body with hot deliberation, slowly stealing the air from her lungs. He grasped her knees and lifted them, then pulled them wide, spreading her to his gaze. His fingers trailed down her calves to her ankles as he sat back on his heels, his gaze hot between her legs, heating her with eyes that had turned silver. Deep inside, she began to tremble with need and anticipation.

His grip tightened, his neck muscles cording, and she sensed he fought an inner battle. A battle for control.

"You're not going to take me." She could see it in his eyes. "Not fully."

"No."

Disappointment plucked at her, hurt trying to wedge its way in. He'd claimed the mating bond didn't matter, that what happened with it, happened. Clearly that wasn't true.

It occurred to her that he must fear making love to her fully would only open the bond further. That twinge of hurt disappeared, washed away in a rush of warmth as she realized what his hesitation really meant.

He feared he couldn't make love to her without his heart opening to her more.

He moved on her like a cat on prey, sliding his broad hands beneath her hips and lifting her to his mouth. Thoughts scattered, wild sensations shooting through her body as his tongue stroked her upper thighs, then moved directly between her legs to that throbbing, sensitive flesh.

As he stroked her and played with her body, she cried out, flinging her head back. She'd forgotten what a talented tongue this cat had. He stroked her nether lips inside and out, one after the other with long, languorous strokes, flicking the nub of her clitoris at the end of each one, just enough to elicit a gasp from her. Then his tongue moved, circling her clit, teasing without touching, yet driving her up all the same.

A flick of his tongue directly on the spot had her crying out, but then he returned to circling.

"Kougar . . ." Goddess she wanted him inside her, deep, driving. *One.* But it was too dangerous.

He did enter her, though not in the way she craved. His tongue slid down into her opening, deep inside, delving and fluttering and licking until she was a writhing mass of need.

Then his mouth closed over her as he tugged on her, flicking her with his tongue until she was writhing beneath him, rising, cresting. . .

She came in a screaming rush of fire and pleasure. And still it wasn't enough.

"More."

His finger dove inside her, and a second, thrusting in and out in a fast, hard rhythm. A sudden pain tore through her skull, a burst of agony that radiated outward like flares of light, leaving her gasping for breath and all but blind.

"Ariana." Kougar's hands left her thighs, one cradling her cheek.

Her brain felt as if it were being wrenched open with a crowbar. Thoughts began to spill across her inner eye, glimpses of people she'd never known and things she'd never seen. Memories that weren't hers.

"The knowledge is coming back."

Her first *awakening* hadn't been painful, she remembered that, now.

Clearly, Morwun and the temple weren't through making her pay.

Chapter
Thirteen

Kougar stripped off his pants, pushing them down over a hard, painful erection, and scooped up Ariana. His body burned with the need to claim her, but it was his heart's need to protect her that drove his actions.

"What are you doing?" She still held her head with one hand, though the pain blasting him through the mating bond had died considerably.

Stepping into the shallow pool, he lowered himself, cross-legged, in the middle, cradling Ariana on his lap. He groaned at the feel of her bare hip crushing his swollen cock against his body. "You said you had to be within the pillars. Maybe the memories will come less violently in the water."

She tipped her head against his shoulder, her

soft hair brushing his chin. "I hope you're right."

He did, too. Tenderness welled as he held her against his heart. Inside, his cat paced and snarled at the feel of her pain. The cat didn't like it any more than he did. Exactly when he'd stopped wanting to see her suffer for what she'd done to him, he wasn't entirely sure, but he had. That piece of him that had always been hers bled to see her hurting.

His fingers slid into her hair, while his other hand stroked her hip, sliding back and forth with fingers that shook with a need to lift her, to fill her. Lily of the valley and warm, soft woman filled his senses, and he wondered at his insanity in taking off his clothes. Wet pants might have helped control the heat raging in his body. Bare flesh to bare flesh just fanned the inferno.

He slid his hand from her hip up to her breast, her beautiful skin healed now from the lightning strikes.

Ariana curved her arm around his neck. As he cupped her breast, she arched into his touch, telling him plainly that it pleased her. He kneaded the soft flesh, then stroked it, his finger and thumb twirling the hard bud of her nipple, pinching and tugging on it lightly.

Her sigh of pleasure changed abruptly to a gasp of pain, her body going rigid, her face tightening in a mask of agony.

Goddess, he hated this. He went back to stroking her hip, wanting to cause her no additional discomfort of any kind.

"Kougar," she said when the worst was clearly past.

He cupped her neck, meeting that brilliant gaze. "Tell me how to help you."

"Pleasure me. Strengthen me. If nothing else, take my mind off it."

Pleasure her. Goddess, it was all he could do just to hold her without taking what he needed. He wasn't sure he had that kind of self-control. Not with her. Anything more, and he'd find himself sinking deep into her body and joining her on that ride to ecstasy.

But he didn't want that, not at all. The more time he spent with her, the closer they got, the better he remembered why he had fallen in love with her in the first place. And the more danger he was in of doing it all over again.

A mistake he refused to make a second time.

Even if he got out of this alive, he knew better than to think a place existed for them in one another's worlds. Ariana would always be queen to her people, their needs coming first. And he refused to be second. Nor could he honestly put her first in his own life. His loyalty was to the Feral Warriors, first and always, and to stopping the Mage who tried to free the Daemons.

Even after a thousand years, he remembered too well what a soul-transforming experience making love to her had been . . . every single time. He feared that if he made the mistake of joining with her in that way, he'd never be able to walk away from her. And they'd only end up hurting one another all over again.

He wouldn't make love to her.

How in the hell was he going to give her the pleasure she needed when he was already struggling, already clinging to every ounce of control?

Goddess, help him.

He slid his hand into the water, between her legs, the springy hair of her thatch brushing his palm as he cupped her. His cock twitched and throbbed, begging for attention.

Think of something else. Anything else.

Tighe's baby in danger of being born without a father. Hawke lost to the world. Humans in Feral House. The burn in his heart that was almost sure to kill him.

But it was the burn in another part of his anatomy that stole all his attention. The need to be one with the woman in his arms.

As he slid two fingers deep inside her warmth, she arched into his hand with a moan of need, ratcheting his own to the level of torture. Stripping away his control. He needed to touch her, to taste her with a desperation that had his body quaking. He lifted her, dipping his head to take one sweet breast into his mouth. As he suckled her, he shoved his fingers in and out of her, meeting the hard thrust of her hips, stirring the water in the small pool until it lapped frantically, spilling over the edges onto the stone floor.

Ariana cried out, arching and stiffening in such

a way that he thought she was in pain but for the intense, rhythmic clenching of her inner muscles around his fingers. When her eyes opened, he realized she'd gotten another memory download right in the middle of her climax.

Gasping, she straightened on his lap, and he cupped her jaw.

"How much have you learned?"

"I'm not sure." Her voice was tight, breathless. "It's a jumble of pictures and thoughts, literally thousands of memories in no particular order." She shook her head, then winced at the movement. "I don't know how I could have missed so much that had been a part of me."

She sat up, sliding her arms around his neck, holding him. And he held her tight against him in return as the tension caused by the pain slowly eased out of her. He felt a small sweet kiss on his shoulder blade a moment before she lifted her head and pressed her lips against his neck in a kiss of erotic sweetness. His hands tightened around her as she kissed him again and again, her mouth trailing down his neck, across his shoulder, down his arm to the edge of his Feral armband, then slowly back up again.

With each touch of her lips, she dissolved a little more of his control until his hands were gripping her too tightly, moving over her back and hip. Shaking from the force of his need to take over and push himself deep inside her heat.

Even as he struggled to maintain control, she slid her hand between them, down over his hard, throbbing erection. The brush of her fingers across the slit in its head nearly made him come. Goddess, how much more of this could he take?

Turning her hand, she trailed her fingers down the length of him and back up again. With a groan, he arched into her touch, shaking with a need as rare as it was terrible. He refused to take her, yet never had he wanted . . . *needed* . . . anything more. Her fingers closed tight around his length, sliding up and down with firmer and firmer strokes, splashing the water between them.

His control shredded. He cupped the back of her head and slammed his mouth against hers, plunging his tongue between her lips, drawing a groan of need and carnal pleasure from her throat. While he plundered her mouth, she released him to slide lower, her fingers slipping between his loosely parted legs to trail across the sensitive skin behind his balls. As her knuckles brushed his tight, hard sac, fire speared into his cock, hardening him nearly beyond bearing. Turning her hand, she gripped his balls, and he knew there was nothing he'd ever enjoyed more in this world than the exquisite pleasure of Ariana's hands on his body.

She returned to his cock, stroking him with gentle roughness until he felt his eyes roll back in his head. With shallow, ragged breaths, the pulse careening in his veins, he kissed her, hotly, deeply, as her hand drove him up. And up.

Kougar's control snapped as suddenly and completely as an overstretched rubber band. All the reasons for not joining with her that had been rioting in his mind fled. All thoughts disappeared but one. Without gentleness, without finesse, he pulled back from her, grabbed her around the waist, and lifted her.

"I need you, Ariana. *Now.*"

Without objection, she swung one leg wide to straddle his hips. Gripping his shoulders, she spread her thighs to take him into her wet and ready body.

With a single, desperate thrust, Kougar drove into her, into heaven. The feel of her tight and hot around him sent him careening over the edge. Tilting back his head, he gave a feral roar of pleasure, of rightness, while inside something shifted, clicking into place.

Gripping her silken hips, he drove into her over and over, harder and harder, coming fast, with a guttural cry.

Not enough. Not nearly enough. Need burned inside him, crazed and out of control. A need that hadn't abated in a thousand years.

He lifted her off him. "I need you again."

"Yes, Kougar. *Yes.*"

Flipping her onto her hands and knees in the water, he gripped her hips, slid his cock between her thighs, and took her from behind, his own hips slamming against her sweet ass as he drove deeper and deeper.

Ariana cried out with her release, her inner muscles contracting, milking him to a second roaring climax. And still it wasn't enough.

Lifting her, he carried her out of the water, laid her on the floor beside the pool, and fell on her, shoving deep inside her as she wrapped her legs around his waist and her hands tight around his neck as if she never meant to let him go. As if this joining was forever.

As he drove deep inside her, the haze of insanity lifted, and he slowed his thrusts, disturbed by the harsh way in which he'd been taking her.

"Did I hurt you?" His voice, rough as sandpaper, hardly sounded like his own.

"No." She lifted her gaze to his, bright eyes shining with the brilliance of blue diamonds, heat in their depths. And something more. Something warm and tender that clutched at his heart, making it ache and swell, nearly obliterating the burn of the poison. "Never."

He kissed her as he drove into her with long, sensual strokes, unwilling to be parted from her in any way but feeling a sudden driving need to give instead of take. Inside, his cat gave a roar of deep satisfaction.

She came with a cry, her inner muscles clutching him tight, and he followed her in an explosion of raw heat and tenderness.

Slowly, his pounding heart calmed, his breathing returning to normal. As he lay atop her soft curves, his hips nestled within the cradle of hers, his body buried deep within hers, he felt right for the first time in centuries. Whole, despite the acid shredding his heart. As if this was all he'd needed. *She* was all he'd needed. If he could have frozen time and remained one with this woman for all eternity, he'd have done so.

The sharpness of the longing rocked him, propelling him up and off her, shattering the perfection of the moment. He turned and strode away, needing distance, struggling for perspective.

He could blame his colossal loss of control on his fucked-up emotions, but that was only a small part of the truth. He'd never had much control when it came to Ariana. From the moment he'd met her, she'd turned his world on end, and it had never righted.

In the aching, throbbing depths of his heart he knew the truth he'd been trying to ignore. Whether she was dead or alive, whether he kept his distance from her or made love to her until they were both breathless from exhaustion, he would never be able to go back to being the man he'd been before he'd known her. All he could do was hope that they survived the next days, and that when this was over, and they'd gone their separate ways, this ungodly need for her would dim to the point he could think of something, anything, else.

Ariana sat on the cool lip of the pool deep beneath the Temple of the Queens and watched Kougar as he paced away from her, pulling on what was left of his pants, his powerful body gleaming, his back rigid with a tension that wouldn't normally be there after the powerful release they'd just shared. In that release, the mating bond had opened almost completely. It still looked like hell, tarnished and shadowed, but no longer was it a shrunken, mangled mess.

And the poison was flowing freely.

The most frightening thing was, she didn't know what the poison was doing. With Hookeye's ability, he could be setting any kind of time bomb inside them, and they wouldn't know until it was too late.

Despite all that, she felt stronger than she had in years, in centuries. Stronger than she had in a millennium. Pleasure strengthened her, but what she'd felt in Kougar's arms went so far beyond mere pleasure as to be atomic in strength. She felt . . . reborn. Renewed.

Whole.

But as she watched him pace, her heart at once throbbed with the rightness of him with her again, and ached with the knowledge that they weren't right together at all. And never really had been. Even in those days when they'd been mated, she hadn't been entirely happy. At times, yes. When Kougar was with her, usually. The moment he'd touched her she'd forgotten everything but her joy in him—the love in his eyes and the gentle power of his body as he brought her to climax over and over again.

But those times they'd been together had been all too few. Even when they were together, there had been a distance between them she'd never been able to fully breach. He'd given her a part of himself, but never all. Never anything approaching all.

Right from the beginning, things had been difficult between them. Melisande's prejudice against the Therians and Ferals had infected her ranks long, long ago, her own attitude toward the shifters formed in the crucible of her friend's bitterness. So when she'd found herself attracted to the Chief of the Ferals, she'd been close to horrified.

The sparks had flown between them from the

start, their courtship more battle than wooing. But in the end, she'd let her judgment be clouded by the excitement she'd found in his arms. And by his own insistence that they were fated to be together, that resisting him was useless. By that point, she hadn't wanted to resist. She'd wanted only to revel in the joy of his rare, earth-shattering smiles, and bask in the pleasure she'd felt beneath his hands.

They'd been joined together deep in the Ferals' ritual cave, surrounded by flaming torches and two dozen naked, antagonistic shape-shifters who'd watched coldly as Kougar had taken her, claiming her in a ritual of blood and sex, forming what should have been an unbreakable cord joining them mind and body—the mating bond. Though Kougar had invited her own maidens to witness the ritual and join in the accompanying feast, only Melisande had been there and, unbeknownst to Ariana, woven magic to keep the mating bond from binding fully.

Even when they'd been married, she'd felt marginalized in Kougar's life. A piece of his world, but only a piece. But she had loved him. Desperately, she'd loved him. With all that had come after—the grief and guilt and anger, then later, the bitter, awful loneliness—she'd forgotten just how much she'd loved him.

And how easy it would be to fall under his spell all over again. But never again would she sacrifice the well-being of her maidens for a man. Any man.

Kougar turned back to face her, his expression closed, shuttered once more. "Have you remembered anything more?"

Ariana lifted a hand to brush her damp hair from her face. "No." She tapped her head. "It's like a dust storm in here. It'll take time for the dust to settle before I can see what blew in."

A strange chill made her shiver.

Kougar stepped toward her. "What's the matter?"

"Nothing." But as a vision rose in her head, she stiffened. *The eyes.* Hookeye's eyes rose in her mind as they had when Kougar removed her moonstones, as they had all those times a millennium ago. In those eyes, she saw determination and triumph. And a raw cruelty she didn't remember from before.

Her pulse began to race with the frantic need to fight or flee, when she could do neither. She tried to close her mind to him, tried to force him away, but he simply watched her with cruel amusement as the chills grew worse.

Kougar was beside her, his hands grasping her shoulders. "Ariana?"

"Hookeye." And suddenly the eyes were gone. The shivers subsided, and she could breathe again. "He was in my head. I could see his eyes." Her hand fumbled for her wrist, her fingers sliding over the moonstone-encrusted cuff. "I'm still wearing the moonstones. How is he seeing me?"

"Did he do anything?"

"No. At least, I don't think so." Her gaze met Kougar's. "He's getting stronger."

"That bastard is going to die." Kougar's hands squeezed her shoulders. "Sooner or later, I'm going to kill him."

"We're going to kill him. But first we have to find him." She frowned. "I wonder . . ."

"What?"

"Maybe I could figure out where he is by walking in his dreams." The thought of meeting that male face-to-face, in any reality, made her skin crawl.

Kougar watched her thoughtfully. "He could be anywhere. And you don't even know who he is."

"No. But we're connected, though goddess only knows what kind of connection I have with that bastard."

Kougar stroked her head. "Once, long ago, you offered to take me with you into another's dreams. Can you still do that?"

"Perhaps." The thought of Kougar at her side as she faced the Mage calmed her uneasiness. And increased it. "He's powerful, Kougar. You've said yourself that the Mage have dark magic, dangerous magic. We don't know what he can do."

"It's just a dream."

She lifted an eyebrow. "I've been in your dreams, Feral. You know better than that."

His eyes heated, and she knew he was remembering just how real some of those very carnal dream visits they'd once shared had been.

She rubbed her hands together, feeling chilled again. To walk in Hookeye's dreams, she had to reach out to him, to find him through the unholy connection he'd formed with her. And she had no idea how to do that. Would he see her eyes rising in his mind as she saw his?

As if reading her thoughts, Kougar took her hand, squeezing gently.

With a deep breath and a nod, she closed her eyes and concentrated on Hookeye, on the poison she could almost see seeping into the mating bond, then followed its trail into total darkness, a wide, empty void.

In an instant, everything changed, and she was tumbling into a blinding chaos and just as suddenly, thrown back out again, Hookeye's furious eyes blazing at her in her mind.

"Ariana!" Kougar's voice sounded beside her, but all she could see were the eyes, copper-ringed Mage eyes glaring into hers.

She was trembling, on the edge of panic, perspiration running down her neck. Her pulse thrummed in her veins as the hated eyes bored into her.

He'd pushed her away. Somehow, she had to do the same.

Concentrating, she imagined shoving him back. For a moment, the eyes dimmed, then popped back into focus, brighter and angrier than before.

No.

This time, she didn't shove. She reached deep, digging up the hatred and grief for all he'd caused her and throwing it at him in a single powerful blast of pure fury.

A moment later, the eyes were gone. "I did it."

The breath shuddered out of her as Kougar pulled her against him.

"What happened?"

"I'm not sure." But she told him what she could, about the eyes and darkness, and that bright chaos. "I can almost still see it." She met his gaze. "I think it's his consciousness. And I think I'm going to know when he falls asleep."

"Good."

"We could be here a long time, Kougar. You might as well get some sleep. I'll wake you when it's time." Pain bolted through her mind, another rush of new memories swamping the first.

Her hands went to her aching head. Kougar's warm knuckles stroked her cheek.

"I'm okay," she said. "Sleep."

"Later." Instead, he took her hand and led her to one of the pillars, sat and drew her down beside him. Gently, he pulled her against him, cradling her head against his chest until the pain finally slid away.

For a long time, they sat like that, quietly, his hand stroking her head, his fingers twirling her hair.

"Tell me about that day," he said finally. "I want to know what happened after you left me on the battlefield. I need to know."

She stiffened, pulling out of his grasp to sit beside him, but his hand followed her, his palm stroking her back in long, gentle strokes, easing the tension his words had caused.

Part of her didn't want to talk about it. Honestly, she wasn't even sure what to tell him.

"I thought we were dealing with dark spirit." She glanced at him, seeing a cautious warmth in the eyes that had blazed with such heat a short while ago. And glimmers of a pain centuries old.

She owed him this. He deserved an explanation, if she could figure out how to give him one.

"They were dying, Kougar. And not just a few. All of them. I returned to the Crystal Realm to find Angelique crazed with evil and in her death throes. She was the first, but as her life cord tore from mine, so did others. Dozens of others. And the maidens around me, maidens who'd been in the Crystal Realm with me, began to show signs of the same darkness. You can't imagine . . ."

His hand lifted to the back of her head, stroking, easing her back from those terrible memories.

"For the first time, I saw the poison in the life cords and how it was flowing into my maidens through me. And I saw it in the mating bond. It was then that Melisande admitted inserting a Mage potion into the bond. I began to suspect the Mage with the hookeye was to blame, that this was all a Mage attack. My maidens were dying around me, and I feared you were about to die, too. Melisande might have caused the vehicle of our destruction, but she'd also given me the means to save you. I severed the bond without a second thought, then turned to trying to save those of my maidens that I could."

She leaned back, Kougar's arm slipping around

her waist as she rested her head back against his shoulder. "The only ones I managed to save were those in the Crystal Realm. And not all of them. Many more died when I turned to mist, before I reclaimed the poison. The palace had never been so silent. I thought I was too late. None of them were moving. All lay on the ground as if dead. Never have I heard such terrible silence.

"Finally, those who'd survived turned to mist, and I knew they'd live. But they didn't move. They didn't waken. I tried to help them, to heal them. I tried to strengthen them through pleasure, singing to them until my voice was hoarse. Nothing helped. I'd never comprehended what true solitude really meant. It was awful."

"You had me. Why didn't you come to me?"

She was slow to answer, uncertain what to say. "I don't know. Those days were a blur. I was numb. Moving in a daze. Shock, grief, depression, I don't know. I started to get weak, having spent too much time corporeal in the Crystal Realm, but I couldn't turn to mist to leave. It was almost too late by the time I found the last remaining moonstone manacle, wove a transport spell into the silver, and locked it around my wrist.

"I traveled to the surface, and sat in the temple until I was strong enough to go back. Over the course of months, I sent my dead friends off to the next world, one by one. And I tended the unconscious ones as best I could. Time ceased to mean anything. Nothing meant anything."

"I'm sorry," Kougar said quietly, his thumb

stroking her ribcage. "I wish I'd known, Ariana. I would have helped you, you know that."

She turned, meeting his pained gaze over her shoulder. "I know. I wasn't the woman you'd loved anymore. I wasn't . . . anyone. I was dead inside. Lost." Settling back against him, she looked out over the small pool and continued. "Finally, the maidens who'd survived began to waken. They were still terribly weak, but they pulled me back into the world of the living. Almost two hundred years had passed by then, Kougar. Two hundred years that are little more than darkness in my mind. It was another eighty or ninety years before my maidens finally returned to full health and strength, able to move freely between mist and flesh. It was nearly three hundred years after the attack that Melisande strapped on her knives and set out to cut out the heart of the Mage sorcerer who'd nearly destroyed our race."

"She didn't find him."

"No. She's hunted him ever since and come so close numerous times, but luck's never been on our side. It's just a matter of time. But I guess time isn't something we have anymore, is it? It wasn't until Melisande began hunting Hookeye that we realized the world thought we were extinct. Once I'd started thinking clearly, I'd wondered why Hookeye had never attacked again. I couldn't be sure, but I thought he could probably reach me again even with the mating bond severed. Now I knew why. Like everyone else, he thought I was dead. We knew we had to keep it that way. As long as he didn't know the truth, Melisande might be able to get close enough to kill him."

"I would have happily killed him for you."

She pulled out of his arms and turned to face him. "I never forgot you. I always intended to find you again, when it was over."

His eyebrow shot up. "A thousand years?"

Ariana flinched. "I never dreamed it would take so long. Melisande was always so close to finding Hookeye. A few more weeks, a few more months, and it would be over. Except it never was."

"And you didn't think you could trust me with your secret?"

"It wasn't that simple." She dropped her gaze to his shoulder. "I don't even know how to explain it. I still loved you, but . . ."

"But?"

Slowly, she lifted her gaze to his. "Hookeye never would have attacked us if not for our mating. What I felt for you was no longer as simple as love. It was a tangle of grief and bitterness, regret and guilt. And so much time had passed. I told myself that someday I'd have to resolve things with you, but not when it could possibly hurt my maidens again."

Emotion flared in his eyes. Anger, or perhaps pain.

Ariana turned away. She couldn't undo the past, however badly she might want to.

"One of your maidens died on the battlefield soon after you left that day," he said, his voice quiet. "She was, as you said, crazed. She told us all the Ilinas were dying. It wasn't moments later that you severed the mating bond. I was afraid it was true, but I had to know. I went to the temple."

Ariana jerked around to face him. "You climbed the Himalayas in the eleventh century?"

"I had to know. The Wind and Horse accompanied me."

"How long did it take you?"

"Nearly a year. We were weak as newborn kittens from lack of radiance by the time we got back to Feral House. But in that temple, which I'd visited with you only once, I found the fires out, the magic gone. No evidence of life, and I believed you were gone."

Remembered pain sliced through his eyes, and, for a moment, she glimpsed the terrible grief she'd put him through. She reached for him, her hand going to his cheek.

"I'm sorry."

The pain in his eyes disappeared, shuttered behind strong male pride. But he lifted her onto his lap and held her, setting up a deep ache in her heart as she wished things between them could be simple.

As she wished he could be hers again.

Wulfe led Xavier into the kitchen, the young man grinning with an untempered emotion most seeing individuals would have long ago learned to mask. With his hand on the young man's upper arm, Wulfe led him to the center island, then pulled up as Pink glanced around from where she was working, mixing ingredients into a bowl.

"Xavier offered to give you a hand, Pink."

The bird-woman stiffened. Though she said nothing, it was clear he'd offended her.

Wulfe cleared his throat. "Let me put it another way. Xavier is human, and blind, and we can't steal his memories."

Pink's bird eyes tightened with understanding.

"Our options are limited." Wulfe shrugged. "I thought maybe you could use an assistant."

He didn't have to spell out the alternative if she refused. Pink might look as odd as they came, but she had a quick mind and a good heart.

"Then I'd be happy for the help, Xavier."

"Cool!" The human felt the space in front of him carefully, then extended his hand in her direction as if wanting to shake. "It's nice to meet you, Pink."

Pink didn't move. As Xavier's smile died, his hand slowly dropping to his side, her gaze flew helplessly to Wulfe.

Hell, just because the kid couldn't see didn't mean he didn't need to know. He laid his hand on Xavier's shoulder and explained. "Pink should have been a shape-shifter, Xavier, but an accident before her birth killed the animal within her and left her an anomaly. She's half woman, half flamingo. Her hands are like ours, but covered with pink feathers instead of skin."

Xavier's smile covered his face. "Cool. If you

don't want to shake my hand, Pink, just say so. I can't read your expression or body language, so *subtle* doesn't work with me. Just tell me what you want me to do, or don't want me to do. Or you can hit me over the head with a rolling pin or something. I've got a hard head. Just ask my sister."

The kid grinned. "You can't hurt my feelings. Believe me, I've heard it all. That I'm too weird, that my eyes go every which way, that I smile too big, and my expressions aren't normal. It's hard to mimic 'normal' when you've never seen it." He smiled a soft, friendly smile. "If you can handle my strangeness, I promise I can handle yours."

Yeah, they were going to have to find a way to keep this kid alive.

"Xavier?" Pink said quietly. "I'd be happy to shake your hand."

The kid's grin widened as he reached out slowly, as if not wanting to startle her. As Pink slid her feathered hand in his, the human's expression changed to one of delight and amazement. Though Wulfe knew both he and Pink were watching for it, he saw not an ounce of revulsion.

"Your feathers feel . . . soft. Really nice."

"Thank you, Xavier."

Xavier released her hand with a laugh. "So, tell me what you want me to do. I'm slow at first, until I learn my way around, but I can do anything. Especially vegetables. I'm great at chopping vegetables."

"Chopping? But . . ." Her voice trailed off.

"Hey, blind people can chop. When you get

going with the knife, you can't tell me you're watching and measuring every cut."

"No. I suppose I'm not." A pause. "Then I'll give you vegetable duty. I've only recently added them back into the menu on a regular basis."

Wulfe grabbed a beer out of the refrigerator and strode through the swinging doors back into the dining room, where he settled his big frame on one of the chairs, out of their way, yet close enough to listen. He wanted to see what happened when he wasn't in the room. Xavier was a talker, and he wondered how long it would take the quiet Pink to tire of it . . . and him. But as he listened, he was surprised to hear Pink's soft words.

"Do you mind if I ask you a question, Xavier? I've never met a blind person before."

"Ask away."

"How do you cook . . . when you can't see?"

Lyon and Jag strode into the dining room. Lyon stilled at the sound of Xavier's voice, scowling. "What's he doing up here?"

"Xavier can cook." Wulfe took a swig of his beer. "I thought Pink could use a little help around here."

"No."

"We can't clear his memories, Roar." Wulfe rose to face his chief, eye to eye. "He can stay here."

"No. It's too dangerous."

"The bird could use some help," Jag said. At Wulfe's look of surprise, Jag shrugged. "Our numbers are growing, and while she lets the women help her, I can tell she doesn't like it. It makes her feel uncomfortable. Like she no longer has a purpose."

"Xavier needs her," Wulfe said quietly. "Just like her, he's stuck here. And he can help her."

Lyon shook his head. "If he escapes, or is even just spotted outside, the human authorities will be crawling all over Feral House before we know what's happened. I don't have to tell you all the ways that could turn into a disaster."

Lyon wasn't budging, and Wulfe was getting desperate. Even though Natalie would never know, he didn't want her brother's blood on his hands.

"We can bind him, Roar. Skye's people might be able to come up with some kind of cuffs like the Mage used on Paenther that will keep him tied to the house and away from the phones and computers so he can't tell anyone he's here."

"Can blind people use computers?" Jag grunted. "Wouldn't they need braille keyboards or something?"

"Not the point," Wulfe growled.

Lyon shook his head. "It's too danger—"

The sound of laughter stopped him cold. A sweet, high-pitched laughter as rare as a blue moon. Pink's.

Jag smiled, cutting Lyon a look that said the chief had just lost, and they all knew it. "Sounds to me like the bird has a new friend."

Lyon's growl was one of pure frustration. "Find a way to secure him. One slip, and he dies. No second chances."

Wulfe nodded, fighting back his own smile. "Yes, sir."

Lyon lifted a brow, then swung away.

Jag's smile was slow and satisfied. "Good job . . . *Dude.*" With a chuckle, he slapped Wulfe on the back, then headed into the kitchen.

Wulfe let his own smile loose. As screwed up as everything else was, at least one thing had gone right. He lifted his finger to trace the newest scar on his cheek. Natalie had given him a gift in her smile, in her laughter. Most of all, in her lack of fear and revulsion.

He'd given her two in return even though, if all went as planned, she wouldn't remember. But he would.

He'd never forget.

Chapter
Fifteen

Kougar woke suddenly, his feral senses and warrior instincts taking in the situation in an instant, telling him they were in no immediate danger. He and Ariana were lying, spooned, on the cool temple floor, her body warm and tensed with pain beneath the curve of his arm. And he knew, now, what had awakened him. She was getting another memory download.

He lifted his arm off her and stroked her hair, marveling that he'd actually slept. Not that he hadn't needed the sleep. He had. But, goddess, they were hardly safe down here, not with the Mage a mere two stories above, trying to reach them.

Ariana had suggested he sleep while she waited for Hookeye to dream, but he hadn't thought he'd actually do it. He hadn't thought he had that kind of trust in anyone but another Feral.

Apparently, he trusted her more than he'd realized.

He continued to stroke her hair until the tension slowly left her body. "You okay?"

"Yes. I'm remembering." The wonder in her voice eased his concern, lifting his pulse and his hopes. "I've remembered something important."

She sounded preoccupied, as if she was watching a movie he couldn't see. Which was probably exactly what she was doing. A movie in her own head.

He relaxed, sliding his hand up and down her arm in slow, soft movements while he waited impatiently for her to tell him.

When she began to speak, her voice was quiet and far away. "The Temple of the Queens was built in the Himalayas for a reason. This mountain actually breaches the Syphian Stream, the same mystical energy stream in which the Crystal Realm was built, although the Crystal Realm is far from here and high above the Earth."

That had always been incomprehensible to him—how a castle had been built in the air, in the clouds. Then again, the women who'd built it were themselves mystical creatures of light and mist. And magic.

"The queen who first discovered the wormhole into the Daemons' spirit trap lived during those dark days of the Daemon Wars. She'd been badly injured in a Daemon attack, unable to live without regular infusions of that mystical energy. Her name was Rayas. And the crystal through which she channeled that energy, much as a Feral's arm-band channels the power of the Earth, kept her alive.

"To reach the Syphian, Rayas stood atop the temple, at the very crown, lifting her hands into the air to draw down the power she needed to survive. One day, while she was up there, she turned to mist and found herself able to merge with the energy stream. She found the wormhole by accident and followed it down into the spirit trap. She'd known the Daemons possessed such a trap, but none had ever known where it was or how to breach it. Now she knew."

"So it's true. Olivia, Jag's mate, seemed to think there's only one actual trap. That it's accessed through various wormholes."

"Yes, there's only one. As the wars escalated, and word came of Mage or Therians who'd been caught in the trap, she went in and pulled them out. Often, she was too late with the Mage. Their souls and bodies were separated quickly. But not so the Therians, who, in those days, were all shift-ers. The separation of animal from body took days."

Eleven days, if the seventeen were anything to go by. Eleven days, of which eight had passed for Hawke and Tighe. The knowledge felt like drag-on's breath on the back of his neck.

Ariana pulled away from him to roll onto her stomach, lifting onto her elbows. Her eyes shone like a pair of gems. "I know where that crystal is, the Crystal of Rayas."

Finally, something was going right. He lifted onto his elbow. "Let's get it."

"It's not here in the temple. It's in the Crystal Realm. And I can't leave the temple until it's through with me. It answered my plea this time, but I guarantee if I walk away now, it won't again. I can't leave until I've retrieved all the memories I've lost."

"You can get into that spirit trap and rescue them."

The light in her eyes died. She sat up, turning her back on him to face the pool. "I still can't turn to mist, Kougar. Now I know what to do once I can, but that's all."

They had one answer but not the other. He sat up beside her. "Still no idea how to solve that piece of the puzzle?"

She glanced at him, her expression pensive. "No. But I can feel the gathered energy still waiting to strike me with more memories. It may take days for me to sort through them all."

"Hawke and Tighe don't have days."

Her eyes softened, saddened. "I know. I'm trying, Kougar. I'm as desperate to defeat this thing as you are."

He reached for her, cupping the back of her neck. "I know." He pulled her toward him. When she turned to him, he covered her mouth, losing himself in the feel of her warm lips against his, her sweet taste and scent. The need to do something, to save his friends, was eating a hole in his gut. But kissing Ariana, he could almost forget anything and anyone else existed.

He stroked her bottom lip with his tongue, and she opened for him, her tongue sliding over his lips greedily. Blood began to pulse through his veins, pressure building in his head, in his chest. He pulled her tighter against him, the need to hold her, to be one with her, a pounding in his body. How had he survived a thousand years without her?

His fingers dove into her silken hair as his lips moved over her cheek, her jaw. Her taste was nectar on his tongue, her soft moan, as he trailed his mouth down her throat, the sweetest of music.

Fire burned inside him, a need as much of the soul as the body. A need to touch and hold, to be one with her.

Soft palms slid over his cheeks, her fingers curling around the back of his neck as she pulled him down to take one perfect breast in his mouth. He drank in the sweet scent of lilies of the valley mixing with Ariana's unique, seductive mating scent as he pulled her to him and suckled her soft flesh.

Some part of his brain warned him not to give in, that he was in serious danger of losing all perspective, of losing himself, if he didn't pull back. But his cat hissed, ears back, urging him to take her, to claim her all over again. And that's exactly what he wanted to do.

Sweeping her into his arms, he laid her down,

his gaze locked with hers, the question asked and answered in a lush, carnal smile.

He told himself to take it slow this time, and he tried. But when she spread her thighs, lifting her arms to him, he was lost.

Holding her gaze, he came to her, entering her, tumbling into the beauty and fire and strength that was Ariana.

Over the next few hours, he made love to her twice more and held her through three more painful memory downloads while she waited for Hookeye to sleep. He was lying temporarily sated in her arms when she tensed beneath him. Not with pain, this time, but excitement.

He lifted off her, and she sat up, her eyes glowing with triumph. "The bright chaos just turned dark. Hookeye's asleep." Her eyes gleamed. "Are you ready for a bit of dream walking?"

Hell, yes. A feral smile lifted his mouth. "Anything I need to do to prepare?"

Her gaze trailed seductively down his body. "He'll see us exactly as we are now. I'm getting dressed." She slid her fingers up his erection. "Up to you."

He purred at the feel of her fingertips on that highly sensitized flesh. It didn't matter how many times he'd come inside her, if she was anywhere near him, he wanted her. Especially when she turned on her siren's charms. Goddess, if she kept touching him like this, he was going to come again, right there in her hand.

If they hadn't waited so long for the bastard to

sleep, he might take her first, but dreams didn't last.

Wrapping his hand around her wrist, he lifted that talented little hand of hers to his mouth and kissed her palm. "Can I shift when I'm in the dream?" He licked her palm and watched with satisfaction as she shivered, her mouth twitching at one corner.

"I don't know. I guess we'll find out." She pulled her hand from his and leaped to her feet to retrieve her clothes.

Kougar joined her, dressing quickly, then sat cross-legged on the smooth stone floor beside her. He eyed her quizzically, feeling a frisson of unease. "How exactly does this work?" Goddess knew how anything worked in the Ilina world.

A hint of a smile played at her mouth. "You'll see." But the smile didn't reach her eyes. As she took his hand, he understood. Her hand was damp, a faint trembling deep in her bones. The thought of facing the creature who'd caused her so much pain had her rattled as he suspected little ever did.

He squeezed her hand, reminding her silently she wasn't going alone.

"Close your eyes and keep them closed," she told him.

He did as she asked, and, a moment later, an odd sensation hit him, a brief moment's dizziness not unlike Ilina travel for him now, a dizziness that was gone almost as quickly as it came. And suddenly he was standing beside Ariana in a firelit cave the size of his bedroom at Feral House. The hair rose on the back of his neck.

Along the walls, corpses hung—five adults and a small one that must have been a child, though he was hard-pressed to tell how many were male, how many were female. They were dressed in the simple, gowned peasant garb of millennia ago, a manner that had been largely unisex. But though their garb appeared unharmed, the flesh of the people had been all but burned away as if they'd died in a fire that had left their clothing unscathed.

The cave was clearly a living space, a cooking pot hanging over the central fire. To one side sat a table laden with bowls and vials and colorful, plastic containers. Kougar frowned at the anachronism of plastic in an ancient cave until he looked at the man standing behind the table, reminding himself he was in a dream.

The man was short, his build slight, his appearance unassuming for one who'd caused so much pain and death. His thin brown hair was cut around his face at odd angles as if he were in the habit of hacking off whatever got in his way with the nearest knife. He was dressed, not as the victims around him, but in the green sorcerer's robes the Mage had taken to wearing in recent centuries. On his wrist he wore a modern black resin sports watch.

The Mage looked up as if seeing them for the first time, then back down at what he was doing as if they were just figments of his imagination.

But in that brief glance, Kougar had glimpsed his eyes. Copper-ringed Mage eyes, one of which had a pupil that appeared to have bled through the iris in the shape of a hook.

Bingo. Hookeye.

Beside him, Ariana's hand spasmed in his, then fell away as she stepped away from him. A knife appeared in her hand, from where he wasn't sure, but a quick glance told him exactly what she meant to do with it.

If she'd felt any anxiety about facing the bastard, it was gone, replaced by a seething hatred.

He grabbed her upper arm. "Wait."

"They didn't survive." Hookeye's tone was conversational. "But they rarely do." He glanced up, his gaze meeting Kougar's. "I'm the poison master, you know. But you know." That gaze turned amused as it flicked to Ariana, then back down at his work.

The scene shifted suddenly, the room and victims changing as if the walls of a Hollywood set had been yanked away, another shoved into place with all the accompanying vertigo. An old castle, this time, built of bare stone. Once more, bodies hung, chained and tortured. The four surrounding them now were covered in the swollen buboes and dark patches of subdural hemorrhaging that reminded him all too well of the dead from bubonic plague.

"You collected plague victims?"

Hookeye smiled absently. "No. This one I caused.

One of my more spectacular successes, though it only affected mortals, which was a shame."

The bastard had caused bubonic plague. Kougar's mind reeled. And how many other devastating human diseases?

It was well known that the Therians had often been the target of Mage poisons, though few had ever died from them. Tighe believed his childhood enclave had been the victim of one such attack, but such successes were rare, or the Mage would have wiped out the Therians long ago.

"You were my greatest failure, Queen of the Ilinas." Hookeye chuckled, but the sound was ugly. "Except you weren't, were you?" His tone hardened. "You just made me think you were."

Ariana stilled beneath Kougar's grip. "You meant to control me."

"Yes."

"Why?"

Hookeye shrugged one scrawny shoulder, still concentrating on the vials and liquids he mixed together like some kind of medieval alchemist.

"To turn you against the Feral Warriors, of course." He picked up a vial and shook it, peering at it closely. "I'll succeed this time, you know." His gaze flicked to her, evil shining in those copper-ringed depths. "You'll bring the Feral Warriors to me."

"Never."

Kougar's impatience for battle cooled with the chilling words. "How will you succeed, Mage?"

He growled. "How will you succeed in capturing the Feral Warriors?"

"The way I always do. I'm the poison master." He turned away, scraping away a bit of flesh from one of his victims into a plastic container.

But as he turned back to his table, the walls of the room shifted yet again. The new ones were eerily familiar, glittering with inlay on ivory-colored stone.

The Temple of the Queens. Kougar's heart began to thud in his chest.

Beside him, Ariana gasped. His gaze slammed into hers as understanding arced between them. To dream of the temple, Hookeye had to have been there. But when?

Recently?

As if in answer, a cat ran through the room. No ordinary cat, but a small, dark-spotted jaguar.

Jag.

Kougar stared at the animal, chills racing over his skin, triumph flaming in his mind. Hookeye had been in the temple when Jag raced through with him a few hours ago.

He's here now. We have the bastard!

"Get us out of here, Ariana," he said under his breath. The moment they were free of the dream, he'd get the other Ferals and attack. This was the break they needed.

Ariana made a sound deep in her throat, a sound of denial, her body tensing to be free of his restraint. Clearly, she'd had enough. She jerked free of his hold and sprang at the man who was little taller than she, lifting her knife as if she would cut out the Mage's heart.

But Hookeye was more aware than he appeared. Before Ariana could reach him, his hand flung out toward her, palm out. Ariana stopped as if she'd hit a brick fence with a guttural cry that was half fury, half pain. And suddenly she shot three feet into the air, her head flinging back, a look of agony on her face.

With a roar of fury, Kougar leaped at the Mage, shifting into his cougar in midair as he soared over the table and slammed into him, his jaws clamping around the bastard's neck. His fangs sank into the Mage's jugular, but no warm blood filled his mouth. He'd forgotten it was dream.

A dream that ended abruptly. He found himself once more sitting beside the pool in the queen's chamber far beneath the temple. Beside him, Ariana collapsed, her hands clawing at her throat as she gasped for air.

Kougar reached for her. "What's the matter?"

"Whatever . . . he did . . . was real."

The pounding of his heart deepened into a sickening thud. "He has you. He's locked onto you with his magic. Can you break it?"

"No."

Dammit. He needed to break out of the lower chambers and go after the damned sorcerer. But Ariana came first.

He shot to his feet, lifting her into his arms. "Then we're getting out of here."

How? He set her back on the floor. "Go, Ariana.

Transport yourself back to the Crystal Realm. Once you're there, I can follow."

She met his gaze, then nodded, her hand sliding over the moonstones as she choked out the magic that would carry her to the Crystal Realm without turning to mist. A moment later, she was gone.

Focusing on her through the mating bond, Kougar curled his hand around his Feral armband and whispered the same incantation. Moments later, he was sitting in the Grand Corridor of the palace in the clouds, Ariana seated on the floor beside him.

Unlike a moment ago, she no longer gasped for air.

"Are you okay?"

"Yes." She took a deep unsteady breath. "He must have known we weren't part of his dream."

"He knew."

Kougar rose to his feet and pulled Ariana up beside him just as Brielle came rushing into the pine-scented corridor.

"Did you reclaim the memories?" Brielle asked, her face radiating a desperate hope he was certain every Ilina shared.

Ariana glanced at him, the truth thick between them that she hadn't gotten them all. And now, probably never would. A truth they would keep to themselves for the time being.

"Yes," Ariana said, glancing at him, then back at Brielle. "Yes, I reclaimed the memories. I'm sorting through them now."

A smile bloomed on Brielle's delicate face.

"Wonderful." She clapped her hands together. "We must celebrate, Ariana. We've not had a true celebration in far too long."

Ariana dipped her head, a small gesture that was all Brielle needed. She hurried away, shouting out names, a four-star general calling her troops.

Ariana turned to him, her eyes at once hard and haunted. "Hookeye has to die."

"And he's going to. Right now. Gather your maidens, six of them, and meet me at Feral House. We're going to need transportation back down to the temple."

Ariana frowned. "What? Wait. You can't kill him. Not until we know whether killing him will help or hurt our ability to destroy the poison." She took his hand. "Wait, please? I may have the answers we need once I sort through this mess in my head."

"He's there, Ariana. In the temple. We can't afford to let him get away."

"Where's he going to go? He's on the top of a mountain in the Himalayas." She gripped his arm. "We can't attack him. Not yet. I *know* that."

"How?"

"I'm not sure, I just know it's true, and it has something to do with my memories. Give me another day to sort through what's in my head. If I haven't come up with the answer we need, I'll order my warriors to transport yours to the temple."

Kougar's teeth ground together beneath the force of his impatience.

"One day, Kougar. I feel like I'm on the edge of something vast. Like the veil is about to be lifted, and I'm going to see what I've been missing all this time. It's going to happen. Tonight." She squeezed his hand. "It's going to make the difference between success and failure, it's that big."

He pulled her into his arms. "Twelve hours. That's all."

"Deal. Then we'll reassess."

Twelve hours. His fingertips itched with the need to draw claws and rip out that bastard's throat, *now.* But Ariana was right. If there was a chance she held the key to the battle in that head of hers, not giving her a chance to find it was a rash, foolish move.

Too many lives hung in the balance.

Fury roared up out of nowhere, ripping through Hawke's mind, white-hot. A vicious rage.

The hawk's anger had become his own.

How long he roared and thrashed, he didn't know. Time held no meaning. But as quickly as the fury rose, it abated, leaving his mind throbbing with pain and the echoes of his hawk's pulsing anger.

He'd never had the relationship with the hawk spirit that his father, the Wind, had claimed to have. Then again, his father had been the hawk shifter for nearly three thousand years until a Confederate mortar explosion ripped his heart out of his chest a century and a half ago. The hawk spirit had flown to the son, but Hawke had never possessed the faith in the wildness that his father had.

The Wind used to tell him that once a man was marked, the animal spirit shared the man's body. It was only fair to give him his head from time to time. And his father had, disappearing sometimes for hours, even days, on a wild flight.

For years after he was marked, the hawk had demanded more freedom, but Hawke refused. The hawk spirit had never entirely forgiven him. But he wasn't giving rein to that kind of wildness again. Not after what happened to Aren.

The last echoes of the fury slipped away, leaving him with nothing but thoughts. And regrets. There were so many things he'd hoped to do with his life. Things lost to him now.

He'd been born with an insatiable thirst for knowledge and had studied the natural world extensively, but there was so much more to learn. So much more to know. The humans were discovering things every year, every day, and he wanted to know them all.

Trapped in that miserable darkness, he thought again of the dream he'd held close for decades. A dream of a mate of his own. He'd never been like many of his brothers, who'd been determined never to be tied to one woman for eternity. Though, of late, four of them had fallen to that fate, hadn't they? It was often like that. Watching that kind of love in another had a way of softening a man's heart. Of making him wonder what it would be like to know that kind of contentment.

He'd always wondered, always hoped he'd someday find the one meant for him. A woman with eyes that flashed with strength and intelligence, and turned liquid with love when she looked at him. Only at him.

Pain turned to agony, stealing his thoughts.

The other animal spirits, too, cried or roared with distress. Were they really in pain, or merely raging against the loss of more Feral animals to the trap?

Were they even there at all?

They were like ghosts in the room, leaving him to wonder if all he was hearing were the echoes of their death cries from hundreds of years ago.

Chapter
Sixteen

Ariana paced the solar in the Crystal Realm, frustration lending a weight to her steps. Why had she expected anything to go right? She'd remembered the Crystal of Rayas being stored in the jewel-encrusted box that sat upon one of the bookshelves that lined the walls of the room. But when she'd opened it, she'd found nothing. Empty.

Dammit.

Kougar stood at the window overlooking the garden as she paced, trying to come up with another memory of where it might have been moved.

Of all the rooms in the Crystal Palace, the solar was perhaps the most Earth-like, with its rows upon rows of books, brown velvet sofas, and plush, vibrantly colored floor rugs. It even boasted a window with real glass. Only the floating crystal lights might have looked out of place in a mortal's home.

The room had been her gift to Brielle more than a century ago, knowing her friend's insatiable appetite for books, an appetite many of her maidens shared.

Those same maidens were turning the palace inside out looking for the crystal while she sorted through the jumble of memories, trying to make some kind of sense of them.

With a frustrated sigh, she went to stand beside Kougar, looking out on the grounds behind the palace, a sea of rocks and waterfalls. She called it the garden, but no plants, no trees, no flowers would ever grow there. It was the Syphian Stream itself that possessed a scent reminiscent of pine.

Kougar's hands gripped the windowsill until his knuckles had turned white.

Ariana slid her hand across his back. "You're thinking of war, aren't you?"

"I'm thinking of all the ways I'm going to kill that sorcerer."

"I know that waiting to go after him is driving you crazy."

"You have no idea," he growled.

A sharp pain pulsed in her temple as another of the myriad memories crowding her head broke through. She groaned at the revelation.

Kougar lifted a brow.

"We can't kill Hookeye, not while I still hold

the poison. It will absolutely ensure I'm never free of it."

Kougar pushed away from the window. "Hell."

"Another queen faced something similar." She turned, talking to his back as he paced away. "The queen sent her mist warriors to destroy the sorcerer. But the poison killed her the moment the sorcerer died. I'm afraid if you kill him, you'll kill me, and possibly yourself, too. If I die, the poison will escape and infect my maidens. We'll all die."

He swung around to face her. "You can't know that. It might not be the same poison."

"No, I can't know for sure, but what she suffered was hauntingly similar to what I'm going through except that the poison she'd taken never spread to her maidens."

Kougar looked at her quizzically. "I thought you said the Mage had never attacked your race before we were mated."

Ariana frowned. "I didn't think they had. I didn't remember." She made a sound of frustration. "There's so much I don't remember."

The memories flitted and fluttered, brushing the insides of her skull like bats fighting to be free. All she could do was hope the answers were already in her head, because returning to the temple was impossible now, with Hookeye waiting to snare her, body and mind.

What she needed to do, as she had in the temple while Kougar slept, was take some time to sort through the new memories, to take each one out and look at it, replaying it fast-forward style. It would take time for the mass of thoughts to filter into her brain and become part of her consciousness. And time was something she didn't have.

Kougar had given her twelve hours to come up with an answer, and only ten remained. But Hookeye could attack again at any time, if he hadn't already. She feared that his insidious poison might be working on her even now, in ways she couldn't begin to guess. How long did she have before it bloomed? The thought terrified her. But she wasn't without warning this time. A thousand years ago, she hadn't known what was happening. She hadn't known she was under attack until far too late.

And by the time she knew what was happening, she'd no longer had Kougar by her side.

Her gaze caressed the man, his strength the only solid thing left in her world. And she knew she wouldn't make the same mistake again. Though she had no illusions that his primary concern was saving himself and his friends, she knew deep down he wouldn't turn away from her when she needed him.

He was her strength, her rock.

"They're lighting the festival lights," he murmured, back at the window. "They think you're on your way to beating this thing."

"Brielle's no fool, Kougar. She knows we're far from safe. But an Ilina celebration empowers us, don't forget. Beautiful lights, music, dancing. All feed the Ilina, body and soul, and we're likely to need all the strength we can come by. Brielle was looking for an excuse, and my renewed memories serve her purpose. We have the possibility of victory locked inside my head. And that's worth a celebration, a badly needed lift of spirits."

He turned to her, his gaze pensive. Thoughtful. Slowly, his pale gaze moved down her body, a physical caress. "Will you dance?" In those eyes, she saw a memory of another time and the echoes of that pleasure.

"Perhaps. Once I find the Crystal of Rayas."

"Once *we* find it."

"I thought you might enjoy watching the celebration."

"I go where you go." He closed the distance between them slowly, moving with the silent grace of the cat he was inside, and came to tower over her, a solid wall of muscle and willful male. He closed his hand around the back of her neck. "Who knows when you might feel in need of strengthening." Though he said the words without inflection, a gleam shone in his eyes.

A smile lifted the corner of her mouth. "You think you have what it takes to pleasure me, Feral?"

The gleam brightened, crinkling the corners of his eyes. "I do." The hand at her neck slid into her hair as his other arm snaked around her back, hauling her against him. He covered her mouth in a hot, luxurious kiss, a tangle of tongues that ended far too soon. But the passion of those few brief moments did, indeed, energize her.

He pulled back, but didn't release her, watching her with a look that questioned, demanding acknowledgment of his skill, if not outright praise.

She smiled at him with a quick roll of the eyes. "You do, Feral. You absolutely do have what it takes."

He watched her with keen eyes, his hand moving to her face, his thumb stroking her lower lip as if he'd forgotten what her smile looked like.

Goddess, how I need this man. "My life would have been so much easier these past centuries if you'd been part of it." She hadn't meant to verbalize the thought, but the growl in Kougar's throat was all agreement.

"You should have told me." The words were more growl than voice, but his thumb continued to play with her lower lip with exquisite tenderness.

"I know. A hundred times I nearly sought you out, once I was myself again. I missed you terribly."

How would she live without him if he died? Even if he lived, she had no doubts that their responsibilities and their lives would pull them in opposite directions even if they wanted to stay together. And Kougar had said he didn't. He'd said that he wanted nothing to do with her when this was done. Whether that was merely anger speaking or the truth of his heart, she couldn't be sure. At that moment, she'd felt the same.

Now, she felt nothing but empty at the thought of them going their separate ways. And yet, at its heart, their relationship had never changed. Kougar was still as closed and contained as he'd ever been. If they tried again, he'd still wind up shutting her out of his world as he always had.

As her mind traveled that dismal path, another memory popped out of the fog, whole and bright.

"The Crystal of Rayas," she murmured.

Kougar raised a brow.

Ariana pulled out of his arms. "Come. I've just remembered where it is. Or another place where it was." She started to turn, to lead the way, then found herself turning back and reaching for his hand.

Their gazes met, his eyes so hard to read, but his hand went around hers firmly, filling her with a sense of rightness as together they walked through the wide doorway and back into the Grand Corridor.

Melisande floated toward them, her body mist, her expression at once demanding and vulnerable with hope. Ariana started to pull her hand from Kougar's, knowing how much Melisande hated to see her with the Feral; but he held fast, refusing to let her go.

Melisande didn't seem to notice either way. She barely seemed to notice Kougar at all, forgetting even to scowl at him.

"Did you really do it, Ariana? Did you learn how to beat that asshole? Hookeye?"

Ariana hesitated, unable to lie to her second, yet hating to dash her friend's hope.

Melisande read the truth in that hesitation. And more. Her expression turned grim. "The situation's that bad, is it?"

Ariana opened her mouth, then closed it again, unable to deny it. "I don't know, Mel. He's attacking me again. We had to leave before I'd finished receiving the memories. And, no, I haven't learned what I need. Yet. But that doesn't mean I won't. I have thousands of memories I didn't have before, but they're still a jumble." She glanced at Melisande's feet. "How long did it take you to get free of that chunk of temple floor?"

Her friend's brows drew together, her expression almost bemused. "About an hour. I tried to turn to mist and couldn't, not with my feet bound. Lyon suggested we wait. If the magic didn't wear off in a couple of hours, he'd call the Shaman. But the magic dissolved on its own, suddenly. One moment my feet were bound in stone, the next, the chunks fell away, littering the chaise and the patio, nearly knocking over one of the pitchers of lemonade. Olivia grabbed it just in time."

Ariana lifted a brow. "Pitchers of lemonade?"

Melisande shrugged diffidently. "They had questions. They wanted answers. It's not like anyone's seen an Ilina in a thousand years."

"So they plied you with lemonade."

Melisande scowled, changing the subject. "What now, Ariana? How do we stop the poison?"

"The answer will come to me, we have to believe that. In the meantime, enjoy the celebration, Mel. Soak up all the pleasure you can."

"While we can?" The words were quietly said.

"Yes."

With a grim nod, Melisande turned and contin-

ued down the corridor. When she was out of ear-
shot, Ariana looked at Kougar. "Tell them thank
you for me. Lyon and Jag for getting Mel out of
there, and Olivia, or whoever offered her the lemonade. Did you notice she didn't scowl at you?"

"I noticed."

It pleased her. Melisande's violent objection to
Ariana's mating a Feral a thousand years ago had
poisoned the entire race's feelings toward Kougar.

Ariana led Kougar up the wide stair to the observatory, then turned right and led him down
a long passageway to the room that had always
been her favorite, the place she'd missed most
during her long absences, forced to live her life as
flesh and blood.

The observatory was round and not overly large,
furnished as it had always been, with a profusion
of pillows in various sizes, covered in bright silks,
the walls long ago painted with a full-sized mural
of a lush, tropical garden, the flowers seeming
real enough to pluck from their stems.

But the thing she loved the most was the ceiling,
for there was none. The Crystal Realm might sit
in the clouds, the sun shining bright and warm,
the stars glittering brilliantly at night. But the air,
air that shimmered with myriad colors, remained
a constant temperature. Never was there wind or
snow or rain.

In the middle of the room stood the great golden
urns of Barse, the fourth queen. And if the latest
memory proved correct, in the middle one, at the
very bottom, lay the Crystal of Rayas.

Ariana released Kougar's hand and strode to the urn which stood higher than her waist. "I think it's in here. Want to help?"

"Of course." With no visible effort whatsoever, he lifted the heavy urn, making whatever was inside rattle and clink, then tipped it upside down over one of the cushions. The crystal she sought tumbled out, the shape of a large faceted teardrop, attached to a thick silver chain.

"Found it. Thank the heavens something's going right."

As she placed the chain around her neck, Kougar set down the urn. "Maybe you've remembered more than you think," he said. "Maybe we should test you."

"Test away." Ariana fingered the crystal settling heavily between her breasts.

"Have there been any other times the Ilinas were poisoned by the Mage? Times the Ilina queen overcame it?"

Ariana tried to seek the answer but hit a tangled mass of thought and backed off. Closing her eyes, she repeated Kougar's question in her mind, concentrating on the question, not the answer. And a pair of memories tore free of the mess with a rip of pain.

She grimaced, the discomfort fading as she examined them. "Yes. Another queen suffered Mage poison twice. A poison similar to the one I'm fighting. Both times she killed it by starving it."

"Starving it how?" Kougar watched her intently,

no emotion visible on his face, but he couldn't quite hide the flicker of excitement in his eyes.

"By not feeding the darkness."

His brows drew together. "Have you ever not fed it?"

"No. The darkness gets stronger when it's hungry. I've always been afraid I'd lose control. But I don't think I will. In fact, I'm sure I won't." Excitement leaped inside her, and she smiled. "This is the answer we've been seeking, Kougar. This is it! The way to defeat the poison."

"Ariana . . ." He came to her, closing the space between them. Sliding his hands into her hair, he tilted her face up to his, his pale gaze embracing hers. "If this doesn't work . . ."

"It will. I'm sure of it. And when it does, once the poison is gone, I'll be able to turn to mist without endangering my maidens. Now that I have the Crystal of Rayas, I'll be able to free your friends. And the death of the poison within me means I'll no longer be feeding it to you through the mating bond. You'll be safe. This is it, Kougar!" Her smile slowly turned to a scowl. "All this time, such a simple answer. If only I'd known."

His thumb stroked her cheek. "If it's any consolation, you might not have been strong enough to vanquish the darkness before."

She lifted an eyebrow. "You think you make me stronger?"

"I know I do." He bent his head and kissed her, his tongue sliding between her lips, stroking her mouth, her teeth, her tongue. When her breathing had turned thoroughly ragged, he pulled back, watching her with hunger and satisfaction. "How long before the darkness grows hungry again?"

"Not long, not the way things have been going. Yours and Jag's fight helped, but even that only satisfied the darkness enough for me to wrench back control. If I had to guess, we have an hour or two. Maybe a little more. In the meantime . . ."

Kougar hooked her around the waist and pulled her tight against him, pressing his hips against her, letting her feel his thick erection. " . . . I pleasure you."

But as his mouth covered hers again, hated eyes appeared in her mind. The voice of her enemy rang in her head.

You can fight me all you want, Queen of the Ilinas. But you'll lose.

Chapter
Seventeen

Ariana jerked back. "*Go away*, you bastard."

Kougar's arms dropped from around her as if she'd burned him.

"Hookeye, not you." But those mismatched eyes had definitely killed the mood.

Kougar's mouth tightened. "You saw him."

"Only his eyes, but as if staring at me wasn't enough, now he's taken to taunting me."

Kougar's pale gaze bored into hers. "Tell me what he said." As she told him, his eyes narrowed. "He's up to something. We know that. I just wish to hell I knew what it was. With the poison flowing to me, now, too, you should be having less trouble holding on to it. Yet you're having more."

"It eased off at first. But then grew stronger, yes. He's definitely feeding more poison into the bond. But who knows what it's doing this time." She reached for him. "It's not hurting you more?"

"It's no worse, just a steady stream of acid eating away at my heart. It's easy to guess he wants me to die. But he'll try to control you this time as he failed to do before."

"It may take time, though. It was two years from the time we mated until the attack. Not for a minute do I think he waited that long. I think his poison takes time both for him to create and to grow inside me. I may not know what he's done to me for weeks or months."

Their gazes met, and locked, with a sick jolt.

"I won't be around by then to help," he said quietly, voicing the thought they shared. "That may be part of his plan."

Ariana sighed, the sound hollow. "He doesn't think we can stop him."

His hands curved over her shoulders. "We'll stop him. If starving the poison is the way to free yourself from it, then you'll starve it." One hand slid down to brush the tip of her breast lightly. "While I keep you strong," he added huskily.

"And then what? Even if I free myself from the old poison, do I dare turn to mist when I know he's still threatening us?"

His hands rose to cup her face. Though his touch was gentle, his eyes were fierce. "We'll beat him. You're still remembering things. Tighe and Hawke still have a couple of days. We'll find a way. Together, this time."

He stroked her face, then dipped his head to

capture her mouth in another searing, tongue-tangling kiss. His mouth slipped to her cheek, to her jaw, as his hands went to the fastening of her pants.

"Start wearing dresses," he murmured against her neck. "Short dresses. With nothing underneath." With a quick slide of her zipper, his hand was in her pants, his fingers sliding beneath her panties and lower, stroking her. As he pushed two fingers inside her, she melted, her knees giving way.

He grabbed her close and nipped at her throat, his teeth scraping lightly, sending excitement bursting in her blood. She came with a guttural cry, rocking against his driving fingers, gasping with the intensity of the pleasure and the accompanying rush of wonderful strength.

As she tried to catch her breath, Kougar straightened, pulling his hand away and fastening her pants again.

She sighed. "That was nice."

He lifted a brow. "Nice?"

She gave him an impish grin, uncertain where the feeling of playfulness came from when their situation was so precarious. "You can practice later."

Without warning, Kougar lifted her up and tossed her down on the middle of the pillows. She stared up at him, watching as he yanked off his shirt.

"I was teasing," she said quietly, as he unfastened his belt. "But don't let me stop you."

His pale eyes speared her. "You won't." He
stripped naked before her, his male body beautiful and powerful, his erection thick and hard.
As he knelt on the pillows, it dawned on her she
could have been proactive, stripping off her own
clothes. Then she thought of nothing at all as the
gorgeous male in front of her reached for her.

He had her pants and panties off her in less
time than it took her to pull off her shirt. Then
his hands were on her thighs, rough and warm,
spreading her wide. Leaning over, he licked her,
a single long, marvelous slide of tongue over her
most sensitive flesh.

"Nice?" he asked, his eyes predatory, his breath
warm against her.

She met that gaze and grinned. With a toss of her
head, she murmured, "Practice, practice, practice."

He growled low in his throat and went back to
work, driving her up with his tongue and lips and
teeth until a monstrous orgasm overtook her. She
screamed with her pleasure, the sound echoing in
her ears as a glitter of Ilina light appeared before
her, followed quickly by the flash of steel.

Melisande stood beside them, blade drawn,
ready to slay her attacker.

"Go away, Mel," she gasped.

The scowl her second gave her was one for the
record books, but she disappeared as quickly as
she'd appeared.

"Again, Kougar. *Again.*"

He brought her to screaming orgasm three
more times before she dug her fingers in his hair

and tugged, gasping too hard to tell him what she wanted. He knew.

He paused for one thick moment, bracing himself over her, staring down into her eyes as she twisted her hips, seeking the relief that pressed against her hipbone.

To her amazement, a small smile lifted one corner of Kougar's mouth. *"Nice?"*

She threw her head back and laughed. How long had it been since she'd laughed? "No. Not nice. Unbelievable. Splendid." She met his gaze, still grinning. "Magnificent."

He smiled and pushed inside her on one hard, perfect stroke, filling her as only Kougar ever had, their gazes locked, laughter and heat and wonder in his eyes. Exactly what she knew he must see in her own.

Laughter. Smiles. Their lovemaking had been like this once. She remembered that, too, now, and not just from seeing it in the dream. Like now, she'd felt as if her heart and lungs and chest would simply burst from the affection she felt.

No. Not affection.

Love.

He drove her hard toward yet another glorious climax. When they were once more still, their hearts pounding, their bodies slick with sweat, she heard the music drifting up from below. The celebration had begun without them.

A smile lifted her mouth. No, the celebration had begun right here—with them.

Kougar lifted his head slowly, his soft beard

brushing her cheek a moment before his lips. Then he pushed off her, his gaze liquid with tenderness as he offered her a hand.

For a long moment, time stood still as they gazed into one another's eyes, remembering. Then he pulled her up, and the moment was over.

As they dressed to the sound of music and gaiety, Kougar rubbed at his chest, just over his heart, and she knew the poison was eating away at him, slowly killing him. The fullness of her heart tumbled into confusion.

She wanted so much, with a need that was almost painful. The safety of Kougar and her maidens, the defeat of Hookeye. The poison gone, her life returned.

And Kougar back in that life.

Side by side, they walked to the open window and the railing that overlooked the garden below. Her maidens looked up, waving to her as they danced in their bright silk celebration gowns, twirling around one another in time with the vibrant music. Ariana felt a bittersweet smile form on her lips.

Kougar leaned on the railing, his gaze turning to her. "I want to see you dance. Here. For me."

"Will you dance with me?"

A smile lit his eyes. "If you'll wear a gown."

A smile played at her mouth. "Wait here."

They were traveling a knife's edge over a pit of disaster, yet she felt almost happy, as she hadn't in centuries. An inappropriate emotion when the man she loved was dying, and so many other lives were at stake. And yet, why not live while they had the chance?

Why *not* feel joy?

He accompanied her to the queen's chamber, one she rarely visited anymore, and watched her strip off her jeans and tee and pull on the deep blue satin gown that was the queen's color alone. The gown was simply made, a wisp of silk that just covered her shoulders then fell to midcalf, lightly clinging to her curves.

As custom dictated, she brushed out her hair, letting it fall freely, and left her feet bare. She turned to find him watching her with eyes of silver, a smile at his mouth.

"Beautiful."

And she believed him. He'd always made her feel beautiful and desired.

Taking his hand, she led him back to the observatory. The moment they were through the doors, she dropped his hand and twirled away, dancing for him, all the desperate joy and love that filled her chest flowing into the music.

He watched her, his gaze a caress that she didn't think she could live without again. In the few short days since he'd stalked back into her life, she'd felt more alive than in the thousand years she'd spent without him.

Any sacrifice would be worth it. Even if she feared she would never truly have his heart.

Wulfe sat on the floor of Natalie's cage in his man form, watching her stir, both glad and not that she was starting to wake. Because it was finally time to send her home.

Her eyes fluttered lightly, her gaze catching on him. "Hi."

"It's time. We were able to get Christy's memories. I can take yours now and get you home."

Her soft movements turned quick with excitement as she sat up. But as she glanced around her cell, she frowned.

"Where's Xavier?"

"Helping out in the kitchen."

She gave a jerk of surprise. "Really?"

Wulfe dreaded this part but couldn't put it off. "He's going to stay here."

"What? No. *Why?*" She scrambled to her feet as if she meant to dart out the open door.

He rose, ready to stop her if she tried. "We can't clear his mind of what he's learned of us. That's only accomplished through the eyes."

Understanding dawned ugly in her own. "And his don't work."

"We're not going to hurt him, Natalie. He'll be well treated here."

"Let me see him."

Her agitation tore at him, and he pulled out his cell phone and called Kara. Less than a minute later, Kara led Xavier into the cellblock.

"Xave!" Natalie rushed past Wulfe, out of her cage.

He let her go to her brother, who enfolded her in a bear hug. "I'm going to be okay, Nat. I don't mind staying. Do you know what they're doing here?"

"Xavier," Wulfe said with a low growl.

"Okay, I can't really say 'cause I'm not supposed to know, but I hear more than I should, and it's big, Nat. Save-the-world kind of big. Really cool shit goes on here."

"You can't *want* to stay here."

Xavier shrugged. "It's not like I have a choice."

Natalie's pained gaze swung to Wulfe, but he shook his head. "I'm sorry. He can't leave unless we find a way to take his memories."

"Do you think that will happen?"

He could lie to her. In a few minutes, she wouldn't remember. But he wouldn't do that to Xavier.

"No."

Her eyes began to glisten with unshed tears as she turned back to her brother, framing his face with her hands. "I can't leave you here. I'll never be able to find you again."

"Nat." The kid gripped his sister's hands, pulling them gently between them, but didn't let go. "You'll think I died, like your friends did. I'm sorry. I know that's going to be hard on you. And Mom." His expression crumbled for just a moment. He visibly swallowed. "But right now you know the truth, that I'm going to be okay. This is a good place, and I can do stuff here that I like. You should meet Pink. She's really cool."

"I'll never see you again." Natalie's voice broke.

Wulfe watched her struggle with tears, hating that she was having to experience this.

"What am I going to do without you, Xave?"

Xavier pulled her back into his arms. "Maybe finally stop worrying about me?"

Natalie's arms tightened in a fierce hug. "I love you, Xavier Cash. I will always love you."

"I know. I'll always love you, too."

Natalie pulled back and looked at him, swiping at the tears that were starting to fall. "If only I had some way to remember this, to know that you're okay."

Xavier pulled a pen from his back pocket, took his sister's hand, and drew on her palm, a circle with a small curved line in it. "A smiley face with no eyes. When you see this, you'll know I'm happy." He kissed her cheek. " 'Bye, Nat." Then he turned away, and Natalie let him leave.

Wulfe watched her, his hands clenching with an inappropriate need to offer her a shoulder to cry on. He might have done it anyway but for the uncertainty of her reaction. It was better to remember her as the one who'd smiled at him, who'd touched his scars without revulsion, than the one who'd backed away when he tried to hug her.

Natalie stood still as stone, tears slipping silently down her cheeks. She whirled on him suddenly, a desperate fire in her eyes. "Promise me you're not going to hurt him, or kill him, or enslave him. *Ever*. He's a good guy, Wulfe. A good man."

"As long as he's genuinely content to remain here, he has a home. I promise."

But if he ever tried to escape, or call the cops, he was a dead man. Wulfe had told Xavier that, point-blank, and he felt certain the kid had understood. At the moment, the kid appeared to be viewing all this as a grand adventure.

Wulfe just hoped that didn't change.

He reached for Natalie, brushing a tumbling tear from her cheek with his thumb. As she met his gaze with damp eyes, he stroked the softness of her flesh for one indulgent moment, then looked deeply into her eyes and snatched control of her mind.

"When you wake, you won't remember anything that happened from the moment you drove into Harpers Ferry. You'll walk into town, go into one of the shops, and call your fiancé. Then you'll look at your palm, see the symbol drawn there, and know Xavier is okay. That he's happy. But for his own safety, you'll never tell anyone that. Nor will you ever try to find him."

Giving in to an urge he didn't entirely understand, he placed a light kiss on her forehead. "Be happy, Natalie."

Then he knocked her out, swung her into his arms, and headed out of the prison block to take her home.

Chapter
Eighteen

Kougar watched Ariana dance with hungry eyes, her beauty making him ache. She was exquisite, her dark hair flying around her shoulders, her brilliant eyes shining. She took his hand and twirled around him, her scent enveloping him in a desire that went far deeper than the flesh. As she met his gaze, she threw back her head, her trill of musical laughter filling his heart.

He held her hand as she danced around him in the circular, roofless room, the walls a living jungle, the music flowing over them from the open balcony overlooking the festivities below. She'd kicked the pillows out of the way and now danced across the sleek golden floor.

With every graceful twirl of her body, the band around his chest tightened, his need to pull her against him and never let her go growing more difficult to resist. Slowly, he was coming to realize that it wouldn't matter how much distance he put between them, he would never be free of her. He would be, as he'd always been, incomplete without her by his side.

With a last twirl, she tugged on his hand and pulled him with her onto the open balcony, to the railing where they could watch the party below. And the Ilinas knew how to celebrate. Ribbons of color danced through the air as crystal lights bobbed and weaved above the maidens' heads in time to the lively music. The women danced, nearly four dozen of them, about half with flesh and-blood-feet on stone, the other half twirling, mistlike, in the air.

To a woman, they were lovely, their hair free, their bodies lithe and graceful, their emotions a tangible force. Joy, excitement, and hope leaped and danced, caressing his senses.

But only the woman at his side moved him, body and soul, making his blood rush with a seductive, carnal need.

This night was a time apart. An island in a churning sea. They had yet to find a clear path to saving Hawke and Tighe, one that wouldn't endanger Ariana and those she loved. But he refused to believe they wouldn't.

He refused to let them die.

And he refused to die himself. Not when Ariana was finally back in his life.

She turned to him, a warmth and depth in her

eyes he thought he could happily drown in. "Do you remember the time you filled the garden with flowers, Kougar? Wildflowers of every color and type."

Of course he did. He remembered better the happiness the flowers had brought to her brilliant eyes. "You liked flowers."

"I loved them. I still do."

"I liked making you smile." Being in love with her had felt so simple then. So right. "It was all I ever wanted—to make you happy." The words came out, low, a whisper from his heart.

"Was it?" She cocked her head, looking genuinely surprised.

He frowned. "You were happy."

She hesitated. And in that hesitation, something died inside him.

"I loved you, Kougar." But she turned back toward the garden and the festivities, avoiding his question. Below, two of the maidens shed their gowns and leaped, naked, beneath one of the small waterfalls, their laughter so at odds with the cold invading his mind.

"You were happy." His voice was starting to sound belligerent, but he didn't care. *I didn't get that wrong, dammit.*

"I was happy," she murmured; but she was hedging, he could hear it in her voice.

"You're lying." The ground was shifting beneath his feet, playing havoc with his balance.

She looked at him helplessly. "I was happy most of the time. At least when we were together."

"I had responsibilities. I came to you as often as I could."

"I know. And we made love, which was wonderful. But . . ." Her hand lifted, then dropped. "I never really knew you."

"We were mated," he snapped. She couldn't just rewrite a thousand years of history.

The look she gave him was starting to spark with annoyance. "Joined, yes, body and soul. But that never gave me access to your mind. I never knew what you were thinking, what you were feeling, unless we were making love." Her brows drew down. "I never knew what made you happy."

"You made me happy. You."

"I don't think you ever told me that."

He glared at her. "You knew." The floor had turned to quicksand beneath his feet.

"You don't get it, Kougar. You never let me in. There was always this wall between us. I could see you through it . . . just as I still can . . . but I've never been able to truly reach you. To this day, I have no idea when or where you were born, or when you were first marked as a Feral Warrior. I loved you, Kougar. But you've never let me really know you."

He stood stunned, silent, his mind reeling. She was rewriting everything he remembered of those two years they'd been together. They'd been happy. *He'd* been happy. Those had been the best damned years of his life. How could she not . . . ?

A thought slammed into him. "That's why you didn't turn to me after you severed the mating bond."

She shook her head, then sighed. "I honestly don't know. Maybe things would have been different if we'd been closer."

If they'd been closer? Goddess, he'd never been closer to anyone. Except his Feral brothers. The Wind and Horse had known everything about him. Everything.

"I loved you." How could she believe he didn't love her? He'd brought her flowers.

"I knew you loved me, in your way. But no, I never thought I had a very big piece of your heart." She turned to him fully, her hand covering his, her eyes pained. "I never thought the rending of the bond would physically injure you the way it did. I'm sorry for that."

The rending of the bond had been the least of his injuries. When she'd died, when he thought she'd died, he'd lost his heart. Even after all this time, the pain was so sharp, he had to close his eyes against the memory of it. A thousand times sharper than the acid destroying him now. How had she not known how deeply he'd loved her?

He stared at the women below, barely noticing that more and more had shed their gowns and were now dancing in the nude, cavorting in the waterfalls and small pools, their laughter ringing gaily over the music. All he could think about was Ariana's words. That he'd never opened up to her.

He didn't talk about his past because it was nobody's business. And yet, just a few days ago, as they'd tried to re-create one of the old Daemon traps, Hawke had asked him questions about the old days, and he'd told him virtually nothing even though the warrior's curiosity had risen thick in the air between them. Even though he'd felt closer to Hawke than he had any of the current Ferals. Even when he knew Hawke possessed a quick mind and an insatiable curiosity, that telling him tales of those old times, of Hawke's own father, the Wind, would be the finest gift he could have given his friend.

Did Hawke even know he considered him a friend? His best friend?

Keeping it all buried had been his way for so long, he wasn't sure he could share the past if he wanted to. But he'd give just about anything to be able to share those stories with Hawke, at that moment.

And sharing himself with Ariana might be his only chance of keeping her in his life. Could telling her his story be any harder than what he'd endured these past thousand years without her? Could it be harder than losing her again?

No. A thousand times, no.

He turned to her, meeting her gaze. "I was born a hundred years before the Sacrifice."

Ariana stared at the man beside her, the man she'd loved for an eternity, with surprise bordering on shock.

The Sacrifice was an old name given to that joining of forces between the Mage and the Therians, both races mortgaging the bulk of their power to defeat the Daemons.

Five thousand years ago.

Kougar stiffened, pacing away from her on the observatory balcony like a caged cat, while the music and laughter of her maidens lifted on the crystalline air from the garden below. She'd hurt him with her honesty, which hadn't been her intent. He was a good man. A strong, honorable warrior who'd probably loved her as much as he was able.

She turned and followed him back into the circular room, feeling the need to touch him, to soften the blow of her words; but his stiffness welcomed no such comfort.

"My father was chief of the cougar clan," he continued, standing before the wall mural as if seeking answers in the lush, painted jungle. "The world was different then—each of the shifter lines a separate community with alliances and enemies, territorial wars and rampant infighting. The cougars' closest allies in those days were the leopards and white wolves. Our biggest rivals were the tigers and the horses, whose chief was a dictator of the worst sort. And the vipers." He glanced at her over his shoulder. "No one allied themselves with the vipers."

He stepped away from the mural, his gaze dropping to the discarded pile of colorful silk cushions, his brows drawn as if he were deep in thought. "But even then, things were changing. Satanan had only recently come into his true power. The Daemons, who'd always kept to the highest elevations and only killed as necessary, were beginning to terrorize the populated regions. They were starting to kill for pleasure and power. Many of their earliest victims were immortals since we took so long to die."

He looked up, his gaze focusing on her briefly. "You know this, or will, when you get your memories from the old queens. The Ilinas had always had little involvement with the other immortal races before that time; but in the century that followed, it took all of us together to defeat Satanan."

As he began to pace again, Ariana clasped her hands together in front of her, awed that he was telling her this, holding her breath as she willed him to continue.

He walked slowly around the room, his unseeing gaze on the floor. "I was still short of my maturity when my mother and one of the other cougar females disappeared. Two years later we found them in a Daemon nest, along with the mutilated bodies of over forty human children. The shifters were still alive, their bodies covered in blood from the tortures they'd endured, but their eyes were empty. The other woman eventually recovered, but my mother never did. She sat in the corner, rocking herself, her mind destroyed. She never shifted again."

Ariana's fingers twisted together as she saw glimpses of the world he'd lived in, flashes of the horrors the Ilina queen had witnessed in that time. The suffering.

Her chest hurt from the pain she was causing Kougar by forcing him to go back there. To remember his own suffering. Part of her wanted to tell him to stop. That he didn't have to continue. But a wiser part of her knew he did. If he didn't want to speak of the past, there was a reason.

"Satanan's power was growing quickly, alarmingly so. Many of the Therian clans banded together and attempted to stop him, but we failed. Many died. The Mage fought their own war against the Daemons; but as Satanan's power grew, their magic was of less and less use. It all came to a head during the winter solstice when I was half a century old. During the week before the solstice, the Daemons captured dozens of shifters and Mage, and at least a thousand humans. We tried to find where they'd taken them; but the Daemons had magic and flight, and even the bird shifters among us couldn't follow.

"Finally, we learned what Satanan was up to—a powerful ritual to create more Daemons, tripling their numbers." He stopped, his gaze spearing her, going right through her. "For centuries afterward, that night was called the Night of Screams." Turning away in the next breath, he moved toward the balcony again, and she followed.

"The situation went from bad to desperate as the Daemon numbers trebled, and it became clear Satanan's goal wasn't survival but domination. Most agree the Daemon Wars started that night, the Night of Screams. And it took another fifty years for the immortal forces to finally band together into one cohesive unit to vanquish him. The Mage were the ones who came up with the ritual to lock Satanan and his horde in the Daemon blade, but the magical energy required was far more than they had, and Ilina energy was ill suited. The Therians had to come on board. All of them. And it was a hard sell. All knew draining their power was dangerous. If the ritual failed, Satanan would easily destroy us all."

Leaning forward, he rested his powerful forearms on the thick gold railing and stared out over the garden as if oblivious to the celebration taking place below. He was caught in another time, and all Ariana could do was stand beside him. And listen.

"What no one knew was that the vast majority of the magic that went into that ritual would never return. It's said that the Therians and Mage willingly mortgaged their power to defeat Satanan, but that's not entirely true. We gave of our power believing it would be replenished in short order. It wasn't.

"The ritual worked. Satanan and the souls of his horde were captured in the blade. But the Mage and Therian alliance severed almost immediately afterward as both claimed the right to guard the blade. Still, celebrations broke out in every corner of the immortal world, until the sun set, and we saw the draden for the first time. While we'd captured the souls of Satanan's horde, small, vicious remnants of them remained. Life-eating remnants that fed primarily on Therian energy. Hundreds of Therians died over the next weeks as we fought to find a way to protect ourselves against them. For nearly a week, no Therian shifted, but we still believed our power would return. The Radiants worked feverishly to pull the energy from the Earth—in those days, every clan had its own Radiant; but they, too, had lost their power and could do nothing. Finally, one of the lions shifted. I heard his roar that day, and it was a glorious sound. It was beginning, we thought. All would be back to normal soon."

He dropped his head. "We were wrong. Others regained the power to shift. One here, another there." He looked up again, his eyes unseeing. "It was days before we began to realize only one from each clan had regained his or her power. But in many of the clans, no one had regained that power and never did. It was weeks before the fear set in that the healing was over. That those who had not been able to shift again never would."

He shook his head, lost in the past. "The anger. The *fury*. I know they were terrified, but . . . *goddess*." A pulse of pure anguish escaped the mating bond, telling her he must be holding the emotions close with an iron fist.

And suddenly she understood. "You were the only one able to shift among the cougars."

Kougar turned to her slowly as if he'd forgotten she was there. "Yes."

"And they turned on you." Ariana fisted and flexed her hands, easing the prickly discomfort of the poison's rising hunger.

His mouth compressed, his gaze glazing over as he once more faced the garden. And the past.

"The first of the jaguars to shift had been attacked by his clan in a jealous rage and killed. Three weeks later, another was marked. Rumor—true, as it turned out—raced through the clans that only one of each line would be marked at a time, another to take his place upon his death. And suddenly we were all in danger. Men I'd lived with, fought with, *my family,* turned on me."

Laughter rang out from below, a sharp counterpoint to the ugliness of the past.

"Three of my clan mates, the closest of my brothers, helped me escape. Together, we fled to a cave the clan often used during hunting, where they promised to defend me, to watch my back until the anger died down." The muscle in his cheek leaped, his mouth taking on a hard, terrible line. "It was a setup. A trap. My father, the clan chief awaited us in that cave, along with the clan's seven strongest fighters. It was his right to be the clan's shifter, he said. A right I'd stolen. And the punishment was death."

As Kougar spoke, his hands moved to the railing. Ariana watched silently as the gold reshaped beneath the fury of his fingers.

"I shifted and fought my way out of there, barely escaping with my life. Never before or since have I run from a fight; but, despite their betrayal, I couldn't kill them. They were my brothers, my family.

"A horse shifter, *the* horse shifter, came upon me as I raced on bloody paws across the valley, badly injured, my clan mates in pursuit. The horse told me to shift and hop on, and I did. He, too, had been attacked. While there had never been any love lost between the cougar and horse clans, we became brothers that day. He was the only one in my life who didn't have a reason to kill me. Over the course of the next few weeks, most of the remaining shifters came together, bound by a common strength and a common enemy—the rest of our race. Almost too late, we found the one remaining Radiant and brought her to us. Then we fled to build a stronghold from which to defend ourselves.

"When it became clear that our combined might could not be overcome, the Therians ceased to attack us. Slowly, over the course of years, the non-shifters lost the power they'd once had, the disparity in strength becoming greater and greater."

Kougar fell silent.

Ariana wanted to move closer, but stayed where she was, his past like a wall between them.

"The only ones you could trust were the Feral Warriors," she said quietly.

"Yes."

And they still were. He might have loved her once, but he'd never fully trusted her because she doubted he could trust anyone but his Feral brothers anymore. And she'd only made it worse by betraying him, too, by severing the mating bond and never telling him she was still alive.

Goddess. How could I have ever thought we might still have a future?

She swallowed hard, struggling to ignore the increasingly uncomfortable prickling in her palms as she wished there was a way to make up for the pain she'd caused him. As she wished she knew how to make it right between them.

She'd wanted the truth. Now, having heard it, she realized how much further apart they were—so much further than she'd thought. She'd wanted him to open up to her, and he had. With his words, his past.

But it was his heart she wanted. A heart badly damaged all those years ago by the betrayal of his clan. Then damaged again by her own betrayal.

If they survived Hookeye's poison, if they had a future to face, she'd offer him everything she had. But if he still believed he'd be happier without her in his life, she wouldn't fight him.

Never again would she willingly cause him pain.

Chapter
Nineteen

Kougar felt flayed alive by the memories of that
time he'd tried so hard to forget. His head ached,
his chest was a coiled rope pulled too tight even
as the poison burned in his heart. Anger bit at
him, a deep frustration that Ariana had made him
dredge it all up again.

But even if she asked for his head on a platter,
he'd give it to her. He'd never stopped loving her.

Below, the celebration continued, the maidens
all dancing naked beneath the moon's glow, the
music lush and beautiful, played by no fewer than
a dozen instruments, many of which he knew to
be unique to the Ilinas.

Beside him, Ariana made a sound low in her
throat. Half growl, half groan. In an instant, the
past no longer mattered.

"What's wrong?"

"The poison. The darkness is growing hungry, and it's annoying the shit out of me."

"Would you normally try to feed it at this point?"

"Yes." She met his gaze. "The battle begins."

"Brielle!" His shout rang down into the garden. A moment later, the Ilina appeared beside him, a naked, mistlike wraith cloaked by a tumble of waist-length dark curls. "Go to Feral House and tell Lyon I need flowers. As many of them as he can get his hands on in the next twenty minutes." Ariana was going to need all the strength . . . all the pleasure . . . he could give her.

Wulfe stood in the shadows between two old brick buildings in downtown Harpers Ferry, spring sunshine warming the sidewalk at his feet. But he barely noticed the sun or the people strolling by, their steps quickening as they caught sight of him. His gaze was fixed on the store across the narrow street, on the window crammed with T-shirts, Confederate soldier caps, plastic place mats with Civil War battlefield scenes in faded colors. And Natalie.

A short while ago, he'd laid the unconscious women on the grass not far from where the Ferals had left the bodies of their friends days ago. Then he'd stayed close enough to keep watch over them until they woke. Until Natalie led Christy into town as he'd directed her to when he took her memories.

Standing in the window, holding a borrowed

cell phone to her ear, Natalie looked out of place, her clothes rumpled, her hair tangled and unwashed. The Ferals had made the conscious decision to return the two women to their world looking like they'd been held captive, deciding their stories of not remembering anything would be far more likely to be believed than if they appeared well cared for.

But even unkempt and a little wild-looking, Natalie exuded an air of calm confidence. And he had a hard time tearing his gaze away from her. She remained on the phone until a silver Mercedes pulled up in front of the store, stopping in the middle of the narrow road with an impatient screech of brakes. A strong-looking young man in a business suit leaped out and ran around the car even as Natalie rushed out the door to meet him, Christy close behind her. The man swept Natalie into his arms and cradled her against him, the sun glinting off the tears on his cheeks.

Wulfe shook out his knotted fists and consciously relaxed his jaw. This was good, the way it should be. Natalie was back in her world with a man who clearly loved her, a man who would stand by her and help her through the tough days to come.

Natalie Cash was no longer his concern.

Ariana watched as a dozen of her maidens misted into her private garden, once more dressed in their festival gowns, their arms laden with blooms of every kind and hue. Gorgeous arrangements in glass vases were set atop sapphire rocks in the small private garden outside the queen's chambers. Beribboned pots were lined up like fragrant soldiers along the crystal walk. And single-stemmed roses, tulips, and lilies were scattered over the rocks and silk pillows, and across the lip of the pool, as if strewn by a gentle wind.

Kougar stood at her back, his arms around her, his chin on the top of her head as his pelvis pressed against her backside, his thick erection telling her he was more than ready for the task ahead.

But amid such beauty, with seduction and passion moments away, all she could think of was blood. The darkness, with its ravenous hunger, clawed at her control, demanding pain. And blood. Anyone's blood.

"Smell," Kougar said, his hand sliding restlessly across her abdomen, down one of her hips and back up again. "Smell the flowers, Ariana."

And she did. The blooms filled the air, a glorious profusion of sweet scents that pleased her Ilina need for beauty of all kinds.

"I'm going to make love to you among the flowers," he whispered against her temple, his hands growing more restless, more needy by the moment. "I'm going to caress your body with rose petals, then follow every inch with my lips."

His words battled back the growing need for violence within her. The flowers themselves warmed her heart—the fact that after all this time, he remembered what pleased her most.

One by one, the maidens left, some walking out, some misting. Only Brielle remained, her hands clasped before her, her eyes unhappy.

Ariana frowned. "What's the matter, Brie?"

Brielle's gaze didn't meet hers but remained fixed on Kougar. "I have a message from Lyon." She glanced at Ariana, apology in her eyes, before meeting Kougar's gaze once more. "The tiger shifter's mate is with child."

Ariana felt Kougar's surprise, his grip on her tightening. The tiger shifter would be Tighe. One of the Ferals in the spirit trap. *Oh, no.*

Brielle continued. "Because his mate is not true Therian, the child appears to be drawing much of its life force from its father. The shifter's mate has been in contact with him and is still able to sense him, but he's lost all consciousness and appears to be weakening quickly. She fears he doesn't have much longer. Hours, not days. Lyon wished you to know."

With each word, Kougar's body turned stiffer, more rigid, until she felt as if she were being held by a man of stone. A stone that was beginning to quake.

"I'm sorry," Brielle whispered, then misted away.

Ariana lifted her hand to Kougar's cheek, turning in his arms to look at him. Raging fury gleamed in his eyes. And a desperate determination.

"We have to make this work." His words were so low as to be almost a growl.

"It's going to work." Her hand on his cheek

began to curl as the darkness inside her clamored for blood. She snatched it away before she could score his flesh.

Kougar grabbed her, sweeping her into his arms. With fast, purposeful strides, he carried her down the stairs and into the middle of the oasis that, for once, looked like a true garden. Almost roughly, he put her on her feet, hauled her into his arms, and kissed her with a passion that rode the edge of violence. And she reveled in it, the darkness egging her on.

As her tongue twisted with his, she gripped his shoulders, her fingernails digging into his flesh through his shirt. Against her will, her grip tightened until she felt the slickness of blood against her fingertips.

Kougar grabbed her wrists and jerked her hands away from him. "Don't give in to it!"

She stared at him. "I need to hurt something. Someone. If only *he* were here." She'd gladly rip Hookeye limb from limb if not for the certainty that doing so would destroy everything she sought to protect. But all that mattered was starving the poison so she could turn to mist.

Mage eyes rose in her mind, sending goose bumps skating over her skin. *Starving the poison is a foolish idea, Queen of the Ilinas.*

"Tough. Shit." She shivered with revulsion.

Kougar lifted a brow.

"Hookeye," she explained.

Kougar grasped both her wrists in one hand and grabbed her jaw with the other, hauling her close. "Focus on me! The flowers. The waterfall. Smell, Ariana. *Feel*."

"I am!"

"Not enough." In the blink of an eye, he released her and pulled her gown up and over her head, tossing it aside. As she reached for him, uncertain whether she meant to grab for his buckle or rake her fingernails down his face, he lifted her and tossed her onto the pillows.

When she tried to get up, he flipped her onto her stomach, pressing her down with a knee to the small of her back.

"*Kougar*."

"Feel."

And she did. *Goddess.* A moment later, a delicate flower brushed against her hip, sliding over her buttocks and down her thigh. A soft, lush sensation in direct counterpoint to the violence struggling inside her. Even as she fought to get up, she shivered from the sensual pleasure of the bloom as it traced her opposite hip.

Kougar curled his fingers around her thigh and pulled her leg away from its twin, opening her to the touch of his flower. The petals slid along her sensitive flesh, drawing a moan of pleasure and need from deep in her throat.

Inside, the darkness growled with hunger and fury.

Without pulling the flower from between her legs, Kougar moved, his hand replacing his knee in the small of her back. A moment later, she felt his mouth on her butt cheek, nipping, scratching with his teeth as if he longed to take a bite and resisted . . . barely. Excitement tumbled inside her, the flower stroking between her legs growing damp and dewy.

Her hips began to rock as he drew the flesh into his mouth, sucked, and nipped. The flower disappeared as his fingers dove inside her, hard, in and out, in and out. She bucked wildly, gasping, then screaming as a blinding orgasm broke inside her.

"More, dammit. More!"

Kougar released her. Moving with his innate agility, he slid onto his back between her thighs and lifted her hips. Wrenching her wide, he pressed her down onto his mouth, shoving his tongue inside her and flicking it over her clit until she spiraled into another screaming orgasm.

The pleasure was almost more than she could bear.

So, too, was the terrible hunger.

She tried to push up, tried to kick free, her hands fisting until she felt the slick dampness of blood in her palms from her own fingernails. "I need to hurt you! Hurt me, Kougar. Hurt me!"

He slid out from beneath her, slamming her back down on the pillows, pinning her with his knee as she heard the rustle of fabric and watched his shirt sail to the ground out of reach. The sound of a belt being unfastened met her ears followed quickly by the slide of a zipper. A moment later the pressure at her back disappeared.

But as she pushed up on all fours, strong hands gripped her hips. She screamed with acute pleasure as Kougar took her from behind, burying himself deep.

This was what she needed! "Stay inside me. Stay. Inside."

He thrust deeper, harder, over and over, then slid an arm around her, yanking her up until she was on her knees. Even as his hips pounded against her, his mouth found her shoulder. He bit her lightly then raked his tongue over the spot and bit her again.

She was out of her mind with passion, sensation, her senses exploding with the smell of flowers and sex. As she rocked back against his hard thrusts, his hand closed around her breast, pinching her nipple nearly to the point of pain. She arched into his hold, wanting . . . *needing* . . . more.

The battle between pleasure and pain escalated into full-out war. Barely conscious of what she was doing, she reached for his face, feeling her nails sink into his cheek before he grasped her wrist and yanked her hand away.

Kougar flipped her around and pushed her back on the pillows without gentleness or care, understanding her need for pain. Then he fell on her, taking her roughly, pounding into her harder, deeper, with every thrust.

Her fingers dove into his hair, too hard, holding him too tight. He captured her with his gaze. In those pale eyes, she saw savage excitement and fierce determination overlaid by a heartrending tenderness. In those pale eyes, she saw the man she'd fallen in love with all those years ago.

Inside her, another orgasm began to build, harder, faster, higher than any that had come before. And building, right alongside it, was the hunger, a seven-headed monster devouring her body and soul. But Kougar gripped her with his gaze, held her together as the war inside her threatened to rip her apart.

As the orgasm broke, she screamed with the glory of it. Then cried out with horror as she felt the bonds she'd locked around the poison all these centuries snap free.

As she turned to mist.

Chapter
Twenty

The orgasm overtook Kougar in a blinding release, his and Ariana's combined—magnificent, brilliant perfection as he sank into her, their bodies merging in a blazing burst of pleasure he hadn't felt in . . .

Realization hit him with a stunning blow. *She'd turned to mist.*

"Ariana?"

For one fleeting moment, he wondered if she'd won. If the poison was gone. But Ariana's horror rushed at him through that open mating bond, and he knew.

They'd lost.

The cry that tore from her throat was part anguish, part fury, and she fled from him, a wraith he couldn't hold.

Kougar leaped to his feet as Ariana's mistlike form, rimmed in blood red, whirled on him, one of his switchblades snapping open in her hand. And he understood. Hookeye's controller spell had been set free.

"Do you belong to him now?" His voice remained calm, but he was roaring inside.

"The poison is trying to control me!"

That she knew that much meant she was still fighting, not lost. Not completely. Though she was mist, he knew she could turn to flesh in a microsecond, the blade becoming deadly just as fast.

"It wants you." Her expression was terrible, her neon blue eyes filled with dread, her mouth battle-hard. "It wants me to hurt you. The *compulsion . . .*" One moment she was there, the next she was gone.

A knife tore through his lower back with white-hot pain. He spun, but it was Melisande behind him, not Ariana. A second later, she, too, disappeared.

Crap. He needed his knives, even if they'd do him little good with the Ilinas turning to mist after every strike. Fighting mist warriors had always been an exercise in futility. And he didn't want to hurt them!

At the next flash of light, he dove for his pants, praying one of his knives was still there. He found it and rolled to his feet only to find the two women circling him, wraithlike, glowing with hot energy.

Neither attacking.

"What are you doing, Ariana?"

"He wants you injured, not dead. We're to take you to the temple. All of you."

All? The Ferals. "The spirit trap?"

"Yes. He wants me to open it for him. To drop you in."

Like hell. And suddenly he understood why the pain in his chest had, if anything, been getting better, not worse. Hookeye didn't want him dead. Not yet. What good was Kougar to him dead when another Feral would only be marked by the cougar? If he tossed him into the spirit trap, no cougar would ever come forth again.

Melisande flew at him, her ghostlike form pure energy as she attacked. She latched on to him, sucking him into her unnatural grip like a science-fiction tractor beam.

He shifted into his cat, the shift difficult and painful with her energy mixing with his; but he sprang away from her to turn and hiss, ears back.

Melisande flew at him again, turning to flesh just long enough to slice the blade deep through his shoulder. If she'd been a Mage, he'd have taken off her arm. He'd had the time. But Ariana . . .

His warrior queen yelled her fury and flew, not at him, but at Melisande. The two pulsing, mist-like figures collided in a spray of energy. Fighting, furious.

He could only watch, uncertain what was happening. What he needed to do was get back to Feral House and warn the others. He shifted back to a man. But as he reached for his armband to whisper the spell, the two Ilinas sprang apart, turning corporeal.

Kougar crouched, expecting another attack, but Melisande swayed on her feet, letting the knife drop from her fingers. Ariana sank to her knees, blood seeping from her pores like drops of sweat.

Goddess.

A wary eye on Melisande, Kougar reached cautiously for his mate.

"Ariana?"

She was doubled over, holding her middle, blood dripping onto the ground. "I beat back . . . Hookeye's control. And took Melisande's poison. It's changed. It's not what it was before. It's darker. Stronger." Her gaze flew to Melisande. "You're okay?"

"Yes." The petite blonde's face had drained of color. "What about the others? Are you taking their poison, too?"

"I can't . . ." Ariana's eyes filled with anguish. "I'm trying, but it won't come!"

Kougar brushed a lock of hair back from her bleeding temple. "He changed the poison so you couldn't take it this time."

"You took mine," Melisande said. "You're going to have to merge with them as you did me."

"Find Brielle. Bring her to me." As Ariana rose unsteadily to her feet, Kougar grabbed her arm, helping her. She looked up at him with fury and devastation. "Starving the poison should have worked!" Her hand went to the silver cuff, tearing it off her wrist and flinging it onto the rocks with a clatter, her face a mask of anguish. "How could I have turned to mist with the moonstones on?"

"The Mage are more powerful than they've ever been." Powerful enough to change the poison already in Ariana. Powerful enough to . . . ?

Kougar stilled. "Ariana, you've seen him in your mind. You've felt something strange going on in your head. What if it wasn't the memory downloads you were feeling, but Hookeye?"

She looked at him sharply. "What do you mean?"

"What if some of what you've remembered wasn't from the queens at all, but false memories planted by the sorcerer? At one time, you were sure the Ilinas had never been attacked by the Mage before. You blamed yourself, blamed us both for Hookeye's original attack after you took me as your mate."

Brow furrowing, she bent down and picked up her dress. "You think my new memories about other attacks, about starving the poison, were Hookeye's doing? For just this reason . . . to make me lose control?" She pulled on her dress, a new horror filling her eyes as she met his gaze. "If you're right, how do I know what's real?"

He grabbed his pants. "Can we kill him?"

"No." The word shot from her mouth without hesitation. Which told him all he needed to know.

"That's what he wants you to think. It's a lie. The only way to get him out of your head is to kill him."

"You can't know that." But as he dressed, he could see her processing his words and watched as hatred leaped past the anguish in her eyes. *"We kill him."*

Kougar nodded. "I've got to get back to Feral House to warn the others."

"It's too late." Melisande appeared behind him. "The maidens have left. The Crystal Realm is empty but for us."

Ariana's gaze collided with his. *Feral House.* She sprang at him, turning to mist and catching him in her energy in a flash of light. Moments later, he felt grass beneath his feet, his head spinning even as he started running for the patio door. He could hear shouts of battle from inside Feral House. Shouts of pain.

Ariana materialized at the door. "Do you want Melisande's help?"

He glanced back to find Ariana's second standing where they'd landed, a wary expression on her face.

"Yes!"

The three rushed through the dining room together. They found the battle in the foyer, Lyon, Jag, and Vhyper in their animal forms, leaping at the mist warriors, attempting to strike during those seconds the maidens attacked with their knives. The floor was smeared with blood. And Wulfe was missing.

"Don't kill them!" Kougar barked. "They've been enchanted. Melisande and Ariana are with me." In a spray of light, he shifted into his cat, leaping at one of the Ilinas as she tried to strike Vhyper.

Melisande flew at Brielle as the latter was about to stab Lyon.

Out of the corner of his eye, Kougar saw Ariana lift her hands above her head. "Mel, hang on!" Then she began to chant fast and furiously. Two seconds later, the Ilinas disappeared, leaving nothing behind but cries of fury.

Even Ariana and Melisande were gone. Kougar searched for her through the mating bond, opened fully once more.

Ariana?

I remembered a warding to keep Ilinas out, Kougar. There was no time to explain. Feral House is safe.

Where are you?

Behind the house.

What of your maidens?

The others took off. Melisande has gone to find them.

Even telepathically, he could hear the devastation in her voice.

I'll be right there. He shifted back to his human form.

"Wulfe and Paenther?" Kougar demanded as the other Ferals shifted.

"Neither was here." Lyon turned to Jag. "Call them. Warn them." His gaze met Kougar's. "What the hell is going on?"

"Come." Kougar strode through the house and out the back door, Lyon and Vhyper close behind him. Ariana waited, her skin and dress streaked with blood, her eyes shattered even as they radiated with a warrior's fire.

Lyon's eyes narrowed as he took in her appearance. "Explain."

"I lost control of the poison," Ariana told him. "My maidens are infected, except for Melisande. They're controlled by the sorcerer who attacked us a thousand years ago. He sent them to capture you with hopes of dropping you into the spirit trap."

"He failed."

"For now." Brittle eyes turned to him, breaking Kougar's heart. She thought her friends were lost to her. That after fighting for so many centuries to save them, she'd failed.

He wouldn't let that happen.

"I'll get your Ferals out of the spirit trap." Her voice was low, vibrating with a pain that sliced what was left of his heart into ribbons. Her gaze turned to him. "Then we go after Hookeye together. I don't care if the entire Himalayan range comes tumbling down." Her lips pulled back from her teeth. "*I want him dead.*"

Even in devastation, the warrior within her rose to the battle. He lifted his hand, an invitation born of a need to hold her, to comfort her, but she gave a small, tight shake of her head. This wasn't the time for comfort.

Her eyes widened, a look of raw doubt shattering her warrior's persona. "What if I don't really know how to save them? What if the Crystal of Rayas is just another thing Hookeye planted in my head?"

"Then we kill Hookeye first."

Melisande appeared in a rush of air that smelled of snow rather than pine. "They're at the temple," she stated without preamble. "The Mage have armed them and set them up as the first line of defense." She looked at Ariana, her eyes almost as hollow as her queen's. "The place is so thick with magic, I couldn't get near it. There will be no misting in. They'll snare us for certain." She scowled. "I don't know what they want with us."

"Hookeye knows we're coming after him." Ariana's voice shook.

Melisande frowned, confused. "Hookeye isn't there, Ariana."

Kougar froze. Ariana's gaze collided with his.

"He's gone?" Ariana demanded.

"He was never there." Melisande shook her head, her brows still drawn. "Why did you think he was there?"

"I *know* he was there, Mel. Why do you think he wasn't?"

"I . . ." Her eyes darted back and forth as if searching for the answer. "I just know." She tilted her head. "Why do I think I know?"

"Shit," Ariana said beside him, echoing his thought. "He's done it to you, too. That original poison must have had some kind of magic in it that would keep us from ever finding him. How many times were you on his trail, then lost it at the last minute?"

Disbelief flashed in Melisande's eyes. "Dozens. Are you trying to say I nearly had him all those times? That every time I got close, the magic kicked in to tell me he wasn't there? *And I walked away?*"

"I'm sorry, Mel. He's stronger than we knew. He's always been stronger."

Melisande's jaw turned to stone. "And now he's taken our people. All of them."

"He probably knows we're going to try to rescue the Ferals from the spirit trap. He's going to make me cut down my own sisters to reach the temple."

"Ariana . . ." Melisande's shoulders bent as if bowed beneath the weight of grief. "They're full of poison, now. They're already dead to us."

Ariana's grief blazed down the mating bond, a cry of anger and devastation that crumbled his soul. Deep inside, his cat let out a howl of answering pain.

Ariana stood beside him, blood-soaked and too pale, her eyes alive with grief and anguish. It was all he could do not to pull her close or, at the very least, take her hand. But the iron in her eyes stayed his hand. Now was the time to fight.

"Mel, tell me about Queen Rayas," Ariana demanded. "I have a memory of her standing atop the Temple of the Queens, channeling the energy of the Syphian Stream through this crystal to access the spirit trap." She lifted the chunk of rock that still hung between her breasts. "Is the memory true?"

Melisande nodded. Kougar knew she'd lived in that time. "Rayas often went into the spirit trap, Ariana. That memory is true, I'm certain of it."

Ariana turned to him. "Your friends are out of time, Kougar. I'll go after them while you track down Hookeye."

"We go together."

"To the temple, yes. I'll need you to help me break through the Mage . . ." Her face pinched. ". . . and my maidens. But once I'm through the gate to the Syphian Stream, you can't follow."

"I'll kill Hookeye."

"Yes."

Teamwork. Something that had been severely lacking in their marriage once upon a time. But history was repeating itself, her maidens attacked, their queen desperate to save them. If they died, as she feared they would, it would once more be because of him. Because he'd ripped the moonstone cuff from her wrist and revealed her to her enemy. She'd blame him. Every time she saw his face, every time he tried to make love to her, she'd remember this day. The tragedy they both feared was about to unfold.

Any thought he might have had of a future with her hung on a very fragile thread.

His gaze captured Lyon's. "The only way for Ariana to reach the spirit trap, and Hawke and Tighe, is through the temple. We're going to need help."

Lyon nodded and gave a shout for his warriors.

Ariana turned to Kougar. "Are you still feeling the poison?"

"Hardly at all. The bastard wants me to survive long enough to be captured in the spirit trap."

"It's not going to happen."

Their gazes met, locked, fierce determination arcing between them. "No. It's not."

Within moments, all within Feral House were outside, gathered around. The Chief of the Ferals began issuing orders.

"Olivia, you're in charge here. I'm counting on you, Ewan, and Delaney to guard our Radiant with your lives."

A soft growl rumbled from Jag's throat, but Olivia's eyes lit like beacons. "You have my vow, Lyon. No one will harm her."

"Good. The rest of us are going to the Ilinas' earthbound temple in the Himalayas. The Temple of the Queens. Arm yourselves." Lyon turned to Melisande. "I need you to pick up two of my warriors and bring them to us. Wulfe's gone to Harpers Ferry. Paenther's on the Eastern Shore. I'll warn them you're coming."

Melisande nodded.

As Lyon pulled out his cell phone, Kougar saw Jag slip his arm around Olivia's neck, pulling her close. "A few days ago, I thought he was going to kill you," Jag murmured to his mate. "Now he puts you in charge of Feral House and his mate."

Olivia looked up at him, her mouth struggling to contain the smile leaping from her eyes. "You jealous?"

A slow grin spread across the jaguar shifter's face. "Hell no, woman. I'm proud. Just don't let it go to your head, Red." He kissed her temple, a slow, gentle kiss that throbbed with love and an aching need to protect that Kougar understood all too well. "Be careful."

"You, too."

A moment later, Lyon glanced at Melisande. "Paenther's ready. Wulfe's finding a place to park the car where his disappearance won't be seen by humans." He turned to Ariana. "Are you able to transfer the rest of us, Queen Ariana?"

"I am."

Lyon's gaze snapped to Kougar. "Anything else?"

"No."

"Then let's do it! It's high time we got Tighe and Hawke home."

Chapter
Twenty-one

The wind whipped at Ariana's thin dress, plastering it against the side of her body, tossing her hair into her eyes as she stared up at the golden temple from the path below. The sun escaped the clouds for one brief moment, setting the ivory temple afire before the shadows doused the brilliance once more.

Ariana felt light, literally, as if with the dissemination of the poison she'd lost forty pounds. And perhaps she had. But her heart felt heavy with grief and the leaden fear that her maidens were going to die.

And Kougar . . . No. She couldn't fear for him, too, or she wouldn't be able to function. The Ferals would win this battle. She had to believe that.

If only she'd called on their aid from the start, the moment her maidens started dying.

Hookeye had always been stronger than she'd realized. At last she knew, from the vantage point of distance and hindsight, that the Ilinas had never had a chance of defeating him on their own. She should have turned to Kougar in those days, not away.

If only.

Instead, she'd put them both through hell. And her maidens were all going to die anyway.

Kougar stood beside her, his shoulder inches from her own. She'd asked him not to touch her, and he'd seemed to understand that if he cradled her now, as she really wanted him to, if he offered too much sympathy, she might crumble, the wild grief inside her taking her down. She had to stay strong. Shoulder to shoulder, he held her up, lending her the strength to fight the battle to come.

Melisande appeared with the last of the Ferals. Wulfe, she thought this one was called. The shifter stood for a full ten seconds before dropping to one knee to retch on the rocks beside the others.

As the Ferals shook off the effects of the travel, Ariana started up the path, needing a moment alone. She reached the spot where she could see the temple yard just as the sun came out again. Flashes of steel glittered across the grounds, the swords held by her maidens, her friends. Dozens of them stood like automatons scattered in rough lines, their eyes blank with enthrallment.

Brielle stood with her dark hair loose and flying around her shoulders in the cold wind. Ariana's stomach felt as if it were being hollowed out with a blade. What kind of monster would force her to cut down her own people to reach him? Then again, as Melisande said, they were already dead. The poison she'd protected them from for so long would steal their lives as surely as Hookeye had stolen their wills.

Her eyes burned, tears escaping to be whisked from her cheeks by the cold wind. Grief pummeled her, leaving raw bruises on her heart that she knew would never heal.

How would she survive such a loss a second time? There would be no one left but Melisande. Two to renew a race. They could do it, of course. She alone could call the magic of rebirth and bring forth new Ilinas upon the Altar of Life, now that she could turn to mist again. She and Melisande would teach them what they needed to know.

But even as her mind set forth what she must do, her heart shattered at the need to do it. How could she go on without Brielle and Getrill and the others? She would, because she'd have no choice.

Goddess, it will destroy me.

The wind raked at her hair and her thin gown, the cold of the air no match for the bitter cold she felt within.

She felt Kougar move beside her, felt his hand slide under her hair to curve around the back of her neck. Warmth. Strength. He gave her both and more, grounding her, pulling her back to the here and now.

Taking a shuddering breath, she felt the cold abyss move away. For the moment.

She could not lose him, too. On the most fundamental level, she needed him. Her life would never be right without him. She knew that now.

But could he ever forgive her for betraying him all those years ago? Could he ever learn to trust her as he trusted his Feral brothers? Could he ever come to love her again as she loved him?

His warm fingers kneaded the tension in her neck. "We'll guard you and get you in there," he said quietly.

"No." She fingered the sword gripped tight in her hand, the sword she'd demanded from him at Feral House. Glancing over her shoulder, she briefly met his gaze. "I'll fight my way in there just as you will."

As she turned back to face the yard, his hand fell away, to be replaced a moment later by a light pressure on the top of her head, the brush of his chin. "My warrior queen," he murmured, barely loud enough for her to hear.

His words strengthened her, his simple, soft use of the word *my* lifting her heart in hope.

"That's the last fucking time I'm traveling by Ilina," Jag muttered, as the Ferals joined them.

"Any sign of Hookeye?" Kougar asked her.

"No." She'd been so focused on her own maidens, she hadn't really looked; but as her gaze moved back to the temple, she saw only a few scattered Mage and none who looked like the one she wanted dead. He was probably tucked safely in his laboratory, in the room where he'd been in his dream, working at his table on whatever magic would best destroy the Ferals.

She glanced at Kougar and found him watching her, pain in his eyes mixed with a deep, caring warmth.

"You're hurting," she murmured.

His knuckles brushed her cheek. "For you."

The constricting band tightened around her chest, pricking her eyes with tears, forcing her to turn away before she gave in to the terrible need to pour out her grief within the circle of his strong arms.

Kougar turned to his men. "No killing. The Ilinas are enthralled and not our enemies. Killing too many Mage could cause an earthquake that would destroy the temple and make it impossible to reach Hawke and Tighe. The only one who dies is Hookeye, and Ariana and I are the only ones who know what he looks like."

"Stay alert," Lyon added. "These bastards have access to a spirit trap, and they want us in it."

"They're not getting what they want," Jag snarled.

Wulfe grunted. "Hell, no."

"Just keep your eyes and senses open," Lyon added.

Kougar palmed the top of Ariana's head, then slid his hand down her hair. "Be careful."

She blinked hard against the flood of warm caring she felt in his touch. "You, too." She couldn't meet his gaze, or the tears would get the better of her. But he gripped her shoulders and turned her to him, kissing her with a quick, passionate meeting of lips.

Through the mating bond, she felt a burst of tangled emotions. Fear and fury, savage determination and aching tenderness.

Unable to resist, she met his gaze and fell into those fierce pale eyes.

"We're going to win, Ariana. We're going to beat him." He kissed her forehead. "Come back to me."

Hope bloomed inside her with a fragrant beauty. "Yes. And you to me."

Beside them, Lyon lifted his arm toward the temple.

"Go!"

Kougar touched her face for one tender moment, then moved behind her, strong and protective at her back. With a fierce cry, the Feral Warriors, Melisande, and Ariana raced into battle.

With one hand, Kougar swung his sword, parrying the blows of the enthralled Ilinas, while with his other he grabbed slender wrists or feminine necks, and tossed his petite assailants far from the field of battle. The falls might hurt the Ilinas, but any injuries sustained would heal quickly enough. And for a few minutes, the women would be out of the way of slashing swords. For once, the Ferals weren't fighting in their animal forms but their human since they didn't want to hurt, let alone kill, their unwilling opponents.

The Ilinas were quick, deadly little fighters, but the magic thick around the temple was holding them all to flesh and blood. Unable to turn to mist, they'd lost the advantage of surprise, their speed and strength no match for the Feral Warriors'. Still, they fought with the single-mindedness of puppets in the hands of a puppet master.

Paenther and Vhyper fought as a team, falling back into the natural rhythm they'd always had. Kougar was glad to see it. Vhyper hadn't been himself since Paenther helped him reclaim his soul. But maybe there was hope for the Feral, yet.

On his other side, Ariana fought, refusing to stay protected within their ranks. She'd always been a warrior, but her skill was a hundred times greater than the last time he'd seen her, reminding him that she'd been a woman on her own for far too long. With her blue satin gown splotched purple with blood, her skin blood-streaked, and her hair a wild tumble around her shoulders, she reminded him of a warrior queen of old, her eyes fierce and glowing.

Never had she looked more beautiful. Never had he loved her more.

One of the Mage sentinels broke through the ranks of Ilinas, his blue tunic rippling in the wind, his sword flashing with the sun's fire. Kougar took him on with a vengeance, funneling his fury into the first combatant he'd been able to fight . . . and hurt . . . without compunction. In the Mage's eyes, he saw no light of battle, no emotion at all.

"Even the sentinels are enthralled!" he shouted

to his companions. It seemed that Hookeye had enthralled even his own.

He fought the Mage in a quick, intense battle, his opponent a skilled fighter even with his will controlled by another. But in moments, Kougar sliced off the man's hand, sending his blade flying. As the man yelled with pain, Kougar grabbed his other hand and cut if off, too. His hands would grow back quickly enough, but he'd be no threat in the meantime.

As the Ferals hacked a path to the temple, Kougar gave thanks that the place was so isolated that the Mage had had no easy way to send up reinforcements in time to defend it properly. Thank the goddess, so far they'd been able to dispatch the Ilinas without anyone's suffering serious harm.

They fought their way up the ivory steps between the great pillars and into the temple's wide rotunda, where the remaining half dozen sentinels and last twelve Ilinas met them beneath the giant golden statue of the first queen.

As the battle resumed inside, the clang of swords echoing off the stone walls, Ariana broke away. Kougar followed, covering her back as she made her escape to find the passage that would lead her into the Syphian Stream and the spirit trap.

On feet as graceful as a gazelle's, Ariana slipped around a corner and started up an open, twisting stair that led to the narrow gallery ringing the curved inner dome, Kougar close behind. When they reached the top of the stairs, he noticed the series of niches that lined the inner wall, perhaps a dozen of which were filled with the life-sized stone carvings of warrior women. Queens? Was Ariana's likeness among them?

He didn't get a chance to find out as she paused beside the second niche, as if searching her memories. She turned to him, her eyes heavier than he'd ever seen them, yet lit with the fire of determination.

"This is it. This is the door. Wish me luck."

He lifted his hand, pressing it to her cheek. Her lashes drifted down as if she absorbed his strength, his touch. Goddess, she was about to travel into the spirit trap. His heart clutched at the danger she was about to face and the knowledge that he wouldn't be there to guard her. He couldn't go where she was going without ending up just like Hawke and Tighe.

Lifting her hand to his, she turned and pressed a kiss to his palm, then turned back to the door niche to call the magic that would let her through.

At least they'd made it there without any Mage trying to stop them.

The thought went through him like a bolt of lightning. *No Mage had tried to stop them.* He grabbed her shoulder.

"Wait."

Ariana glanced at him. "What?"

"It's too easy. *This* is the trap."

She turned slowly back to face him. "I have to go through if I'm going to save them."

"Hookeye knows we're here to breach that spirit trap, and he controls every Mage and Ilina in the room. Yet no one tried to stop us."

"Maybe he doesn't know this is the door."

"Regardless, no one followed us. He wants you to go through that door."

Her lips pressed together. Slowly, she nodded. "You're right. But what are we . . ." Her gaze flicked behind him, eyes widening. "Kougar, look."

He whirled toward the battle, seeing immediately what had caught her attention—the glimmer of firelit magic circling the floor around the statue of the first queen. Enclosing the Ferals.

He lunged for the balustrade. "Trap! Out of the temple! *Now*."

But his warning came too late. Even as he shouted the words, the magic shot up, arcing over the statue to form a glimmering, gleaming bubble. A bubble trapping all five Feral Warriors and nearly twelve Ilinas, including Melisande and Brielle.

The moment the trap snapped closed, all the Ilinas except Melisande fell unconscious, as if the one calling the shots didn't want the Ferals harmed. As if he wanted them alive for what came next.

The Ferals leaped for the bubble, fighting to break through with knives and claws, but their efforts were futile.

Disbelief and denial tore through Kougar's mind like shock waves. "The spirit trap."

"Yes." Ariana grabbed his arm, her hand trembling. "I can feel the magic."

"He's going to send them all in." The Ferals wouldn't die for days. But Ariana's friends would be dead the moment they hit the trap.

Below, the Mage sentinels and those Ilinas not caught within the bubble turned in perfect unison toward the stairs beneath where he and Ariana stood. As if they shared a single mind. And they did, didn't they?

Hookeye's.

*Chapter
Twenty-two*

Mage poured into the upper gallery from the two hall passages on the far side of the dome. Triple the number of sentinels that Kougar had believed were in the temple. They split their forces, circling in both directions, coming at Ariana and him from either side as more started up the stairs.

Surrounded.

Ariana glanced at him, her knives at the ready. "I don't suppose you have a plan."

"Only one. Find Hookeye and kill him." Which conveniently left out the part about fighting their way through several dozen Mage sentinels—Mage they shouldn't kill.

"Right," Ariana muttered. "All this time I didn't dare turn to mist. And now that it no longer matters . . . I can't."

"At least I can shift." But as he called on the power of his animal, as the magic swept through his body, nothing happened. The sparkling lights flashed and spit, then went dark, like electricity shorting out. "Scratch that. The Mage magic in this place has us both stuck in human form."

"You cannot stop me, Feral."

At the sound of the familiar voice ringing out across the dome, Kougar's gaze jerked toward the other side of the gallery as Hookeye stepped out from behind the advancing sentinels to stand at the railing.

"Opening wormholes into the old Daemon spirit trap is a difficult task," the sorcerer said, his expression preoccupied, as if he were talking to himself. "Mystery caught two Ferals. I've caught the rest. Except you." He nodded. "I'll catch you, too."

"Don't count on it."

Hookeye blinked in surprise. "The Ilina won't save you. Don't think she'll save you. She can't survive that trap any more than you can."

As the first of the sentinels reached them, Kougar drew his sword. If Hookeye said anything more, it was lost in the clang of metal on metal.

Out of the corner of his eye, he saw Hookeye lift his arms high above his head, his eyes closing, his mouth moving as if he intoned some chant.

The spirit trap. He was opening the spirit trap!

"Stop him!" Ariana cried, coming to the same conclusion.

Kougar lunged into the fray like a madman, hacking at limbs and tossing sentinels over the balustrade in a desperate race to reach the soulless sorcerer before he completed his spell and took the lives of their friends.

Below, Lyon and the others watched, listening to the chant that spelled their doom, fury on their faces. Only Vhyper's face held little but the same flat expression he'd worn since he returned. As if he couldn't gather the will to care that his life was about to end. Or the lives of his brothers.

Kougar's stomach twisted with sick fury. If the sorcerer succeeded, there would be only two Ferals left. Himself and whoever the goddess marked to take Foxx's place. Unless Hookeye was lying, and Ariana was in no true danger from that trap and could free them.

And if Hookeye was telling the truth?

Goddess help us all.

The rage had become Hawke's constant companion. His only companion, leaping up out of nowhere to consume him for minutes or hours at a time in a berserker's haze. If he were able to move, he was certain he'd find his fingers and mouth dripping with claws and fangs. And blood.

The pain had left him at some point in this endless night; but so, too, had the hawk spirit, or at least his sense of him. He wasn't sure how long it had been since he'd last heard him or felt him. Time had no meaning anymore.

Even the other animal spirits were gone.

Was this how the seventeen had died, then?

This lonely, angry death? He'd always imagined them fighting together to find a way out. Perishing together, brothers in arms. Now he knew the truth. They'd died in darkness and isolation.

Just as he was about to.

Several of the seventeen had been mated, one with a young son. How much harder to be unable to reach the ones who would suffer most at his dying.

How much harder this must be on Tighe.

In between bouts of rage, he drifted in and out of consciousness, unable to tell sleep from awake. People ran through his mind, people he'd known long ago. His father. The friends of his youth.

Were they spirits come to deliver him to the beyond?

No! There had to be a way out!

Within his mind, he struggled against bonds he couldn't feel. Slowly, painfully, the fight inside him drained away. There was no fighting the dark. There was no way out this time. His animal spirit was all but lost to him. His own spirit nearly gone, too.

His life was ending, and he couldn't stop it.

When the fury blind-sided him yet again, blasting through his head, he let out a war cry that would have rattled the windows, had there been any. If he'd still had a voice. As that white-hot haze swept through his mind, stealing his sanity, his last thought was that perhaps it was better he never escaped like this.

Goddess knew what kind of damage he'd do in this state. What kind of carnage he'd cause, lost to the fury of a mindless, vicious rage.

Kougar fought like a berserker, Ariana at his side. Both hacked off limbs right and left, Mage and Ilina, alike. No longer were they careful not to hurt the Ilinas. Limbs would regrow. And if they didn't reach Hookeye before he completed chanting his spell to open the wormhole into the spirit trap, Melisande, Brielle, and nearly a dozen other Ilinas would die.

And goddess only knew how many Ferals.

Even through the clash of swords, he heard the rest of the enchanted army closing in on them from behind.

"I've got them." Ariana turned and they fought back-to-back as he pressed forward, desperate to reach Hookeye in time.

Sweat rolled down his back, despair licking at his nerves as he hacked through the attacking Mage. The sorcerer's chanting carried faintly through the clang of metal and the screams of the injured. A quick glance told him the magic wasn't done. But he had no illusions. He was out of time.

With a Feral war cry that rang throughout the dome with an animal ferocity, Kougar stabbed and slashed, heedless of the damage he caused, focused on only one thing. One person. One unimposing bastard of a Mage.

Dismembered hands and arms flew this way

and that in a rain of blood that splattered his face and clothes, the metallic scent igniting a hunger inside him. In his cat form, he enjoyed the warm rush of blood in his mouth. But the only blood he craved now was Hookeye's.

The floor grew slick beneath his feet, but he pressed ahead, the sentinels unable to stop his forward charge and the Ilinas no challenge at all.

But as the Mage troops between him and his quarry thinned, something caught his eye on the floor in front of him—a shiny black substance that was beginning to bubble up with a sound like popping corn and a smell like rotting eggs. The hair rose on the back of his neck with the certainty this was another of Hookeye's plagues—one Kougar wasn't going to like at all.

Within seconds, the black ooze covered his boots and slid onto his bare calves beneath his pants like a cool, sticky goo. A goo that hardened within seconds of contact even as it continued to climb.

He stomped his feet, hearing the crack of the hardening tar. But more climbed his boots to take its place.

All around him, movement slowed as the vile tar attacked all equally—him, Ilina, the Mage.

"Goddess!" Ariana cried behind him, and he glanced at one of the Mage he'd sent sprawling to watch the black ooze slide over the man's head and cover his face. "Is this some kind of poison?"

The downed sentinel clawed at his face but couldn't seem to break the goo's deadly hold.

"Keep moving!" Kougar called to Ariana. "Don't let it harden."

As the dozen Mage between Kougar and his quarry yelled their own frustration, Hookeye continued to chant, his expression one of cool satisfaction. At any moment, the spell would be complete, the wormhole would open, and his friends would be gone.

Kougar struggled forward, every step more difficult as the tar crept over his knees and slid up his thighs. Sweating with effort, he broke through the constricting ooze over and over, forcing his legs to move, swinging his blade against the Mage still in his path, still trying to stop him.

The air shifted suddenly, a charge of electricity making the hair on his arms stand on end. The air pressure dropped, the light in the temple dimming.

They were out of time.

If only Ariana could turn to mist! But if she tried, she'd almost certainly become trapped in the floor as Melisande had.

A thought pierced his despair, an idea blooming with a burst of adrenaline.

"Ariana, turn to mist!"

"I'll sink into the floor."

"You'll sink *where you land.*"

The clang of his own blade drowned out her response, if there was one. A moment later, the shimmer of mist high above Hookeye's head caught his attention, and he knew she'd caught his meaning.

The temple grew darker as Hookeye's magic sucked the very light from the room. The sorcerer stood with his hands straight in front of him, his eyes closed as he fought to pull open the gates to the Feral's personal hell. He didn't sense the Ilina hovering above him until it was too late.

As the bottom of Ariana's feet grazed the top of the sorcerer's head, she turned solid. Hookeye jerked, trying to duck away, but it was too late. His own magic had the now-corporeal Ilina sinking into the surface where she stood.

Sinking down into Hookeye's skull.

The sorcerer screamed and flailed, grabbing her ankles and trying to pull her loose. But the magic was too strong. Her feet slowly disappeared inside his head.

Hookeye collapsed, unconscious, Ariana falling with him. She crashed into two half-frozen Mage, knocking them down even as they broke her fall.

Kougar struggled forward, the black ooze reaching his waist. The air in the temple began to blow in a spinning wildness as the vortex prepared to open. The spell had been completed, the magic engaged.

He reached Hookeye just as the bottoms of Ariana's bloody feet emerged below the Mage's jaw. Ariana struggled to sit up as the black ooze climbed her shoulders. But the fire in her eyes as she met his gaze was pure bloodthirsty triumph.

"End it, my beast."

With a roar that melded with the wild wind's,

Kougar sliced through the bastard's throat, through windpipe and spine, and cut off Hookeye's head.

At once, the black ooze fell away, sinking back into the floor, leaving only the acrid smell of sulfur behind. Murmurs of confusion and cries of fear rose with the din as the Ilinas emerged from their enthrallment and the Mage sentinels, no longer bound by their leader's poison, turned toward Kougar, raising their knives to renew their attack.

"Roar!" Kougar yelled as he took on four Mage at once, standing over Ariana, who was unable to stand herself.

"We're free!" Lyon's voice carried to him on the roar of the wind.

A quick glance over the balustrade told him what he needed to know. The bubble was gone, the floor glowing, but not yet open. He caught sight of Ilinas stumbling free of the circle, while Ferals snatched others, slung them over their shoulders, and ran.

An unnatural, earsplitting scream nearly blew out his eardrums as a red glow erupted inside the temple, and the wind blew gale force, piping hot.

He didn't have to look to know what he'd find—a spinning vortex in the middle of the floor. A wormhole straight into the spirit trap.

"To battle," Ariana cried, her voice a command ringing over the vortex's howl. A command to her maidens. "Fight the Mage!"

The few Ilinas on the gallery walk shook off

their confusion and turned on the sentinels they'd fought beside moments before. As two Ilinas dove in to draw off Kougar's attackers, he scooped Ariana into his arms, Hookeye's bleeding head still dangling heavily from her feet.

She slung her arm around his neck. "Get me to the door so I can save your friends."

"Wouldn't diving into the vortex be quicker?"

She looked at him askance. "Hookeye's vortex? No thanks. I'm going in the way that won't get me killed."

"The way he wanted you to go."

Her eyes narrowed. "He's dead. And your friends will be, too, if we don't hurry."

"True enough." Kougar turned and pressed through what was left of the battle, four of Ariana's maidens taking up guard positions around him.

"The poison?" he asked. "I can't feel it any longer."

"It's gone." Ariana's voice rang with a relief as deep as her eyes. "It's over."

That part was over. His own life no longer hung in the balance, and neither did Ariana's maidens'. But Hawke and Tighe were another matter. As, he feared, was Ariana herself. Not until he saw her emerge from the spirit trap would he breathe freely.

As he neared the second alcove where Ariana had said the door was located, Lyon and Wulfe barreled up the stairs.

Lyon eyed Ariana's feet with a lift of a brow.

"We're going after Hawke and Tighe," Kougar

told his chief. Ariana was, at least. He'd help her as far as he could.

Lyon's gaze swung to Ariana, but words seemed to elude him.

Ariana reached out and touched Lyon's arm. "I'll bring them back to you."

Lyon dipped his head. "And I'll be forever in your debt. We all will."

Kougar ducked inside the alcove, nearly bumping his head. Ariana reached deeper, around the statue. As she pressed her palm against the back wall, she began to sing, her soft, musical tones calling a curling trickle of magic. Moments later, the wall beneath her hand began to shimmer.

"Let's go," she urged.

Kougar eyed the wall skeptically. "The statue?" There was no way in hell he could squeeze past it.

"Walk right through her."

Right through stone. Damn Ilina magic.

Taking a deep breath and forcing himself to let go of logic, he stepped forward, pressing through a statue and wall as if they weren't even there.

One moment they were being buffeted by the hot tempest of the temple, the next, a frigid wind whipped at his face, sending Ariana's unbound hair flying. They stood on the temple's celestial roof, looking out over the rugged, snowcapped peaks of the mountains. Surrounded by the sudden silence and stillness, but for the biting wind, the battle that raged within the temple might as well have been a world away.

"Up there." Ariana pointed to the small spiral tower rising from the top of the dome like a crystal stair to the heavens.

"We need to free your feet." He started up the stair. "Can you turn to mist, yet?"

"No, Hookeye's magic is dissipating, but too slowly. I'll open the wormhole, then once I do, I'll need you to throw me inside. I'll turn to mist in there and free myself from these macabre shackles."

Kougar continued up, the crystal stairs ending in a small, open platform.

"This is it," Ariana breathed. "The spot where Queen Rayas used to stand to call the magic that opened the passage into the spirit trap. Set me down, Kougar."

"Even you can't balance on a head."

Their gazes met, a shared moment of amused disbelief that they were having such a conversation. "Help me to my knees."

He helped her kneel, then stood beside her as she lifted her hands above her head, closed her eyes, and began chanting the musical magic of the heavens, the cold wind blowing her hair in a tangle around her head.

Kougar could feel the magic gathering, riding his skin, until finally it leaped at Ariana in the form of a slim bolt of lightning, diving into the crystal that hung between her breasts. The Crystal of Rayas. The force of the blast knocked Ariana back against his knees. He reached out and steadied her, then released her as she continued to chant. If the blast had hurt her, she made no indication.

Moments later, a prism of colors erupted around her, flowing and twisting with power. The air parted to reveal a seething, pulsating mouth of dark crystal.

His heart began to pound as he stared at the death trap that held Hawke and Tighe, a path Ariana intended to travel.

Goddess, if only I could go myself and leave her safely behind.

"Now, Kougar." Ariana reached for his hand. "Throw me in. You can't touch it, or it'll pull you in, too."

The blood pounded in his temples. The last thing he wanted to do was toss her in there. *She'll be fine,* he told himself. *She's the Ilina queen, the only one who can do this. The only one who can save Hawke and Tighe.*

But as he swung her up and into his arms, his hands clasped tight around her, and he didn't think he could let her go.

Ariana cupped his face with her hands and placed a gentle kiss on his mouth, then pulled back to meet his gaze. "Trust me," she said simply. And he did.

It was the damned Mage still attached to her feet that he didn't trust.

But there was no choice, was there? She was willing to risk her life to save his friends. His heart melted beneath the weight of that gift.

The least he could do was let her try.

With immense effort, he returned her kiss, then pulled back. "Be safe."

Love warmed her eyes as she released him and tucked her arms against her chest. "Do it."

With a deep breath for courage, he did as she demanded and heaved her into the yawning maw. She didn't fall, as he might have expected, nor did she turn to mist midflight, as he'd counted on. She landed as one might in a pool of water, sinking down a short way before bobbing back to the center.

He caught his breath, waiting for her to move, to turn to mist.

Nothing happened. She just lay there.

His heart stopped beating.

Slowly, she began to spin in a slow corkscrew and he saw her face. Her eyes were closed, her expression lax as if she slept.

As if the act of entering the wormhole had rendered her unconscious. She was still corporeal!

His heart turned to dust.

"Ariana!"

This was what Hookeye had intended to happen all along. He'd set this trap, ensuring that Ariana wouldn't turn to mist. And the moment she hit that spirit trap corporeal, her soul would flee. She'd die. With the Queen of the Ilinas dead, there would be no one to free the Ferals.

His heart jackhammered in his chest, his head pounding, *No, no, no!*

The breath tore into his lungs like broken glass, ripping him to shreds from the inside out. She was gone. Into the wormhole, floating toward the spirit trap.

His precious Ariana, back in his life for only a handful of days.

Gone.

While his cat shrieked its rage in his mind, Kougar threw back his head and shouted at the heavens, "You're not taking my heart!"

In an act of pure insanity, with a roar of desperate grief, Kougar dove into the wormhole after her.

Chapter
Twenty-three

The wormhole was like some kind of freak-show thrill ride, the dark crystal walls lighting every few seconds, breaking the pitch-blackness, as the force of the energy within spun Kougar in a slow spiral, pulling him inexorably to his death.

The cat inside him growled with approval, sharing the fierce need to protect his mate that consumed him. He wasn't letting Ariana go again. Ever.

Ever.

If by some miracle they got out of this alive, he would offer her everything he could and take whatever she was willing to give him in return; but he would *not live without her again.*

If they got out of this alive.

The energy pricked at his skin, stinging like ice

crystals. And maybe that was what they were, because damn it was cold in there. Even half-frozen,
perspiration broke out on his brow, his heart beating against his ribs as he searched the weaving
tunnel ahead for Ariana and got no glimpse of
her. If he couldn't reach her, and wake her, and get
her to turn to mist before they fell into the spirit
trap, they were all dead. Ariana, Hawke, Tighe,
their three spirit animals. And him.

*Goddess, I'm out of my mind for following her in
here.*

"Ariana!" His voice barely carried in the wind's
tunnel-like roar. Ahead, he could see nothing but
more twisting curves. But Ariana was up there.
She had to be.

Kougar began to swim, propelling himself forward with hard sweeps of his arms, praying he
wasn't simply accelerating his own rendezvous
with death. Though what difference did it make?
Unless he could reach Ariana, none at all.

Over and over, he swam forward, his pulse
pounding with adrenaline, his mind narrowed,
focused on only one thing. Finally, as he turned a
corner, the dark light flashed, and he saw her. She
was still spinning slowly, bonelessly, her dark hair
floating out around her.

Unconscious.

"Ariana!" Kougar gave a hard pull with his
arms, gliding forward. Hookeye's sightless eyes
stared at him as he drew close, her feet and their
burden trailing her as she floated headfirst toward
the trap.

Another push forward, and he was able to grab hold of her leg. With a massive sigh of relief, he pulled her into his arms, but he was moving too fast, the force of his momentum propelling them forward. *Too fast.* Kicking hard the other way, Kougar tried to slow them down. He might not be able to see the spirit trap yet, but he knew it was there, waiting to send them to their deaths.

When he'd done all he could to slow their forward motion, Kougar pulled Ariana against his heart, stroking her ice-cold face, his chest seizing with his need to save her.

"Wake up, Ariana. Wake up, my love." When she didn't stir, he lifted her face to his and kissed her, sliding his tongue along the crease of her unresponsive lips. Sweet, sweet lips that no longer possessed even the slightest tang of darkness. She was finally free of the poison that had consumed her life for so long. It almost killed him that she might never have the chance to enjoy that freedom.

The light flashed again, revealing a throbbing, malevolent darkness no more than a dozen yards away.

The spirit trap.

His heart stopped, then thundered like a herd of horses. At the rate they were traveling, they had mere minutes before they reached it. Before it was over.

"Goddess, Ariana."

He felt a light pulsing in the mating bond, the soft glow of connection. Inside, his cat began to growl and hiss, urging him to do . . . *something*. A picture flashed in his mind, the cougar at the end of the mating bond, scratching at it as if trying to get in. As if he wanted him to open it.

What the hell? The mating bond was already open, like an untwisted straw. That was the reason the poison had been able to reach him.

Except that wasn't what his cat was asking of him, he realized. If the bond was a small, mystical tube running between them, heart to heart, at either end was a cap. Or perhaps a fine mesh filter. A small separation allowing each of them a measure of privacy. It was *that* that the damned animal wanted him to do away with. He wanted him to open it completely.

Hell no. The mating bond was open enough. He already felt Ariana's strongest emotions bursting through from time to time. A man needed some measure of solitude.

His cat growled.

Inside, he began to quake as he remembered Ariana's accusation, that he'd never opened himself to her.

Yes, but she hadn't been talking about the mating bond.

Of course she'd been talking about the mating bond. About opening himself completely, mind, body, heart, and soul. Holding nothing back. Nothing.

The thought of it made his hackles rise. He didn't share himself like that with anyone.

And what if I do? What if let her in, fully?

He waited for that sick feeling to punch him in the gut, but felt only a warm wash of love and rightness at the thought of pulling her inside him, tucking her into his heart, and never letting her go.

It was what he wanted.

Goddess, that's what I have to do. I have to open that bond. Then, maybe I can reach her.

But how?

The answer, he knew, lay inside. In his heart and the mating bond.

He pulled her tight against him as they spun through the wormhole, cradling her head on his shoulder and thought about how much he loved her, how much he'd always loved her. How much he needed her.

But nothing happened.

Fuck. How was he supposed to open the thing?

Dark lights flashed around him, illuminating the pulsing blackness of the trap.

They were nearly there.

His pulse thudded in his ears.

He had to find a way to open his heart! He imagined ripping the end off the bond, much as his cat had, clawing at it to reach Ariana. Inside, he felt the bond throbbing, felt his heart cracking. Just a little. Not enough!

I'm a warrior, dammit!

Give him a blade or fangs, and he could battle anything, but this was beyond him.

Goddess.

If only Ariana could help him. She'd know what

to do, he felt certain. *Ariana*. Desperation to save her pounded in his mind.

Love for her surged inside him, thicker, blinding, swelling until it threatened to break his ribs. For a moment, he thought it had, as he felt the walls of his chest crack. No, not his chest.

His heart burst open, the mating bond wrenching wide, flooding his mind and body with warmth, and with a light he thought might be bright enough to make him glow.

Love flowed into him with the nectar-sweetness of Ilina song. Ariana's love.

The mating bond glistened and sparkled like a crystal rainbow, casting away all the dark shadows inside him. He drank of her love, letting it seep into his cells and his bones, blending with the overwhelming love he felt for her, then he poured it back into the bond, into her.

"Ariana, come back to me."

The light flashed behind them. In front, lay nothing but the black void of the trap.

"Ariana!"

Kougar? Her voice sounded thin and distant in his head, but his pulse quickened with hope.

"Sweetheart, you must wake up, or you're going to die. We're both going to die."

What did you do? Her voice was stronger this time, closer, and filled with wonder as if she, too, were looking at crystal rainbows.

"I love you, Ariana. Completely. Heart and soul." His pulse thundered, his hands shaking. "Wake up, sweetheart, and turn to mist. Now!"

Beneath his touch, she stirred. As he held his breath, her lashes fluttered gently, and rose.

If he'd been standing, his knees would have buckled beneath him.

"Turn to mist, Ariana. Quickly!"

Confusion clouded her eyes. "Kougar?"

He gripped her face, his hand shaking with urgency. "Ariana, we're in the Syphian wormhole, about to enter the spirit trap. And you're flesh. You must turn to mist, or you'll die!" She met his gaze. "We'll both die."

The confusion cleared, her face taking on a mask of concentration as she lifted her head. As they reached the dark void of the spirit trap, Ariana dissolved, turning to mist in his arms. And then she was inside him, wrapping him in her Ilina energy, filling him with elation.

The darkness swallowed them, stealing his sight and senses, but for Ariana. He felt her energy caressing him and her love filling him, flowing through his blood and dancing through his mind, embracing him inside and out.

His cat leaped, sensing the other animals nearby. He tried to talk, but he could no longer feel his body even to do that. The trap had stolen his ability to move. All he could do was trust Ariana to get his brothers and him out of there. And he did trust her, he realized. Implicitly.

Though he could feel nothing, his cat roared inside with anxious excitement. Time ceased to exist. And suddenly, he was moving again at a startling speed, the lights of the wormhole once more pulsing around him. As they shot into a blast of cold Himalayan air, he saw Tighe and Hawke caught fast in Ariana's energy glow. They were unconscious, at best, their big bodies hanging lifeless on either side of her.

His gut clenched, then released slowly as he heard two faint, thready heartbeats. They weren't too late.

A Feral shout of triumph exploded beneath them, then slowly went silent as Ariana set them on the ground among their brothers and the Feral wives. Melisande must have gone to get the women from Feral House.

The Ferals surged forward, catching Tighe and Hawke out of Ariana's energy grasp, then laying them on the ground as Ariana released Kougar and turned to flesh beside him.

He grabbed her to him with shaking hands, kissing her with joy and relief and the love that had burst inside him as they'd joined within the mating bond. A brilliant light that showed no sign of abating. Ever.

"You did it," he murmured, pulling back.

A smile broke over her beloved face. "We did it."

He smiled. "Yes, we did." But when he would have lost himself in her eyes and told her again what was in his heart, she pulled away.

"I have to see them." Her maidens stood on the other side of the yard, watching her with a mix of worry and relief, confusion and pain, as many suffered the growth of new limbs.

With difficulty, he released her and watched her

hurry away from him, to her people. Watched as they surged around her.

He swallowed and turned back to his own. Delaney clung to Tighe, while Lyon pulled her gently away, calling for Kara's radiance and asking for Skye to try to help their animals.

Kougar's gaze returned to Ariana. Like a mother with her children, she touched and embraced and murmured soft words to the women he knew to be her life and heart. While on the other side of him, Kara administered radiance, glowing like a thousand-watt bulb, and Skye danced the dance of a Mage enchantress, drawing on her rare skill as a caller of animals to help heal his friends.

He stood between the two groups, needing Ariana, yet unable to walk away from his own any more than she could her maidens.

Was this to be their world then? Together, yet destined always to be apart? No, not always. Once the threat of Satanan's rising was quelled, he'd have more time to spend with her. And he would spend every moment he could. The situation wasn't perfect, but he knew it didn't matter.

He wasn't losing her again.

He wasn't living without her.

Kara released the radiance, and Delaney rushed in to hold her still-unconscious mate.

Moments later, Skye stopped dancing and walked to Paenther. "Their animals are suffering, but they're alive and still minimally connected to the men. Tighe's is the stronger of the two."

Everyone looked at her in surprise.

"I thought the babe was killing him faster," Lyon said.

"He might have been, but Tighe had an advantage Hawke didn't have. Tighe had Delaney to help keep him tethered. Hawke had no one. I've done all I can for now."

"Are they strong enough to transport back to Feral House?"

Skye nodded. "Yes, thanks to Kara's radiance. We'll continue to strengthen them as we can, but ultimately it's up to the warriors."

"They'll fight their way through this." Lyon's voice commanded it be so.

Growls of assent filled the air. The alternative was unthinkable.

Lyon turned to Kougar. "We'll need the Ilinas' assistance to get home."

Kougar nodded, joining him. "What about the vortex? And the Mage?" Though the wind was whipping it up, Mother Nature was far from throwing a tantrum as she would have if they'd killed many more than Hookeye.

"The vortex closed on its own a few minutes after you left," Lyon said. "As for the other . . ."

Jag chuckled. "Had us a little Mage-throwing contest, right off the mountain. Sorry you missed it, Kougar-man."

"I won," Wulfe said.

Jag scoffed. "No way, Dog. It wasn't how many you could throw at once, it was how far you could throw them."

"I won." A smile twitched at Wulfe's scarred mouth. "And don't call me *Dog*."

Kougar left them to their good-natured argument and started toward the throng of Ilinas and their queen. A low, warrior-type cheer went up from the women, and Ariana turned away from them, starting toward him.

They met halfway between the two groups, Ariana's eyes once more laser-bright and clear of the grief and worry of the past hours, her cheeks flushed with a health he hadn't seen in her since she'd been poisoned all those years ago. If possible, she was even more beautiful than before.

As she reached him, her eyes filled with a love his heart couldn't contain. She reached for him, and he took her hands, but neither spoke, their eyes sharing all that was inside them.

"I'd thought I loved you," Kougar said quietly, breaking the warm, full silence. "And I did, but with my heart all but closed, that love was a shadow of what it should have been." He released her hands and took her face in his palms. "A shadow of what I feel now. Be my mate, Ariana. For now. For always."

She met his gaze with eyes swimming in love. "Yes."

He grinned, a swift, fierce, triumphant baring of teeth. "You're mine, Ariana. I refuse to live without you again."

"And I, you."

They stared into one another's eyes, and he felt

as if he were drowning in love, in the rightness. And yet some things hadn't changed. Some of his happiness slipped away.

"We're at war with the Mage. I can't forsake my brothers. And I know your maidens need you; but when it's over, we'll be together. Somehow, we'll be together even if I have to . . ."

She lifted a single finger and pressed it against his lips, silencing him. "We'll be together now."

His heart clenched. "I can't . . ."

"But I can. I realized something today in the midst of all this. All these years, I've believed my mistake was in thinking I could be both queen to my people and mate to you. I thought that if I hadn't tried to be both, none of this would have happened. I thought I had to choose one or the other. And being queen isn't a choice."

"And now?" he asked quietly.

"I've realized my mistake wasn't in trying to be both. It was in not learning how to do it well. I need you, Kougar. I'm not giving you up again. It's not even in the best interest of my race to do so. In the coming war, the Ilinas need strong allies, and there are none stronger than you and your men."

"What are you saying?"

"I'm saying that the Ilinas can help in this war, and you're going to let us this time."

A smile softened her words, but the steel in her eyes told him there would be no talking her out of it. And, truthfully, he didn't want to.

"I'll be fighting at your side, Kougar, living at

Feral House, if your chief will have me. Melisande and Brielle have been ruling the Crystal Realm for centuries. They don't need me for that. And, unless I'm mistaken, I'm needed here." She reached out and placed her hand over his heart. "With you."

Kougar felt his mouth stretch, widening into a fierce, primal smile as his world righted itself, finally. Completely.

He hauled Ariana against him, still grinning, loving her with his eyes as he leaned forward to kiss her. Lilies of the valley filled his senses, love singing its Ilina song in his head—the most beautiful sound he'd ever heard aside from Ariana's sweet voice. His heart overflowed on a rush of love that cleansed him, inside and out.

"You're needed," he murmured against her soft lips. "By the Ferals, but more, far more, by me. Be my mate, Ariana. Renew the mating bond in the ritual with me. Be mine for always."

She pulled back to look into his eyes, her own shining with the same endless well of love and glistening tears.

"I always have been yours, Kougar. And I always will be. Always."

In the ritual room deep beneath Feral House, Lyon intoned the ancient rite of mating as he dribbled the combined blood of the Ferals in a circle around the mating altar, a job that was usually Kougar's. That night Kougar played a different role. As the chanting continued, he drove into the woman beneath him, the glorious love of his life, her bright blue eyes shining with love and heat and power as they joined in this most elemental way, opening minds and hearts and souls to the power that would bind them for eternity. This time, without the interference of her maidens.

The room was nearly full to overflowing, the Ilinas acting as a privacy curtain as they circled the altar, their backs to the mating pair, a shimmering curtain of energy. Beyond them, the Ferals stood, their own power riding the floral-scented air, for before the mating ritual, Kougar had filled the room with flowers.

The chanting ended. Without looking, Kougar knew Lyon had poured the last of their mingled blood into one of the ritual fires. The resulting burst of power barreled through him. As one, he and Ariana came with roars of unbridled joy, and he sank into the beauty of her essence as she turned to mist.

Inside, the mating bond, which had already been all but fully renewed, transformed in a brilliant arc of light that flared out into the room from their joined bodies in a beautiful crystalline glow. A bond so much deeper, stronger, and far more beautiful than the original, than he'd ever thought possible.

Ariana, her gaze locked with his, began to laugh, and he joined her, euphoric, then pulled out of her to kneel on the altar and adjust his clothing. She turned back to flesh and sat up, lowering her ritual gown to her knees.

The Ilinas moved away, and Kougar leaped off the altar, swinging his bride into his arms.

A cheer went up from his brothers as they moved forward, congratulating him, embracing his mate, the wariness with which they'd always treated him at bay, if not entirely gone. Which wasn't necessarily a bad thing. Someone had to keep this lot on their toes.

As the Ferals gave way, the Ilinas gathered around Ariana with soft touches and presses of cheek to cheek. They were happy for their queen and friend, but their wariness of him and the rest of the Ferals wasn't altogether gone. Not by a long shot.

"Where's Melisande?" Kougar asked, when the last of the Ilinas had stepped back, giving them some room. He knew Ariana's second had been there during the mating.

"She left."

"She was hoping you'd end it with me once and for all."

"Melisande's coming around." With a soft smile, she shrugged. "She not only didn't try to stop the mating, she attended . . . and didn't try to kill anyone."

"I see your point. I guess that's the best we're going to get for now."

"For now."

"Tighe!" Delaney's cry sent the room into a spiraling silence. Tighe and Hawke, both still unconscious, had been placed on pallets along one wall and blooded with the rest of the Ferals. The Shaman had urged them to include the pair in all possible rituals, hoping to draw them back into the world. Delaney had spent the ritual sitting on the pallet at Tighe's head, stroking his hair.

But at her cry, all hearts clutched with fear, Kougar's included. Until he saw Tighe's eyes blink open, a dimpled smile lifting his mouth as he stared up at his mate.

Kougar let out a deep breath of relief. *Thank the goddess.*

"Did I dream you're carrying our baby, D?" Tighe's voice was hoarse with disuse but possessed a thread of strength that told Kougar he was going to be fine.

"You didn't dream it." Delaney cried out again, this time with laughter, as Tighe pulled her down on top of him and kissed her thoroughly. The Ferals numbered seven active warriors again and would soon number eight, even without Hawke. The new fox shifter had made contact and should be arriving in the next few days.

But one of the bands around Kougar's chest remained too tight. His gaze went to Hawke, lying alone, still lost to the darkness. Kougar had to believe that his friend would recover. He'd already made it his mission to talk to him for long hours—stories of the past, and the Wind. Stories that might stir his mind and encourage him to return to them.

And when Hawke finally woke, he'd tell him those stories again. He'd tell Hawke everything he wanted to know.

He turned back to find Ariana shaking her head softly.

"What's the matter?"

She nodded to her maidens, crowded against the wall farthest from Tighe and the Ferals.

"Opposite sides of the room, as if we've brought together warring factions," she murmured, curving her arm tight around his waist. "It doesn't need to be like this."

But even as she said the words, Kara and Skye approached Brielle with smiles and hands of friendship.

Kougar stroked Ariana's beloved head. "It's going to work out. Eventually."

"I suppose."

He turned her until she faced him, his arms loose around her back. "Trust takes time, Ariana. More time than it should for some of us. But when it happens, the Earth moves."

A smile lit her beautiful face. "I love you, Feral. Have I told you that?"

"You have." He kissed her. "But tell me again. And again. And again," he said, punctuating each with another kiss. "I love you, Ariana. More than I'll ever find words for." He pulled her against him, pressing her head to his heart as emotion nearly got the better of him. All those years of thinking her dead, of grieving for her. Of missing her.

Having her in his arms again was a miracle he would never stop giving thanks for. Not only was she in his arms, and in his life, but she was his as she'd never been before. Because he'd learned to give to her completely.

Across the room, his gaze caught Jag's as the jaguar shifter held his own mate against his chest, his eyes gleaming with suspicious moisture. An understanding Kougar wouldn't have thought possible even a few weeks ago passed between them.

Jag clenched his fingers behind his mate's back,

his hand forming a thumbs-up. Kougar felt his mouth twitch with a smile and mirrored the move.

Jag threw his head back and laughed, drawing a chuckle from Kougar. His heart felt lighter than it had since he was a boy.

Ariana looked up at him, her eyes dancing. "You laughed."

"You make me happier than I've ever been."

A loving smile wreathed her face. "Then my life's goal is complete. And Kougar?"

"Hmm?"

"I feel the same."

Inside, his cat purred with satisfaction. And his heart gave a triumphant roar.

They are Feral Warriors—
an elite band of immortals
who can change shape at will.
Sworn to rid the world of evil,
their wild natures
are primed for release . . .

Missed any of
PAMELA PALMER's
dark, sexy series?

Turn the page for a glimpse of more
of her untamed romances

from

Avon Books!

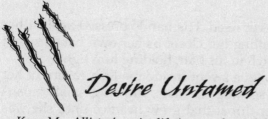

Desire Untamed

Kara MacAllister's quiet life is transformed forever the night a powerful stranger rips her from her home, claiming she's immortal and the key to his race's survival. Lyon arouses a fierce, primal hunger deep within Kara—beyond anything she ever imagined. But when their lives are threatened by an ancient evil, Kara and Lyon realize they have found a love they would risk their souls to claim . . . and a powerful desire that could never, ever be tamed.

The relief and welcome in her eyes as he approached nearly drove him to his knees. His hands shook with the need to pull her into his arms. For once he didn't have to fight the urge. He cupped her bare shoulders and pulled her against him, his passion igniting and flaring into a wildfire with the first brush of his heated flesh against her silken skin. Her breasts pebbled against his bare chest. Her scent rose up, clouding his mind, ensnaring him in a haze of lust that was almost too thick to breathe.

When he covered her mouth, reason fled. Her sweetness drugged him, stealing all thought but the certainty she was the only sustenance he would ever need. His hands pressed against her back, pulling her closer as her own hands swept up to catch in his hair, holding him tight.

His tongue swept inside the lush cavern of her mouth, seeking its mate, drawing small moans from her throat that grew in force until she was rocking against him. In a far, distant corner of his mind, he remembered where they were. Remembered they stood within the circle of his fellows. He should let her go and step back.

But his beast roared, *Mine!* and he increased the pressure of his tongue strokes instead, marking her, his beast daring the goddess to ignore his claim. In a trembling rush, Kara came apart in his arms, clinging to him as soft whimpers escaped her throat.

Lyon continued to kiss her, drinking in the heady taste of her release until the torrent passed, and she clung to him. Slowly, regretfully, he released her mouth and held her tight against him until she could stand on her own.

Sweet goddess, he wasn't letting her go. She had to be his. His logical mind took up the cry of his beast. *Mine.*

But she would only be his if his fingertips glowed in the mark of the true mate.

His scalp began to tingle with cold realization. Glowing fingers would have triggered a shout. A cheer. The only sounds that met his ears were the crackle of the fires and the stunned and utter silence of his brothers. He knew. Before he ever pulled away from her and looked at his hands, *he knew* there would be no glow.

Mine! his beast roared in anger and betrayal. But he lifted his hands and stared at the traitorous normalcy of his flesh.

Kara wasn't his.

Obsession Untamed

Every time FBI agent Delaney Randall closes her eyes, she suffers yet another nightmare. A brutal serial killer has found his way inside her head, and she lives each murder through his soulless eyes. Tighe, a dangerous Feral Warrior, needs Delaney and her visions to help stop the rampages of an evil fiend. As the two join forces, Tighe—who has little use for humans—falls for the intense beauty and becomes wild with an obsession as untamed as his heart . . .

"I'm not getting married without underwear. Or without my gun. Not with wild animals on the loose."

He took a step toward her, his mouth compressing dangerously. "You'll do whatever I tell you to do."

She threw the gown on the floor. "Go to hell."

He lunged for her, grabbed her arm, and hauled her roughly against him. "I don't like this any better than you do, but it's either bind yourself to me or die. I gave you the choice already. You chose this. You chose me."

"I was delirious."

His jaw went hard as he released her with one

hand and flicked open a switchblade three inches from her face.

"It's not too late to change your mind." The tightness of his mouth spoke of barely leashed violence, but in the agitated flutter of those angel wings in her head she sensed an unhappiness as raw as her own. He was being forced to tie himself to a woman he didn't love.

No, not forced.

He could have let her die.

Her fury ebbed as her heart began to ache for him almost as much as herself. "Would you really kill me?" she asked quietly. She already knew the answer.

The anger drained out of him as he retracted the blade and shoved it back in his pocket.

"No." He released her along with a sigh that echoed with pain. "But if you won't go through with this, I'll have no choice but to step aside while someone else does. The survival of our race is too important." He shook his head. "Not just to us. If we die, there will be no one left to keep the Daemons from returning. Imagine thousands of creatures terrorizing the human population. Creatures worse than my twin. A dozen times worse."

She shuddered and stared at him, her mind struggling to accept round after round of evidence that the world was so much more complex than she'd thought. "So I really don't have a choice?"

His mouth turned rueful. "You really don't."

"But you do. A human death can't mean that

much to you. Why bind yourself to me when you could have let me die? When you don't want me?"

His mouth turned up in a wry half smile. "Who says I don't want you?"

As she stared at him, he bent down and picked up the gown, then met her gaze again, his expression softening just a little. "Come on, D. Let's get this over with."

It wasn't quite the marriage proposal she'd dreamed of, but there had been something in his expression, something in his words that eased the ache inside her. Not much, but maybe it was enough. Especially since she clearly didn't have a choice.

"I need to get cleaned up."

He handed her the gown and nodded toward a door in the corner. "Bathroom's in there. I'll see if I can find you a brush or something."

She nodded and took the gown from him. As he started to turn away, she stopped him. "Tighe?"

He turned back to her.

"Thank you," she said softly. "For not letting me die."

His gaze seemed to search hers for several moments, then he lifted his hand and traced her cheekbone with his thumb in a feather-light touch. "You're welcome." Then he turned away.

Passion Untamed

Though the Mage witch Skye has a gentle heart, demonic forces have enslaved her, forcing her to kidnap Paenther, a powerful and dangerous immortal. Even chained and naked, he is a cunning prisoner who seduces her, turning captive into captor. Despite Paenther's fury over her treachery, Skye's gentle beauty calls to his soul, calming the wild chaos within. But when evil threatens, their only chance at survival is to trust in one another . . . and the power of love.

Paenther scented violets even before the witch stepped into the room. She returned without her animals, her hair wet as if she'd just showered, her eyes hollow. Without a word, without meeting his gaze, she crawled up beside him, between his body and the wall, and lay down, curling against his hip. He could feel her trembling.

As much as he hated her, he'd always had finely honed protective instincts toward women and children, and they rose now. Something had hurt her. He reminded himself he didn't care. But as he felt her slowly calm, her breathing evening out in sleep, the tension eased from his own body.

He wasn't sure when he'd drifted off, but he woke to the sound of water dripping from the stalactites into the puddles scattered across the room and the feel of the witch's silken head on his chest. She had one arm wrapped around his waist, the other hand tucked against her neck. That second arm was nearly within reach of his mouth. But he'd lost the desire to hurt her. Her gentle touch and her acceptance of his fury had taken the edge off his need for revenge.

He blinked, feeling . . . strange. Almost . . . relaxed.

With disbelief he realized what was wrong. Or what was right. The rage, the ever-present rage he struggled to contain day and night, the rage burned into his soul by Ancreta nearly three hundred years ago, had inexplicably left him.

How? Was this simply more magic?

Did he care?

Chained atop this cold stone, deep in the bowels of a second Mage captivity, he felt more at peace than he had in years. Eased. Whole in a way he hadn't felt in centuries.

Had she somehow, miraculously healed him? Or was her nearness affecting him in a way he'd never imagined anyone could?

The implications rocked him. He almost hoped it was just enchantment. Just a lie. Because if it wasn't, if this easing of the torment he'd lived with for centuries was somehow coming from her . . .

A witch.

Heaven help him. The last thing he wanted was to need her. More than he did already.

Rapture Untamed

The most combative and tormented of the Ferals, Jag is a predator who hunts alone. But when daemons terrorize the human population he partners with Olivia, a flame-haired Therian temptress as strong as she is beautiful. As their sensual dance heats up, a dark force sets its sights on Olivia, threatening to destroy everything she's vowed to protect—and the only one who can save her is the arrogant shifter she lusts for but dares not love.

"Did you love him?"

"You know the answer to that. As a friend, yes, but you know I didn't return the feelings he had for me." Her elbow slammed into his solar plexus. "But so help me, if you think I shouldn't care that he's dead . . ." Her heel drove hard into his knee. "If you think I can just forget the sight of that monster stripping his face away one strip of flesh at a time . . ." Her voice cracked. "So help me, Jag, I'm going to beat your cold ass to hell and back."

The bed collapsed beneath them with a crash. He rolled onto his feet, but Olivia followed, spinning and slamming her heel into his knee again, splintering his kneecap. With a roar, he collapsed onto his other knee just as the door burst open wide.

Tighe and Wulfe pushed inside, then halted in the doorway, staring at the wreckage of the bed, him on his knees, blood running down his face and his fire demon of a partner standing over him about to drive her elbow into his skull.

Jag grinned. Goddess, but he loved a strong woman. He wiped the blood from his mouth and gave Tighe a jaunty salute.

Olivia whirled on the pair in the doorway, her eyes blazing with unholy fire. "Unless you want to join the fight, get the hell out of here."

Tighe lifted his hands in quick surrender. "I'm gone."

Wulfe, the bastard, grinned. "Don't kill him."

The respite had given his knee a chance to heal. As Wulfe pulled the door closed behind him, Jag shot to his feet, ready for another round. He loved a good fight, and this one had gotten his blood pumping, and at the same time given him an outlet for the awful tension that had been riding him ever since that goat fuck of a battle.

But Olivia's eyes showed no such relief. Deep in those gray depths, he could see her shattering. His heart clenched in his chest as he understood. She fought the grief and her own emotions more than she fought him. And while he'd gladly let her beat the crap out of him if it helped her, he could see it wasn't helping at all.

The emotion needed another way out. The sheen in her eyes told him that.

She launched herself at him again, but even as she did, tears began to run down her cheeks, seeming to make her madder. He let her get in a couple of good punches, then he grabbed her in a bear hug and pressed her face against his chest as she struggled.

"Let it out, Liv," he said quietly. "You're not going to get rid of it until you give in. Just let it out."

She fought him a moment more, her fists pummeling his shoulders until the storm overtook her. Sobs wracked her small body, her fists opening, her fingers clinging to him as grief swept her away.

He felt a deep and sudden need to comfort her and didn't have a clue how to do it. He'd always been great at causing anger. Soothing raging emotions was beyond him. He could always use the calming touch of his hand, but he sensed that wasn't what she needed right now. She needed to get it out.

He patted her back awkwardly.

She buried her face tighter against him, clinging to him harder, as if his attempts weren't that awkward at all.

He lifted his hand and cupped her small head, holding it tight against him. Deep inside his chest, he felt a cracking of the ice that had for so long encased his heart.

He didn't want that. Didn't need it. But even as the thought went through his head, his arms enclosed her in a vise of a protective cage through which nothing would ever harm her again.

Next month, don't miss these exciting new love stories only from Avon Books

A Borrowed Scot by Karen Ranney
Agreeing to rescue Veronica MacLeod from making the biggest mistake of her life, Lord Fairfax of Doncaster Hall takes the Scottish beauty as his wife in order to help her avoid scandal and disgrace. But will Fairfax's mysterious past keep him from getting close to Veronica? Or will passion overcome all?

The Welcome Home Garden Club by Lori Wilde
Iraq war vet Gideon Garza returns home to Twilight with just one thing on his mind: Caitlyn Marsh, the girl he left behind. However, upon his arrival he finds Caitlyn mother to a son who greatly resembles himself, and is stunned to learn he's inherited his estranged father's cattle ranch. With the help of the Garden Club, can Gideon overcome the past and claim the family he craves?

Secrets of a Proper Countess by Lecia Cornwall
Lady Isobel risks losing everything she holds dear when an innocent flirtation at a masquerade ball leads to a steamy tryst in a dark garden with the infamous Marquess of Blackwood. But tantalizing passion isn't enough to unmask Isobel, only furthering her lover's unrelenting pursuit. Will her secrets ignite his desire?

Captured By a Rogue Lord by Katharine Ashe
Alex Savage, Earl by day and pirate by night, uses his alter ego to steal from the rich to help the poor. When a band of smugglers ravages the beautiful Serena Carlyle's estate, Savage can't help but don his captain's hat to woo the ingénue. But falling for Serena could be trouble, as his identity hangs in the balance.